ASSEMBLING ELLA

Emma G. Rose

Imperative Press

HAMPDEN, MAINE

Published by Imperative Press Books, LLC

Imperative Press
Hampden, ME
www.imperativepressbooks.com

Publisher's Note: This is a work of fiction. Names, characters, places, and incidents either are the product of the author's imagination or are used fictitiously, and any resemblance to actual persons, living or dead, business establishments, events, or locales is entirely coincidental.

Book Layout © 2017 BookDesignTemplates.com

Assembling Ella/Emma G. Rose – 1st edition
ISBN 978-1-7339079-7-2

To everyone who has ever lost a sibling

&

To my cousins, thirteen years and we're still learning to live with it

CONTENTS

ACKNOWLEDGEMENTS

I didn't mean to write this book, but everyone who read *Nothing's Ever Lost* loved Ella so much that I couldn't help it. I had to know what happened to her.

Of course, no author brings a character into the world alone. Thank you to my beta readers: Deb Fernandes, Brian Fernandes, Veronica Green-Gott-Potvin, Lauren Platt, Jeanne Hargett, Roger Hammons, and Kay Hightower.

To my Mom, who has been my editor, proofreader, cheerleader, business manager and all around supporter for four books now. This book would not exist without you.

Special thanks to the student at Fort Kent Community High School who told me about losing her sister when she was a little girl.

And to my coworkers at the Chrysler Museum of Art in Norfolk, Virginia. I only worked with you for a year, but in that short time, you deepened my love for art. I'm pretty sure Ella wouldn't be the same without you.

Finally, thank you, reader, for reading Ella's story. Stay tuned for more from Owen.

ASSEMBLING ELLA

CHAPTER ONE

Dreamscape

PhiTau paused for a moment in his work. He straightened his bent back as best he could and settled his leathery wings more comfortably against it. His eyes looked out toward the horizon, surveying the seemingly endless fields of Dream. Straight rows of dream plants stood knee-high between well-trodden furrows. Translucent web-like dreamstuff erupted from the unharvested plants in complex tangles. The harvested plants looked naked by comparison, all greenish-brown and trembling.

Looking out over the nearly unbroken rows under the broad expanse of purple sky, PhiTau sighed. He knew in his soul of souls that there was no place in the worlds more boring than the Dreaming.

His fellow oneiroi bent and picked, bent and picked. They raked up dreamstuff with their long fingers, freeing the plants from their cocoons and gathering the wispy harvest into soft bundles. The only sounds were their footsteps and the susurrus of plants shivering together.

PhiTau clenched and unclenched his bare toes. He felt sticky and unreal from such labor. Bits of dreamstuff clung to the fur on his arms and the backs of his hands. No matter how thoroughly he rubbed his fingers, they were never quite free of it.

Aside from the boredom, this was the main hazard of the job. Constant handling of the dreamstuff would eventually make parts of his body insubstantial. Hands were often the first to go. It was a fate that befell every harvester in the Dreaming eventually. You could spot the very oldest among them by what they'd lost. Missing fingers. Hands with palms worn through. Arms, hips, knees and toes permeated by the dreamstuff. Somenight, PhiTau would be one of them. The thought made his throat constrict. He coughed to clear it. He had to speak, if only to distract himself.

"Do you ever wonder what happens to all of this?" He held up a tuft of dreamstuff. "Like this piece. Will it be a moon, or a plant, or something we can't even imagine?"

Most of the other oneiroi ignored him, but BetaZeta, the foreman and oldest member of the crew, with fingers blunted and thin from a near-eternity of harvesting, shook his head at PhiTau. "Your job is not to imagine. Keep to the task in front of you."

"I just think—"

"It's not your job to think either," BetaZeta interrupted. The foreman's voice was as thin as his fingers. It wouldn't be long before he faded away completely. "Do your work and in due time the Lord may reward you for your diligence."

PhiTau had heard that line before. It was what the

long-timers always said to any youngster who asked too many questions.

PhiTau had never heard of anyone being rewarded by Morpheus, but everyone knew about his punishments. Periodically, while harvesting up their row, PhiTau's crew would come across a group of other harvesters working the neighboring furrow. When that happened, the foremen would allow the work to slow enough that gossip and tales could flow between the crews.

In this way, PhiTau had learned that some harvesters were not left to fade decently away after a lifetime of work well done. Some simply disappeared all at once while their fellows worked on around them. These were always referred to as having been "taken by the Lord." The more hopeful harvesters claimed that he had another task for these chosen ones, but most believed that they had been unmade as punishment. For what, no one could say.

Maybe both punishment and reward were nothing but stories made up by bored harvesters.

"How?" asked PhiTau.

BetaZeta blinked rapidly at him. "What do you mean, how?"

"How will he reward me?"

BetaZeta's lips curled, revealing a flash of yellow teeth. "It is not for you to ask such questions," he said. "Your purpose is to harvest. If you do it well you may be rewarded. That is all you need to know."

Harvesting was the whole point of an oneiroi's life. In

fact, it was practically the whole of their lives. Supposedly Lord Morpheus, master of the Dreaming and all within it, had created oneiroi specifically to harvest the dreamstuff. He used the dreamstuff to weave unthinkable creations, which were sent into the minds of creatures called humans. As PhiTau understood it, the humans needed dreams and the Lord needed dreamstuff to make those dreams. The harvesters, therefore, did a very important job.

Secretly, PhiTau wasn't sure he actually believed all that. He'd never seen Lord Morpheus. Although he had heard of people who had supposedly seen him. PhiTau had never even seen where the dreamstuff went. For all he knew, it was dumped into a pile somewhere and left to rot. He'd certainly never seen a human, and doing a thankless task for a creature you'd never seen from the moment of your creation until you faded away to nothing didn't seem like a rewarding life to PhiTau. It would be nice to know that there was something else to strive for. He tried a different tack.

"Has he rewarded you?"

The other harvesters shied away, as though the Lord himself might appear to punish PhiTau's inquisitiveness. He didn't, of course. But BetaZeta did wrinkle his nose, as though he'd been confronted with something foul.

"I have faith."

"Faith," PhiTau echoed.

"Shut up, PhiTau," someone muttered.

A spattering of nervous giggles rippled through the

group. PhiTau turned, but couldn't tell who had spoken. All of the other harvesters were bent to their work.

"Of course, punishment is much easier earned than reward," BetaZeta said.

BetaZeta was content with the bend and pick, just like everyone else. Only PhiTau seemed to wonder about things, to question, to hope that the next moment would be different from this one. It hadn't happened in PhiTau's lifetime, but someday it would. It had to.

CHAPTER TWO

Prime and Pose

Ella had hoped to wriggle out of it, but there was no escape. Apparently school shopping was some kind of social imperative. When she protested that she was too old, Mom countered that most 17-year-old girls would be thrilled to spend a day at the mall.

"Have you seen the mall lately?" Ella pushed away her cereal bowl.

"There are other stores in Bangor," Mom answered. She snagged Ella's dishes on her way out of the dining room.

"I basically wear the same outfit every day."

"Wouldn't it be nice to wear something new for your senior year?" Mom said just before Ella heard the dishes clatter into the sink.

Ella didn't say that senior year was already the beginning of something new and what was so great about new things anyway? She preferred old things. Sometimes even broken and discarded things. She made them into art, constructing sculptures out of the dregs from other people's toy boxes and treasures found at Goodwill.

Mom turned on the water and gave Ella another idea of how to talk her out of this dumb shopping trip. Maybe the mention of a costly home repair would make Mom rethink the whole idea of buying school clothes.

"When are those guys coming to dig up the septic tank?" she asked.

"Not until next week," Mom said. She came back into the dining room. "Get your shoes on. We should head out soon."

Ella made a last-ditch effort, as she climbed into the back seat of Mom's Jeep. "We could just go to Wally World."

They had a Wal-Mart right in town, and there were only so many clothes available to try on there. Mom couldn't possibly stretch the trip to more than an hour or two.

"We're going to the mall," Mom said. "It will be fun." Then in the same cheerful tone she added, "Hey, why don't you sit up front?"

Ella ignored this, because it was a stupid question. She clicked her seatbelt into place. Mom sighed and adjusted the rearview mirror.

It had been years since Ella rode in the front seat of a car. There was a time when she'd scream and cry if Mom drove faster than she thought was reasonable. Reasonable being defined as something like 20 miles an hour. She'd gotten better about it in the last couple of years. These days, she could avoid a full-on panic attack as long as she kept herself distracted and tried not to think about how, while she was much safer in the back seat, Mom was in the front with nothing but a glass window between her and any oncoming projectile.

Still, she avoided looking out the windows if she could help it. It wasn't like there was anything worth seeing anyway. Her hometown of Corinna was a smear of houses bisected by a lazy river. Long before she was born, the area had been declared a Superfund site. The EPA had spent millions of dollars to filter woolen mill contaminants out of the water, leaving behind a sanitized nothingness that looked like every other backwoods town in Maine. Except for the crooked intersection that always seemed like an accident waiting to happen.

Newport lay alongside it. Bigger and more bustling, but not really much better. Dad's apartment building hid behind tall trees down one of the side streets. Ella couldn't have seen it even if she had been willing to look out the window.

And then they were speeding down the highway in what passed for Saturday traffic on Interstate 95 south of Bangor. Which is to say that, when Ella glanced up, she actually spotted a few other cars on the road. Cars and SUVs and 18-wheelers. All driving too fast, all full of people not paying attention to the other vehicles. As though they were the only ones. As though nothing bad could ever happen to them. Watching them made her heart pound. She slouched lower, propping her knees on the back of the passenger seat, and looked down at her phone.

"Who are you talking to?" Mom asked.

"No one," Ella said.

"What are you doing?"

Ella sighed. "Just looking."

She'd been scrolling through Instagram. Among the hundreds of artists she followed, someone was always posting some new piece that made Ella feel like her stupid plastic sculptures were just piles of broken toys. She looked anyway, partly out of low-key masochistic tendencies and partly hoping to absorb a little bit of their genius by looking long and hard enough.

It wasn't as though she could spend her weekend at a museum. Maine wasn't exactly a world center of sculptural art. Or any art really. Someday, she'd go to New York City and see the Guggenheim and MoMA in person. She'd stand in front of a Calder sculpture for hours and just soak it in.

But all that was a daydream, one that would require riding in cars or buses or planes to reach. For now, she had Instagram and YouTube.

If only someone would invent teleportation. Then Ella could hop to New York, or Paris, or Amsterdam, see the art, and get home again without having to ride in any death trap of metal and speed. Her best friend, Liv, was on track to do something mathematical and amazing with her life. Maybe she'd be the one to invent it, and Ella would be right in line as a beta tester.

When they reached the mall, Mom parked under a streetlight in front of JCPenney. Ella prayed she'd done it out of habit and not because she expected them to be there until dark. It was only 10 a.m.

Inside, Mom dragged Ella from store to store. She was doing that cheerful Mom thing. The one where she tried, through sheer force of smile and tone of voice, to convince Ella that they really were having a wonderful time. Watching her, you'd think clothes shopping was the most exciting adventure in the whole universe. Personally, if she had to shop, Ella would rather do it at a thrift store, where she could spend as little as possible on clothes and then use the surplus to buy whatever random bits and pieces called out to be included in her next assemblage.

Thankfully, before the end of the second hour, Mom's patience started wearing thin. She kept grabbing cute shirts with butterflies and flowers on them, and Ella kept gravitating toward black sweatshirts and skinny jeans, which was literally all she ever wore. Why Mom thought senior year would suddenly make her a different person was beyond her.

In the dressing room Mom said, "Ella, put your phone away. You're supposed to be looking at clothes, not texting."

"I'm not texting," Ella said. There was no one to text. Liv and Owen were on some kind of end-of-summer, last-hurrah trip with their parents, which meant they were basically forbidden from looking at their phones. She slipped hers into her back pocket.

"Do you like any of these?" Mom asked.

Ella stared at the array of cutesy blouses. Why did it matter what shirt she wore to school? She never took off her sweatshirt unless it got in the way during art class. Then whatever she had on underneath was likely to end up covered in paint, glue, or other random art supplies. It would be smarter to take her school shopping money and invest it in a stain remover company. And maybe some kind of fabric dye company for all the times she'd spilled paint thinner, bleach and other assorted chemicals on her clothes. Still, Mom seemed determined not to leave the dressing room until Ella picked something, so Ella caved.

"That one." She pointed at a dark blue short-sleeve shirt with tiny silver stars.

Mom squinted at it as though she'd never seen it before, even though she had picked out literally everything in the dressing room. "It's awfully dark."

"I like it. It's like wearing the sky."

"Great." Mom smiled. "Let's look at pants and we'll be done."

Ella rolled her eyes, but only after Mom had turned to gather up the pile of rejected shirts. She knew Mom was trying, but it would be better if she didn't. If she actually wanted to make Ella happy, she could have stopped to ask what Ella wanted instead of assuming her own daughter was a walking stereotype.

Finally, Mom took her receipt from the cashier and handed the shopping bag full of sort-of-okay clothes to

Ella. Then, she took a deep breath. Ella noticed the way the lines at the corners of Mom's eyes had deepened. It must be all the squinting from looking on the bright side all the time.

"Alright, I think we've accomplished something here," Mom said.

Ella didn't really think so, but before she could say as much, Mom added, "Do you want frozen yogurt?"

"Um, yes?" Ella said. Was it possible to not want frozen yogurt? Besides, it would get them out of the mall. Sweet Frog was up the street in front of Wal-Mart. The walk to the car took longer than the drive.

They sat at one of the tiny round tables that always seemed to sprout like mushrooms inside of frozen yogurt shops. Ella imagined they weren't made, but grown from the shiny white tile. Just spread some frozen yogurt on the floor, sow some sprinkles, and in three to six weeks, your tiny tables would begin to grow.

Mom chose a demure coffee fro-yo with chocolate chips on top. Ella had a blue cotton candy and creamsicle monstrosity topped with every type of candy they served, except for sour gummy worms, of course. Ella had just started to eat, when Mom smiled in a way that made her look like her underwear was too tight.

"So," Mom said, too casually, "how are you getting to school on the first day?"

Ella felt sweat prickle along her chest. She should have known Mom had an ulterior motive for this little adventure.

"You're taking me," Ella said, as though saying it out loud would end the argument before it began. No such luck.

"Honey, I have to work." Her mother stabbed at the frozen yogurt with her spoon.

"Liv will take me then. It doesn't matter."

"What about the bus?"

"The bus? They don't even have seatbelts on the bus."

"You're a senior now, don't you think—"

"No," Ella said.

They'd had this argument a dozen times or more. Mom couldn't seem to understand what was so obvious to Ella. Driving was dangerous. Being a senior had nothing to do with it. She could be ninety-nine and it would still be dangerous.

"You know, if you had a driver's license—"

"No."

Ella wanted to scream. Why couldn't her mother understand this? It was so simple. Driving was dangerous. She did not drive. End of discussion.

"Honey, I know you're scared but—"

The legs of Ella's chair squealed against the tile floor as she stood up. She snatched her frozen yogurt from the table. Mom just sat there, looking sad, like she wasn't the one who'd started this whole thing.

"I want to go home now," Ella said.

Mom avoided her gaze. "Well, I want to finish my frozen yogurt."

"Fine."

Her mother could be so stubborn. Ella stomped away. Outside, she dropped into one of the bistro chairs that were cluttering up the sidewalk. She didn't know why they bothered to put the stupid things here. It wasn't like anyone wanted to eat frozen yogurt while sucking in exhaust fumes and gazing out over the scenic parking lot.

She shoveled a heaping spoonful of frozen yogurt into her mouth and sputtered when whipped cream somehow made its way up her left nostril. This was all her mother's fault. She'd tricked Ella into coming on this stupid shopping trip. "I want to buy you new school clothes we can't afford." Right. As though some new clothes would make Ella say, "Oh yes, these metal death traps that killed my brother are totally safe and I would like to operate one please." If Jack had drowned, nobody would be trying to force her to become an Olympic swimmer. But for some reason everyone had to have a driver's license. It was stupid and unfair.

By the time her mother came outside, smiling as though nothing had happened, Ella's frozen yogurt was a melted soupy mess. She threw it in the trash can, but pocketed the neon green plastic spoon. She could see a use for it later.

CHAPTER THREE

Dream Come True

After the argument with BetaZeta, PhiTau went about his work silently. He couldn't afford to draw any more attention. He already wasn't the most popular oneiroi. Even when he wasn't talking back, he worked slowly and his attention tended to wander. Which is why he was the first to notice a spot of color off in the distance, a flash of blue.

It was a small spot, but moving closer at a speed no oneiroi could accomplish on his bent and bandy legs. Fascinated, PhiTau paused in his work. He couldn't help it. All around him, the other harvesters continued to rake dreamstuff from the plants and put it into their baskets and dump the baskets into carts. PhiTau did not. He could not. His eyes demanded a look at the only anomaly that had ever graced this landscape.

Under the purple sky, over the red-brown fields, between the rows of dreamstuff, something was moving.

Whatever it was, it was coming closer. PhiTau tried to make sense of what he was seeing. It was not an oneiroi. It was not a cart. That exhausted every reasonable option, which left him with only the unreasonable. There was nothing else in the Dreaming that could move unless the plants had sprouted legs and learned to dance. Except . . . could it be?

PhiTau held his breath. He stared until his eyes ached, afraid that if he looked away the blue spot would disappear and his world would once again empty of all interest. And that was how PhiTau, of all the harvesters in all the Dreaming, happened to be standing idle when the Lord of Dream strode up between the furrows.

The spot of blue had been the fabric of his robe, which billowed around him as he walked. The fine woven belt showed off the leanness of his figure. This was all PhiTau had time to notice before the Dream Lord stopped, barely more than an arm's length away.

Never had PhiTau been so close to greatness. He felt rooted in place. He knew he should bend to his work, show the Lord that he was a diligent harvester who did as he was told, but he could not. Instead he tilted back his head so he could look into the face of his god.

Lord Morpheus loomed, hands on his hips and head held high. The Dreaming was his. His six-fingered hands had shaped every part of it, the plants and the carts, and all the oneiroi including PhiTau. PhiTau had doubted this before, but now he knew it, knew it to the core of his soul. It would have been impossible to look at Morpheus and not see that he was the lord and master of all that he surveyed.

As Morpheus' green eye roved over the workers bending and plucking, his blue eye stared out over unseen lands. PhiTau had heard that Lord Morpheus wore the shape of a human. This was impossible to confirm since PhiTau had never seen one, nor had any of his fellow harvesters. One thing was certain, Morpheus with his straight limbs, wingless back, and dark hair that grew only on his head, was no oneiroi.

PhiTau observed all this, and then, in a fit of audacity, looked into Morpheus' green eye, drinking in the strangeness, the newness of a god in their midst. For a moment the green eye alone stared back at him. Then the blue, recalled from wherever it was wandering, turned on him as well.

PhiTau lowered his gaze. Too late.

"You." Lord Morpheus pointed one long finger, pale and delicate where PhiTau's were rough and weathered. "Come with me."

The voice was rich, musical, full of possibility and the knowledge of things as yet unimagined. PhiTau felt his hearts jump into his throat. If he did not move right now they would escape from his chest and run off after the Dream Lord without him.

Apparently satisfied that his command would be obeyed, Morpheus turned without another word. With the Dream Lord's eyes no longer pinning him to the earth, PhiTau felt able to move. That was a good thing, because the Lord's long legs carried him easily across the fields. PhiTau had to scurry to keep up. He didn't so much as glance back at BetaZeta and the other harvesters who had populated the entirety of his life so far. His mind was too full of possibility to spare a thought for what was being left behind.

What could Morpheus possibly want with him? Was this the reward that BetaZeta had talked about? If so, it couldn't have gone to a less deserving oneiroi. PhiTau knew himself to be lazy, slow to harvest, and quick to distraction. Perhaps this was not a reward at all, but a punishment. Maybe he would be interrogated, beaten, unmade. These thoughts should have scared him, PhiTau knew, but another feeling, stronger than fear, had him in its grip—curiosity. What came after this didn't matter, because for the first time in PhiTau's long and dreary life, something new was happening.

"What is your name?" The voice startled PhiTau so completely that he almost tripped. His eyes had been so full of Morpheus that there had been no room for anyone else. But now that the voice had drawn his attention, PhiTau noticed a tall oneiroi, slightly less bent than PhiTau and his fellow harvesters, hurrying along behind Morpheus. In one hand, he held a board with a sheet of paper clipped to it. In the other, he held a stick of graphite. PhiTau looked at these tools with wonder. He'd heard of writing, a way of passing knowledge with shapes, but he'd never actually seen it done. All of PhiTau's knowledge had been passed by word of mouth between the harvesters.

"I asked your name," the tall oneiroi said.

"PhiTau."

Watching the tall oneiroi scratch graphite against paper, PhiTau was so fascinated that he ran himself knee-deep into a dream plant. Buds and dreamstuff tangled in his leg hair. Not wanting to be left behind, he pulled himself free. The tall oneiroi somehow managed to walk and write at the same time without running into anything, and PhiTau couldn't even keep himself moving in a straight line.

"Where are we going?" PhiTau asked, keeping his voice low.

"You have been chosen," the writer said.

"For what?"

"A new assignment."

PhiTau's hearts swelled in his chest. He had been chosen for something new. Never had he dared hope . . . well, that was a lie. He had hoped every day of his life that something, anything would happen. But he'd never dared to believe that such a thing could really happen to him. Now, here he was, following the Dream Lord to a new destiny. BetaZeta would be livid.

CHAPTER FOUR

Diptych Plus One

On the first day of school, Ella's stomach was clenched up tight. Eating breakfast seemed impossible. So she grabbed Jack's old backpack, the navy blue L. L. Bean one with his initials on it that she'd carried since second grade, and went out onto the porch to wait for Liv. The air was cooler than she'd expected. It felt like autumn had arrived overnight and a soft breeze drew a lock of blonde hair across her face. She pulled her sweatshirt sleeves down over her hands.

Around the edges of the yard the trees whispered to each other. Ella liked the trees. Three months out of the year they blocked the view of the road, protecting Ella's little world from the traffic of the outside. Yes, the lawn might be mostly weeds, the paint on her childhood playhouse might be faded, and the farm pond at the edge of the woods might be nothing more than a mosquito breeding pit, but Ella still saw them with a child's eyes.

Liv's Civic thumped over a pothole in the driveway, snapping Ella out of her reverie. She waited as Liv turned the car around in the widest part of the driveway. The dirt road in front of Ella's house wasn't exactly a major highway, but Liv knew that backing into even imaginary traffic made Ella nervous. She avoided doing it when Ella was in the car.

Ella ran down the steps and opened the rear passenger door to find Owen sitting in the back seat.

"Push over," she said.

"You can sit in the front you know," Owen said.

"Not going to happen."

Liv looked at Owen in the rearview mirror. "Told you. Now get up here. I'm not a chauffeur."

Owen clambered out of the back seat. He was wearing a faded Kings of Leon tee shirt and a pair of khaki pants that looked like they'd never been in the same universe as an iron. A breeze tousled his hair carrying the scent of Old Spice and coffee. Owen had a four-cup-a-day habit. Ella wondered how he ever managed to sleep.

He held the door open for her and waited as she slipped inside the car. Hand on the doorframe, he bent down to say, "That's an idea actually. When you go off to New York you can just hire me to be your driver."

Ella made a face at him. "With all my vast riches? Sure. I'll get right on that."

Owen grinned and slammed the door shut. As he settled into the front seat, he added, "You'll have to buy something nicer than a Civic though."

"Don't hate on Beverly, or you'll be walking your ungrateful asses to school," Liv said.

"Dude, this is technically my car," Owen said.

Liv's parents had handed down the clunker when Owen got his license, but he almost never drove it. As far as Ella could tell, he'd ceded complete control of the vehicle to Liv. She seemed attached to it. She'd even named it. Ella didn't understand how anyone could feel affection for a death trap, but Liv did.

"You love us," Ella said. Then she hunkered down in the back seat so Liv could drive without distraction. Aside from Mom, Liv was the only person Ella felt semi-comfortable riding with. She always kept her eyes on the road and turned the radio down low. Ella had never seen her so much as change the station while she was driving. But that might be because Owen was a natural copilot. He seemed to know what Liv needed before she did. It was some kind of sibling telepathy.

Owen and Liv weren't twins, although almost everyone at school had forgotten that by now. They looked practically identical, especially since Liv had started cutting her hair super short. Which looked amazing of course. If Ella tried that she'd look like a 12-year-old boy, but Liv looked like a green-eyed Joey King.

Owen had the same eyes and the same over-long dark eyelashes. His shoulders were a little broader and Liv was slightly curvier, but if someone told you they were twins you wouldn't have thought to question it.

Owen was actually older by 17 months. He should

have been in college already, except that he'd been held back in the second grade. He and Liv had been in the same class ever since. And because Liv was Ella's best friend, Owen ended up being her second-best friend by proxy.

She sometimes wondered if Jack were alive today, would he and Ella be as close as Owen and Liv were? When she was little she thought they would be, but now she knew better. Jack would be twenty-seven by now. He might even have kids and stuff. How weird would that be, to be an aunt? She imagined the art projects she could do with Jack's imaginary children.

"El, you awake back there?" Liv said.

Ella blinked. They were pulling into the school parking lot. It was the same rambling old maroon and brick monstrosity that Jack had attended 11 years ago. But that was about to change too. Hers would be the last class to graduate here. The town had built a brand new building up the street that would house both the high school and middle school students. It made her sad to think that this building would just be torn down, discarded, a useless shell.

"Yeah, I'm awake."

Owen turned around and proffered his travel mug. "Need some coffee?"

"I don't drink coffee."

"Weirdo."

"Spaz."

"Oh my god, you two," Liv said. "Is this senior year or

second grade?"

Ella stuck her tongue out at Liv. Owen, still twisted in his seat, saw it and laughed. Liv didn't see it, so she glared at Owen like he was the one being immature. She got out of the car and straightened her black vest. Trust Liv to actually dress up on the first day of school. Well, dress up might be stretching it a little. But she looked a hell of a lot more put together than Ella did. She was wearing a soft green tee shirt and long bronze necklace under the vest. Her jeans were clean and dark. She carried an oversized shoulder bag instead of a backpack.

Ella scrambled out of the car. Owen didn't hold the door for her this time. He was busy juggling his phone, coffee, and the cheesy Ninja Turtles backpack he'd picked up at Goodwill the last time they'd all gone together. How he fit any books into that tiny thing was beyond her. It looked like it was made for a preschooler to carry his juice box.

Grabbing her own backpack, Ella rushed to catch up with Liv who was already walking toward the school.

"I wish it was second grade," Ella said when she reached Liv's side. "I'd take addition over Algebra II any day."

"You liked geometry."

Ella shrugged her backpack higher on her shoulder. "Geometry is just shapes. That's not real math."

"You're better at math than you give yourself credit for," Liv said.

"Sure."

Liv, of course, loved math, and physics, and basically everything else that required hours of study time. So she and Ella had exactly zero classes together. Ella and Owen both preferred art and their schedules often overlapped.

Ella watched a group of girls greet each other like long-lost friends, complete with squealing and hands thrown up in the air. She rolled her eyes. There was something to be said for being unpopular, at least you didn't have to act like everything was the most exciting thing that ever happened.

"Senior year, woot woot," Owen said, his tone flat.

Ella shuddered. "I should have just failed geometry so they would keep me back."

"And let us graduate without you?" Owen said. "Hard no."

Liv put her arm around Ella's shoulders. "Smile, you. It's going to be a great year. We're finally seniors."

Ella clenched her teeth in the cheesiest smile she could muster. Even Liv didn't really understand how badly she didn't want to be a senior. Everyone thought senior year was some big milestone. Something to get all excited about and throw parties over. But Ella couldn't stop thinking about how Jack had never made it to senior year. He'd never gone to those parties or worn one of those stupid square graduation caps. She felt like she'd spent her whole life walking along a trail he'd marked for her and the markers had suddenly disappeared. She was alone in the forest, but nobody knew it.

If only she could spend the rest of her life in the art

room, assembling sculptures until they filled the halls and spilled out into the driveway. People would buy tickets to see the Eleven Hundred and Ten Assemblages of Ella Elizabeth Pratt. She'd have to do something about that name though. Pratt didn't exactly roll off the tongue. Better to have something alliterative. Maybe Ella the Enigma? No, too cheesy.

"What's a good word that starts with E?" Ella asked as they passed through the front doors and into the familiar echoing hallway. The place was already a traffic jam.

"Ella," Owen said, immediately.

"Eclectic," Liv said. "Esoteric, euphoric."

"Ooh, esoteric is a good word," Ella said. "Doesn't that mean snobby though?"

"No, it means a thing that not many people can understand."

"That's perfect."

"Perfect for what?"

"Just thinking," Ella said. "Let's get to homeroom."

"Exceedingly excellent enigma," said Owen.

Liv rolled her eyes. "Embarrassing."

Ella led them into the crush of teenagers, smiling despite herself. Maybe this year wouldn't be all bad.

CHAPTER FIVE

Gate of Horn

PhiTau's new life was full of firsts. First number one: he had seen the Dream Lord with his own eyes. First number two: he had been chosen for something other than punishment. First number three: He had somewhere to be, somewhere that was not between two rows of dream plants. As he hurried through the fields of Dreaming he watched his fellow oneiroi bend and bob to rake in the harvest.

That life, which had so recently been his, now seemed as remote as the moons above. Had he really once bent and toiled like these poor creatures? Had his world been as small as that? How could that be when he was on the way, at this very moment, to a new life beyond his imagining?

Of course, oneiroi weren't known for their imaginations. The tall oneiroi, the one with the power to write, had tried to explain what would happen next, but it had all seemed far-fetched to PhiTau. All he really understood was that he would get to see what some of the dreamstuff he'd harvested over the years had turned into.

Now as he approached the Horn Gate, he worried that his legs might buckle beneath him. His face felt hot, his hands tingled. The combination of excitement and anxiety was almost too much to bear. This was another pair of firsts, twined together like plants—PhiTau's first day at his first new job. Oh, he supposed that sometime, hundreds of moon cycles ago, he must have had a first day as a harvester, but all that had been so long ago he couldn't even remember it. He might as well have been harvesting since before he was created. Perhaps he had been.

The Horn Gate loomed suddenly into view. It was tall enough that Morpheus could have walked through it without stooping, broad enough that he could walk back out again without crossing his own footsteps. It made PhiTau feel tiny. It was impressive. Not just the size, but the brassy shine, the complex curves, the strange vine-like tubes and overly symmetrical buds that grew in perfect lines. The whole structure gleamed in the moonlight.

He reached out to touch one of the circular buds. It was cool and smooth, more like a stone than a plant. PhiTau wondered what this gate was made of and why his ears detected the faintest wail of wind through the opening. He hadn't noticed any wind until now.

PhiTau paused a moment outside the gate. It was just a free-standing arch marking one section of field from the next. He could see no difference between this side and the other, but he felt as though passing through it would mark the beginning of a whole new life.

Finally, he stepped through . . .

. . . and found himself in a long low building with benches in rows all facing an open space in the front. He spun and looked behind him at the Horn Gate, which was now set into a wooden wall. He touched the wall. It felt real and solid under his hands. How could this be?

He thought about walking through the gate again, to test whether it would lead him back into the Dreaming or into another world all together. But he hesitated, his hand still on the wall. What if the gate somehow closed behind him and he was trapped in the boredom of his old life forever? He couldn't bear that. Not now, not when he was standing on the cusp of something new.

"PhiTau," said a voice behind him. "Good, you are here."

PhiTau spun again. In his initial shock, he hadn't even noticed he was not alone. Nearly a dozen oneiroi sat on the long benches nearest the front of the room.

The voice belonged to a small oneiroi with a broad face. He was even less bent than the writer, although he was shorter, and walked with a confidence that PhiTau had rarely seen in another oneiroi. And unlike other oneiroi, he wore a garment. A belt with a sort of pouch that hung at his hip.

"I am AlphaBeta and I will be your instructor. If you would take a seat, we will begin."

PhiTau, hearts pounding, dropped onto the nearest bench and waited for the lesson to start. He'd never been in a place where the sky was so low and held up by visible supports. He wondered where the material to build it had come from. Was this what dreamstuff turned into? Or was it another plant altogether?

AlphaBeta made his way to the front of the room. PhiTau watched his eyes roam over the small group of oneiroi in their seats. PhiTau had no idea what he was thinking. Was he pleased with this group or disappointed?

"You have been chosen for a very important role," AlphaBeta said, clasping his hands behind his back. "There are roughly seven point five billion humans on the earth. Each of these people spends one third of their life asleep. And nearly all of that time is spent dreaming."

He began to pace. The group listened, rapt. "Not in the Dreaming, where you have lived and worked, but in the wild border country where the human mind and the Dreaming overlap."

PhiTau leaned forward, enraptured. AlphaBeta went on, oblivious or perhaps simply accustomed to the effect his words were having on the gathered oneiroi. "Humans need dreams. It is our role and our responsibility to see that they get what they need."

Here he drew a handful of glittering flakes from the pouch at his waist. The shimmer fell from one of his hands to the other as he talked. "But dreams are delicate things, easily dissolved by the human world. A tender is required to hold the dream together. This is your new purpose."

PhiTau shuddered. He never could have imagined this, not in a thousand moon cycles. He, PhiTau, former harvester and long-suffering servant, would finally glimpse another world, or at least the edge of one.

One of the oneiori raised his hand. "How?" he asked.

"That is what you are here to learn," AlphaBeta said.

He plucked a pinch of the glittering stuff from the palm of his hand and threw it to the floor. Something exploded upward, something PhiTau had never seen before, a group of elongated creatures flapping their flat, stubby arms. They rose toward the top of the room and went through the roof without leaving a mark.

"Those were flying fish," AlphaBeta said. "And they are just one of the billion forms that dreams can take."

PhiTau leaned forward in his seat. Curiosity blazed so hot it made him feel like his limbs were on fire. He wanted to know every shape of the dream.

"We will start with something familiar," AlphaBeta said, "the lifecycle of a dream plant."

PhiTau relaxed. He knew this. It was basic history. In the time before the first moonrise, Lord Morpheus planted the endless fields of Dream. Then he made the first oneiroi to bring in the harvest. The oneiori spent their lives harvesting the dreamstuff, loading it into carts to be sent to Lord Morpheus' workshop where he processed it into dreams. How exactly that happened had never been clear.

AlphaBeta reached his hand into the bag and drew it

out again. "This is the result of his labors. Processed dreamstuff. Think of it as the seeds of a dream."

Turning to the oneiroi closest to him, AlphaBeta said, "Hold out your hands."

When the student obliged, AlphaBeta rewarded him with a handful of dreamstuff. "Look closely," he said, "and see what you can see."

Then he walked around the room, depositing dreamstuff into each upturned hand. PhiTau was surprised to find that unlike the cloudy wisps he'd harvested for most of his life, the processed dreamstuff was hard and formed into shapes. Squares with rectangular holes. Tiny figures with the same general outline as Lord Morpheus. Things that looked like plants, and other complex shapes for which he had no names. Each in a form so tiny that the details were hard to discern. He stirred the little pile with his fingertip. What could this dust become?

CHAPTER SIX

Suggestions for Emulation

By a heroic act of will, Ella managed to keep herself awake through first period Algebra II. Whoever thought that 8 a.m. was an awesome time for math class should be nailed to a plinth by their ear. This did not bode well for the rest of the semester.

Fortunately, the next class was art—the one class that made coming to school worthwhile. Ella strolled into the art room and immediately felt herself relax. The familiar aroma of paint and turpentine and drying clay seeped out of the walls, almost entirely masking the musty musk of too many teenagers in too small a space that permeated the rest of the school. Rainbows shimmered against the ceiling from prisms set high in the windows to catch the sun. Under the sound of students finding their seats, she could hear the soft guitar music that Ms. Beaudry, the art teacher, often left playing in the background.

Most importantly, Ms. Beaudry herself stood in the

center of the room, wearing her paint-streaked artist smock, black jeans, and orange croc shoes. A wide cloth headband in guacamole green held her short curls back from her forehead. Hands in her pockets, she rocked on the balls of her feet and smiled at the students streaming into the room.

Ella grabbed her favorite seat, right under the window where the light fell sideways across the desk in the afternoon. A girl with bright pink hair and a nose ring sat next to her. Ella couldn't remember her name, probably because she'd never heard the girl actually speak. She did recall that miss bubblegum drew mostly in an anime style. Sure enough, she immediately bent her head over a drawing of a big-eyed girl in a short skirt. The pink hair fell down to hide her face.

Ella nodded to Owen, who had claimed his own favorite seat, directly across the room in the corner closest to the supply shelves. Owen worked in mostly 2-D art but liked a range of media—paint, ink, pencil, crayon. He would draw with pretty much anything. Being close to the supply shelves saved him valuable seconds of walking across the classroom, at least that's what he claimed.

Ms. Beaudry greeted them with a cheerful "Goooood morning artists." She raised her chubby hands and clasped them together. Somehow she already had a smudge of blue paint on her arm. Ella wondered if she'd been painting before everyone got there. What kind of art did Ms. Beaudry make in her spare time? She always had example pieces for the class, but it had never occurred to

Ella to wonder what she made for herself. Bright blobby animals on abstract fields of color probably. Or complex mandalas that took Zen-like patience.

"I am so pleased you've all chosen to share your senior year with me."

It would have sounded ironic coming from anyone else, but Ms. Beaudry had this way of making you feel like you were just as legitimate as any artist with a Soho gallery show. It was something about the way she listened intently when you talked and looked carefully at what you made. If all her teachers were like this, Ella might have managed more than a barely B average.

"This semester is going to be a little different," Ms. Beaudry said. "Since you're all seniors, I'm going to consider this your capstone. I've introduced you to all different kinds of art styles and a range of art history topics over the last three years, now I want to see how you put them to use in your own work."

This was the kind of class Ella could get excited about. She was going to be allowed to just make art. That was practically the whole point of living as far as she was concerned.

"Now, we will still have to cover a bit of theory so I have something to quiz you on." Groans echoed around the room. Ms. Beaudry raised both hands to hush them. "But all of the creation time will be yours to use as you see fit. All I ask is that you create one project or collection that you're truly proud of by the end of the semester."

Ella's mind was already in overdrive. She had a pile of

sketches at home with ideas she'd love to build, but just hadn't had the time or materials. Maybe this assignment would convince Mom to kick in some extra money for art supplies. It wasn't like she needed dozens of fine canvases or anything. Even twenty or thirty dollars could go a long way toward assembling something truly awesome.

"And, I want to encourage each and every one of you to start thinking about a piece to submit to the Maine Regional Scholastic Art Awards."

Ella knew all about those. She'd entered last year, and the year before that, and the year before that. Any work that made it into the regional exhibition automatically got entered into the Congressional Competition with the possibility of being shown in Washington, D.C.

Despite her serial submissions, she hadn't gotten so much as an honorable mention. Not even last year when she'd assembled a 1/100 scale model of the Statue of Liberty out of the prize toys she'd collected from years of kid's meals at fast-food restaurants. She'd spent hours and hours on it. Yet some watercolor of a dog wearing a tutu had won a prize. The day they'd announced the news she'd spent the whole evening dismantling her sculpture for parts.

But this year would be different. She was going to do something completely original. Something that would stagger the judges. She had to win this time. Or at least place. Ella knew her stuff was good. At least, she was pretty sure. Most days.

The rest of the class was mostly talky-talk. That was the problem with the first day of school. Every teacher wanted to tell you all about their agenda for the year as though you were actually going to remember it. Even Ms. Beaudry couldn't seem to repress that impulse. At least it gave Ella plenty of time to daydream about her masterwork.

As they left the art room, Owen asked, "So, what are you going to make for the contest this year?"

Ella had plenty of ideas, but none of them felt like something worthy of a Congressional award.

"I don't know yet, maybe something with an environmental message, you know, like the Washed Ashore project? But I don't know, that might be too derivative."

Owen nodded. They'd had several conversations about those sculptures, which were made out of trash pulled from the ocean. The point was to remind people that the stuff they threw away didn't just disappear. That was Ella's point too, more or less. Except she also wanted people to think about maybe not throwing that stuff away at all. Like, just because something was broken or old or worn didn't mean it was useless. She'd have to work on her artist statement.

"It is an important message," Owen said.

Ella noticed that he didn't say anything about whether it was derivative, which probably meant that he thought it was.

"But I want to win this year," Ella said. "Or at least

place."

"Place that right back in the dumpster," said a voice from behind them. She hadn't spoken loudly but Kristen Lund's voice had the kind of nasal whine that tended to carry. Ella would have recognized it anywhere. She started to turn, intending to tell Kristen exactly where she could shove her opinion. But Owen caught her sleeve.

"Don't give her the satisfaction," he muttered under his breath.

Kristen brushed past them. Which is to say, she brushed past Owen. Even though there was plenty of space for her to just walk by like a normal person, she made sure to lean toward him so her hair swept across his upper arm as she passed. Owen shuddered. Ella rolled her eyes. They both kept quiet until Kristen was out of earshot.

"Ugh," Owen said. "I think she has a crush on me."

"Uh, really, you think so? Only since like fifth grade."

Owen made a face like he smelled something foul. "But she's so mean," he said, as if no mean girl had ever looked lustily at a boy, "and what is her deal with you?"

Ella shook her head. "Don't know, don't care. Some people think it's not real art unless there's an urn in it somewhere."

"What is your obsession with urns?"

"Or a plinth," Ella added, trying to keep the conversation moving. It did bother her that Kristen thought her work was literally trash and not just made out of it. Anytime anyone disliked her art it triggered an inner monologue that went something like this: *She doesn't like my work. Of course she doesn't. Why should she. It's trash, literally trash. What do you expect when you make art from junk?*

"You should make an urn out of empty paint tubes and put it on a plinth made out of canvases and call it 'Shut up Kristen,'" Owen said.

It's not even like you're actually an artist. You barely know how to draw. Kristen Lund could draw better in the fourth grade than you can now.

"How exactly would I make a plinth out of canvases? Last time I checked, plinths were solid."

"I don't know, you're the sculptor. I just draw and paint stuff."

And painting, we won't even talk about painting. No. You're basically just a kid playing with toys and you know it. At least kids grow out of it eventually. What are you going to do? Go to New York and get discovered? Please. You've never been further south than Portland in your whole life.

Ella tried to ignore the internal spiral while her mouth spouted silly observations. It almost worked. Shifting her focus would have been a lot easier if Owen would have just let it go.

"Then you take a photograph of it and you set the actual sculpture on fire . . ."

"Now I'm Baldessari?"

". . . and put the photo in a museum. You call it, 'Seriously, Kristen, Shut up.'"

Owen chattered away while they walked to the cafeteria, got their food, and found seats next to Liv. Ella thought he might be over caffeinated, or possibly under caffeinated. Either way, he didn't have the exact right amount of caffeine. And it showed.

He told the whole story to Liv, complete with an impersonation of Kristen that was basically just a high-pitched whine.

Liv licked pudding off her spoon. "She's jealous of Ella."

"She should be. Ella's great," Owen said.

"Ass-kisser," Ella muttered.

"No," Liv said. "I mean, yes, obviously Ella is awesome, but she's jealous that you and Ella spend so much time together."

"What?" said Ella.

"Why?" said Owen.

Liv wiggled the spoon back and forth between them. "She thinks you guys are a thing."

Ella dropped the French fry she'd been holding. It splatted into her ketchup. "Eww," she said.

Owen gave her a rumple-eyed look. "Hurtful."

Ella punched his shoulder. "You know what I mean. You're practically my brother."

She'd always thought of Owen like a brother. When they were little, she used to imagine that Jack hadn't died in a car accident when she was six, but had instead, done some kind of magic spell to transform himself into someone closer to her own age so they could grow up together. In this fantasy, Owen actually was her brother, he just looked different so no one would be freaked out.

Obviously, she didn't actually believe that, but she'd held on to the fantasy way longer than was probably healthy. The idea of dating Owen, holding hands, kissing. It was unthinkable.

"Yeah, well, while you two fantasize about becoming the next Picasso, one of us is actually paying attention to what goes on around here, and the rumor is that the reason Ella refuses to date anyone is because she's secretly in love with you."

"Yeah, no," Ella said.

"Understandable. I'm very charming." Owen grinned. "Not to mention handsome."

"You have something in your teeth there, stud muffin," Liv said.

"What exactly is a stud muffin?" Ella asked, happy to shift the conversation away from awkward rumors and her lack of a love life. Which she didn't even want anyway. She generally found guys kind of icky. "Anytime someone says that I picture a bedazzled breakfast pastry."

"Oooh, Ella, you should make one of those," Owen said.

"You could use a Cupcake Surprise doll instead of a muffin," Liv added. "That would be more on brand."

"A what?" Owen asked.

Liv rolled her eyes. "Ask the internet."

Ella wondered if real artists got as many unsolicited suggestions as she did. Did people walk up to Andy

Warhol and say, "Dude, loved your soup can thing. You should totally do that again, but you know, with dish soap and maybe like, add a cool filter?" Or "Hey Vinny, the ear cutting was pretty impressive. Maybe you should do a toe next." She thought not.

Ella became aware of a hand waving in front of her eyes. "Hey, El, you in there?" Liv asked.

"Sorry. I wasn't listening."

"I noticed. I was just saying I've got to go."

Ella looked at the big clock bolted to the wall above the soda machines. "We still have five minutes."

"I want to get to Calculus early. I have questions for Mr. Grishom."

"It's the first day!" Ella said.

"The early bird gets the tomato," Liv said.

"It really doesn't," said Owen.

Liv grabbed the apple off her tray and shoved it in her mouth. Holding it between her teeth, she picked up Owen's tray with one hand.

"Hey!"

Then slid hers underneath with the other. She took the apple out of her mouth. "Thanks, brother."

Ella watched her walk away. "Your sister is weird," she said.

"They both are," said Owen. Which made Ella look down at her tray so he couldn't see how wide she was smiling.

CHAPTER SEVEN

Rules of Reverie

PhiTau stood in a small field with the other tenders in training. This was the first time they'd left the classroom since their training had begun. PhiTau looked around with interest. He'd never seen a field like this before. There were no rows or furrows, just a wild gathering of unkempt greenery, each stem no thicker than the leaves of a dream plant. They grew straight out of the ground and reached the level of PhiTau's knees. AlphaBeta had told them it was called grass. That was just one of the many new words PhiTau had learned in the course of his studies. He'd also learned the word fence, which was what surrounded the grass at about knee height.

The fence forced the trainee tenders to stand close together in their loose semicircle around AlphaBeta, as AlphaBeta reached into the pouch on his hip and drew out a handful of glittering dreamstuff.

This was nothing new, PhiTau had seen it many times

before, but he still marveled at the beauty of it. Processed dreamstuff seemed to consume light and return it a hundred fold. Look at it too closely and your eyes would dazzle.

"Today, we will visit a dream in the mind of a human named Edward Wells." AlphaBeta looked around at the semicircle of students. "Who can tell me how we cross into a human mind?"

UpsilonChi's hand shot up. PhiTau wasn't surprised. UpsilonChi was always the first to volunteer. If someone had said, "Who wants to be slapped?" UpsilonChi's hand would be in the air before they finished the question.

AlphaBeta ignored the eager hand. "How about PhiTau?"

PhiTau's toes cracked in embarrassment. "I'm sorry, what?"

"Please tell us how you would cross into a human mind."

"You um . . . I mean, I would take a pinch of the dreamstuff from that bag there and then sprinkle it on the ground in a circle." He mimed the action as he talked, then realized he probably looked like an idiot and clasped his hands behind his back.

AlphaBeta was nodding, so PhiTau continued. "And then you just step into it."

"Oo, you have to wait until the grass turns dark," UpsilonChi added.

"Correct, PhiTau," said AlphaBeta, ignoring UpsilonChi's interruption even though it was right. You had to wait for the ground to turn dark because that meant your dreamer was asleep. PhiTau had a sneaking suspicion that their instructor found UpsilonChi as annoying as he did.

At their feet, the ground went dark, as though the moons cast a shadow on the grass. AlphaBeta sprinkled the dreamstuff in a rough circle. "Now," he said, "I will step into the circle and you will follow in an orderly fashion. When we are in the dream, I expect you to be on your best behavior. Remember, this is someone's mind and you will treat it with respect."

He turned, and disappeared. There was a soft chattering from the group. PhiTau and his classmates had heard this procedure described, but they'd never seen it done. Of course UpsilonChi was the first to follow. A few others went along after him. Soon it was only PhiTau and a quiet oneiroi named SigmaSigma.

SigmaSigma turned to look at PhiTau. "Are you afraid?" He asked in a gentle voice that said he wouldn't blame PhiTau if he was.

That softness gave PhiTau the courage to tell the truth. "No, not at all. It's just . . . this is so new, but when I've done it a hundred times, a thousand times, it will be no different than the bend and pick. It will be normal. I just want to make sure I remember this first time forever, because I'll never do this for the first time ever again."

SigmaSigma smiled and nodded like he understood. PhiTau stepped into the circle . . .

. . . and found another world.

A writer of pictures had come to class to show them drawings of some of the common items they might encounter in a human dream. Those illustrations had not prepared PhiTau for the noise, or the color. In the Dreaming most things were brown, white, or black. The sky was purple, of course, and Morpheus wore blue, but almost everything else was drab.

Not here. Here everything was colorful. Frilly pink fabrics hung around what PhiTau suspected were windows. Tiny pictures of flowers adorned the walls. Even the floor was soft and blue. A blue floor. Incredible.

But the most amazing things of all, were the people. They had talked about humans in class. How they walked upright and came in many different colors. How they wrapped themselves in woven plants and sometimes in the skins of other animals, which had made PhiTau's stomach turn. How they tended to travel in groups, especially in their dreams. But PhiTau had never seen a real human before.

Yet here he was, surrounded by them. Dozens of them clustered around the room. Most were chattering and talking. It took him a moment to realize that the few silent staring ones were his classmates, altered to fit the dream. PhiTau looked down at his own hands. They were hairless and short-fingered. He touched his arms and chest, which were wrapped in some soft material. He hoped it wasn't the skin of some animal.

A tiny human, one-quarter size at best, bounced against PhiTau's leg. PhiTau shied away, but the tiny human didn't notice. This was the dreamer. PhiTau knew it. He didn't know how he knew it, but it was somehow perfectly obvious. The dreamer appeared ineffably more real than the dreamworld around it.

The tiny human had liquid leaking from his eyes. PhiTau tried to remember the word. Tears. They were called tears.

"Mommy?" the tiny human said.

He bounced against another pair of legs, "Have you seen my mommy?"

None of the dream people took any notice of the tiny human as he staggered around the room. PhiTau felt sorry for him. How lonely must a human be before it was forgotten even in its own dreams?

One of the dream people raised its hand in a familiar way, and PhiTau realized it was AlphaBeta in a human shape. He wore reflective circles over his eyes and the pattern on his shirt was difficult to look at. There were too many colors. Guiltily, PhiTau realized he probably should have been paying closer attention to AlphaBeta instead of letting himself be distracted by the trappings of the dream. Had he missed some important part of the lesson?

"We must be going now," AlphaBeta said to no one in particular. He went to the door and opened it. UpsilonChi walked through first, followed by the rest of the group. PhiTau hung back, wanting to take in every detail—the horizontal surfaces covered in tiny models of humans and other creatures, the glittering lamp that hung from the ceiling, dripping shards of what looked like processed dreamstuff. The colors. There were so many colors. He wanted to burn it deep into his memory.

But AlphaBeta was staring at him. He was the last student in the dream. PhiTau walked through the door, and found himself standing with his classmates in the empty field. The dark green grass and purple sky looked bland against the memory of the dream. PhiTau closed his eyes and saw the glittering pinks and blues again. He would treasure that memory forever.

AlphaBeta appeared beside them, adjusting the pouch at his waist. PhiTau thought his face looked oddly naked without the glass circles in front of his eyes. Something about them had suited him.

"That's enough for now," AlphaBeta said. "Dreams are intense experiences. You may feel some slight dizziness or even a sense of euphoria. These should pass momentarily if you breathe deeply."

PhiTau looked around and realized for the first time that some of his classmates seemed to have taken the transition badly. A few of them had a bluish tinge to their lips. SigmaSigma was blinking rapidly. PhiTau sidled up beside him.

"Are you okay?"

"Yes. I'm sure I'll get used to it eventually. Did you see all of those colors?"

"Yes! It was amazing."

SigmaSigma looked at him like he'd just called the Lord bowlegged. "Did you actually enjoy that?" SigmaSigma asked.

"Of course. Didn't you?"

SigmaSigma shook his head and shifted his stance so he was facing slightly away from PhiTau. PhiTau frowned in confusion. What was wrong with everyone? That was the single most exhilarating thing that had ever happened to him, including looking Lord Morpheus in the eye, and everyone was acting like they'd just found a field of rotting dream plants.

"Who spotted the dreamer?" AlphaBeta asked.

"The tiny human," PhiTau said.

"Very good, PhiTau."

"I knew that," UpsilonChi muttered. He kept talking, clearly uncomfortable with someone else getting all the attention. Or any attention. "When we left the dream must have collapsed. Right?"

"Indeed it did," AlphaBeta said. He began walking across the field. The others, mostly recovered, straggled along behind him.

"Won't the human notice? Aren't they supposed to spend a long time dreaming?"

"This particular human has a condition known as dementia. That means he spends large portions of his life on the border of the Dreaming. He will not notice that he has slipped out of the dream."

"He gets to spend all of his time there?" PhiTau said. "That must be wonderful."

AlphaBeta shook his head. "The humans do not think so. Most believe that dreams are meaningless concoctions of the human brain. Spending too much time in dreams is considered a handicap, not a reward."

"But dreams are wonderful!" PhiTau said.

UpsilonChi whispered something in the ear of the oneiroi next to him. The other oneiroi laughed quietly. PhiTau saw this, and drew his wings closer against his back.

AlphaBeta looked over his shoulder at PhiTau. "Do you think so?"

"Don't you?"

"They are certainly more interesting than the harvest," AlphaBeta said.

PhiTau didn't think that was fair. The dirt under his toenails was more interesting than the harvest.

CHAPTER EIGHT

Found Object

Ella was exhausted by the time she got home from school. Maybe it was because she hadn't slept well. Maybe senior year was just going to suck. Who could know? In the car on the way home, Owen had been a bouncing ball of cheer. He'd even managed to draw Liv into a conversation, *while she was driving!* If this kept up, Ella was going to have to start riding her bike to school at least until the first snowfall.

Mom wasn't home yet. She didn't get home from work until around 4:30. Ella intended to grab a glass of water and a bowl of grapes and then lie on the couch watching YouTube videos on her phone until then. It was Wednesday, and @Trash_Art always posted a new video on Wednesday. He'd been promising a glimpse at his work in progress, which Ella was eager to see.

She dropped her backpack by the door and went to the sink. While she waited for the water to get really cold the way only well water pulled from deep below the earth could, she just happened to glance out the window at the backyard.

Normally that view would include a strip of green grass, a garden shed, and the tree line. A squirrel would not have been unusual, or even a blue jay. The hole big enough to bury someone in was new though.

Ella remembered that the contractor was supposed to start work on the septic tank sometime soon. That presumably involved some digging, so the hole didn't bother her much. It was, if not what she had expected to see, at least what made sense to see after she'd thought about it. Just a hole in the ground in her backyard, nothing to worry about. So why did it make her sad? A hole in the ground shouldn't make you feel anything. Especially if you weren't the one who had to fill it up again.

She stuck a glass under the stream of now frigid water from the tap. She was about to look away, down at her glass to monitor water levels, when something caught her eye. It was a bit of bright red in that pile of brown dirt. Ella saw it, and even though she couldn't possibly see details at this distance she knew what it was. She knew instantly. And at the same time, she knew why the hole had made her sad.

When she was six years old, just a few weeks after Jack died, she'd accidently knocked his old action figure off the shelf. He'd had it for years before handing it off to her, and the plastic must not have aged well, because the helmeted head had popped right off the broad armored shoulders. She vividly remembered the sight of his bright red and yellow plastic body decapitated on her bedroom rug. Six-year-old Ella had decided he was dead, and she'd done what you were supposed to do with dead things, she'd held a funeral and buried him. It had made perfect sense to her at the time.

Her fingers were freezing. She looked down and realized that water was overflowing the glass, pouring over her fingers and back down into the sink to disappear down the drain. Ella set the glass down gently on the counter to the right of the sink.

She reached out, feeling as numb as her fingers, and turned off the faucet. She felt like she was underwater. The water had overflowed not just her glass, but the sink, and the kitchen and the whole house, immersing her and everything she knew in chilly isolation. She couldn't hear anything except her heart pounding in her ears, and that too sounded submerged.

Ella waded through the kitchen and her memories, toward the back door. Opening it, she half-expected a wave to wash her out into the yard and right into the hole the contractors had left. But there was no wave, because there was no water. The air was dry, with that slight underbite of coolness that meant the leaves would start to change soon. Still, the yard seemed oddly silent as she walked across the grass toward the open hole and the pile of dirt.

She stopped beside the pile. She had been certain, when she caught the glimpse of red from the kitchen window, that she was seeing Maximus Tron exhumed after eleven years of peaceful slumber. Up close, she wondered how she possibly could have known. The visible bit of plastic was smaller than a postage stamp. Irregularly shaped and smeared with dirt, it could have been anything, but she had known, known that it was Maximus Tron back from the dead.

Now, she reached out to brush the dirt away, and revealed a red and yellow plastic arm about three inches long with a clenched fist at the end. Anger flared and burned away her numbness. They had come in, without so much as asking, and just dug up her yard, disrupted her space, uncovered her past, and then just left the work half-done.

She clawed at the dirt. It was cool and slightly damp beneath her hands. The smell brought the scene back to her clearly, digging the hole with her mother's garden trowel. She'd known at the time that graves were supposed to be six feet deep, but she didn't know how deep that was. She'd just dug and dug until she was tired, and these, these, assholes, had come along and just scooped up all her work like it didn't matter.

She reached toward the toy, "Mint condition in the box," she practically heard Jack's voice echo in her mind. "Shit condition in the ground," she answered. She plucked the toy from the dirt, then hugged the dirty plastic against her chest and went inside.

When Mom came home half an hour later, Ella was back in the kitchen.

"Ella, what in God's name?" Mom asked. "We just bought that shirt."

Ella looked down at herself. She was streaked with dirt in various shades of brown and gray. A half-circle of rustlike red had appeared just under her left breast, or where her left breast would have been if she wasn't as flat chested as a 12-year-old boy. It was the shirt her mother had insisted on buying her at the mall and then insisted she wear on the first day of school because it was "cheerful".

Ella shrugged. "It'll wash."

"That's not the point," her mother said. "And look at the floor."

Ella looked. She'd tracked dirt from the front door across the dining room and into the kitchen.

"What have you been doing?"

"When will they be done digging up the backyard?"

Mom's eyebrows jumped. "I thought they were starting next week."

"They started today." Ella levered her shoes off using the toes of the opposite foot. "Unless we have a serious mole problem."

Mom went into the kitchen and Ella went to put her shoes down by the front door. How had she gotten them so dirty?

Even from the next room, she could hear her mother's sigh. "They're digging in the wrong place."

"Seriously?"

"The septic tank is on the other side of the shed."

There was a pause. "Damn it."

Ella stopped halfway across the dining room. Had Mom noticed Maximus Tron in the sink? He should have been hidden by bubbles. And why would she care even if she did see him? Ella was always bringing home random toys and bits of plastic. An eleven inch, headless action figure in her dishpan wouldn't be a huge surprise. Unless she recognized Maximus Tron and remembered he'd originally belonged to Jack. Mom didn't like things that reminded her of Jack.

"What?" Ella called.

"It's too late to call them. I'll have to do it in the morning."

"It's only 4:30." She opened the hall closet in search of a broom.

Another sigh, this one more tired than frustrated. "Yes."

Ella started sweeping. The sooner she got all of this cleaned up, the fewer questions she'd have to answer. Mom came back through the dining room, a box of crackers in one hand and her cell phone pressed to her ear with the other.

As soon as she crossed into the living room, Ella leaned the broom against the wall and went into the kitchen. Maximus Tron was still submerged in the sink beneath a layer of suds. There was no way Mom had seen him. Ella quickly pulled him to the surface and patted him as dry as she could with a dish towel. He was still oozing water from somewhere so she bundled him in a second towel and peeked around the kitchen door.

Mom was still in the living room. Ella could hear her voice raised in annoyance. Either it wasn't too late to call and someone was getting an earful, or Mom was leaving the world's longest voicemail rant. Either way, now was Ella's chance to get Maximus Tron up to her room without a lot of questions. She darted through the dining room, around the corner, and up the stairs.

It took less than a minute to shoulder her bedroom door open, deposit the still dripping action figure on top of a box of random toy pieces in her closet, and slip back downstairs. By the time her mother was done on the phone Ella had swept up most of the dirt and gotten out the mop. With any luck, the whole thing would be forgotten within the hour.

CHAPTER NINE

Somnambulance

PhiTau and his classmates sat in four neat rows on the benches while AlphaBeta threw questions at them rapid-fire. He pointed one knurly finger at a random student.

"Why do humans need dreams?"

"To work through conflicts."

AlphaBeta's finger whipped toward another student. "And?"

"To practice living."

AlphaBeta nodded but he was already pointing at UpsilonChi. "What is your purpose?"

"To hold the dream together."

"Where must you never go?"

"Through the Ivory Gate."

The finger moved to PhiTau. "What must you never do?"

They'd drilled these questions hundreds of times since the start of their training, but even so, PhiTau stumbled over his answer. "Inter-interfere with the dream."

"Correct."

The students sat in tense silence until AlphaBeta's finger dropped. You never knew when he might add another question to the mix. One you'd never heard before, or asked in a slightly different way.

"You're ready."

PhiTau looked at SigmaSigma, who shrugged one shoulder as if to say, "I don't know what that means either."

AlphaBeta met the gaze of each student in turn. "Theory can only teach you so much about dreams. The only way to truly test what you have learned is to put it into practice. Today, you will get your new assignments."

PhiTau's hearts leapt. A dreamer of his very own. That meant he would be allowed to spend as much time as he wanted inside the human mind where there were lights and colors and everything was new.

SigmaSigma raised his hand. "Excuse me, AlphaBeta, but I don't think I am ready for this assignment."

"Nonsense. Your first few solo dreams can be overwhelming. Even frightening. But the best way to overcome your discomfort is to do the work in front of you. It will get easier with time."

"I was a good harvester," SigmaSigma said.

"And you will be a good tender, SigmaSigma. The Lord chose you for this role and the Lord does not make mistakes." He looked out over the group. "You were each chosen for this job by the Lord himself. You have completed your training and I have no doubt that you will do yourselves proud. When in doubt, you can always come to me with questions or concerns. I have taught hundreds of thousands of tenders before you and by now there is nothing I have not seen. Remember, you were chosen for a reason. Trust your instincts and your training. Both will serve you well."

AlphaBeta reached into the pouch at his waist. PhiTau wore a pouch like that himself, now, issued by AlphaBeta at an earlier class. It held his small store of dreamstuff, just like AlphaBeta's usually did. Except that this time, AlphaBeta drew out something new. It wasn't dreamstuff. It was too big, and dark. He walked among the rows, handing one object to each student. PhiTau examined his immediately. It was a black seed as long as his pinky finger, shiny and tapered at one end. He wondered what it would grow. He had never seen such seeds in the dreaming, nor in any of his lessons.

"What is the seed for?" UpsilonChi asked.

"Be patient and I will explain," AlphaBeta said. "But first, we must go outside."

He led them, not out the Horn Gate through which PhiTau had passed so long ago, marveling at its shining splendor, but instead out a wooden door set into the wall.

They emerged into an unplanted field divided into squares about three paces wide. Around each plot was a small fence that reached the level of PhiTau's knees. The fences were all different. Some were white and spiky. Others were formed from interlocking diamond shapes.

One seemed to made out of blades of grass woven tightly together. Each was divided from its neighbors by a walkway that crunched underfoot. It was made of small, hard chunks, none much bigger than PhiTau's thumbnail.

AlphaBeta gestured to the new gardens. "Each of you will be assigned a plot of land, and on that plot you will plant a seed. From this seed will grow a plant. Think of it as a record of the dreams you and your human share."

"How can a plant be a record?" someone muttered, but UpsilonChi spoke over him.

"There's one thing I don't understand."

"Just one, UpsilonChi?" AlphaBeta asked.

UpsilonChi was too eager to ask a question to notice that he was being teased. "Where are the other tenders? You told us there were seven-and-a-half billion humans alive in the world. Surely we can't guide all of their dreaming."

AlphaBeta chuckled. "No, surely you cannot. There are other tenders in other fields all around the perimeter of the Dreaming. Each one has its own garden to tend. For now, you must care for this one plant, but in time, others may be entrusted to you. Does that answer your question, UpsilonChi?"

"It does, thank you."

"Very well. Now to your gardens. Your dreamers will be needing you anytime now."

He showed each of them to a plot of land. PhiTau's plot was surrounded by shards of color, haphazardly placed, as though someone had walked around the perimeter and thrust a collection of random objects directly into the ground. They hardly seemed like a fence at all. They certainly formed no real barrier against even the tiniest of intruders.

SigmaSimga's plot was right beside his, neatly encircled by black fence posts, all uniformly spaced. They each stepped over their fences and into their gardens. PhiTau felt a lump rise in his throat. Never in his life had he had a place of his very own, and now he did, and it was here. Tight against his belly he pressed the fist that enclosed the seed.

SigmaSigma raised his hand. "How will we know what to do?" he called out.

AlphaBeta smiled and walked back down the row of gardens toward them. The walkway crunched with every step. "You will know. You were made for this."

"I was made to be a harvester," SigmaSigma muttered under his breath, but so quietly that AlphaBeta almost certainly couldn't hear him over the sound of his own footsteps.

After AlphaBeta had gone, PhiTau knelt in the soft soil. He picked a spot right in the middle, where the plant would have plenty of room to grow. With curved fingers, he scooped a shallow hole just a bit deeper than the seed was thick. It was strange to think that with all his experience harvesting, he'd never once planted anything. PhiTau pressed the seed into the hole. Then he paused, trying to imprint the image in his memory. This was the most precious thing he'd ever held, and he was burying it in the ground. Gently, he smoothed dirt over the seed until it disappeared from view. Then he sat back on his heels, brushing away the dirt that had caught in the fur on the backs of his hands.

He waited. Nothing happened. He waited a bit more. Still nothing. A swell of panic rose in his throat. Maybe he'd done it wrong. He looked over at SigmaSigma's plot to find the other oneiroi watching him.

"Nothing's happening," SigmaSigma said. "How long does it take plants to grow?"

"I don't know. All the plants I've seen were already grown," PhiTau said.

"AlphaBeta could have told us what to do," SigmaSigma said. "He could have given us some sort of directions. When I was a harvester, I always knew my next task. Bend and pick, bend and pick. Easy."

"Boring," PhiTau muttered, hardly realizing he'd said it out loud.

"Yes! Boring, predictable, simple. My life was simple," SigmaSigma said. "Now it's this." He swept one arm in an all-encompassing gesture that nearly toppled him.

PhiTau looked down at his own little patch of dirt. Still no plant. He stood up so he could look around at the other gardens. All of the other tenders were on their knees in the dirt. No one had figured out how to make their plants grow.

Someone crunched toward them on the path. They heard him before they could see him.

"Do you think it's a test?" UpsilonChi asked.

SigmaSigma shrugged.

PhiTau smoothed the fur on his arms, teasing it straight. He didn't think it was a test. Maybe AlphaBeta just wanted to see if they could figure it out on their own. The idea excited him. He'd never really had to figure anything out before.

Since no one had really answered him, UpsilonChi kept talking. Of course, he probably would have kept talking either way. "Should we go find AlphaBeta? He said we could come to him if we had any problems."

"No," PhiTau said. He hadn't meant to say it so firmly. The other two stared at him. "I mean, not yet."

He tried to ignore them and think about the problem. It was possible that seeds grew very slowly and they simply had to wait, but AlphaBeta had said that their dreamers would be needing them anytime now. That didn't sound like something you had to wait for. What did plants need to grow? He wasn't sure. But he didn't think AlphaBeta would have left them here unless they had what they needed.

He reached his hand into the pouch at his waist and drew out a pinch of the glittering dreamstuff.

"What are you doing?" UpsilonChi asked. "You can't enter the dream until the ground changes color. AlphaBeta told us a thousand times."

"I'm just trying something," said PhiTau. He sprinkled the dreamstuff on the dirt directly above the seed. The ground darkened. PhiTau smiled. He sprinkled a little more, just to be safe. Then he stepped into the circle and fell into the dream.

CHAPTER TEN

Atelier Appropriation

Ella half-expected Maximus Tron to have disappeared when she went up to her bedroom after dinner. She imagined kneeling on the carpet, reaching both hands into the closet, and pulling away the dirty clothes to find nothing but a small pile of dirt.

But no. Under the damp dirt-streaked dish towel she found Maximus Tron with brown dirt packed into the joints and crevasses of his armor. Ella ran her fingertips across his shoulders and felt the jagged place where his head had been. She hadn't found it in the dirt. But it must be out there somewhere, disembodied in the dark.

For a long moment she stared down at the action figure, remembering. Maximus Tron had been Jack's favorite toy when he was little. He'd told her that the day he'd called her in while he was cleaning his room. He'd handed the doll to five-and-a-half-year-old Ella and said, "Take care of him for me." Maximus Tron had been the last toy Jack had given her.

And then she'd broken and buried him. She blinked rapidly and stood up, Maximus Tron still in one hand. She carried him across the hall to her studio. It was in the room that had once been Jack's bedroom.

She set Maximus Tron on Jack's old desk next to the pile of random sketches she'd amassed in place of a sketchbook.

The action figure looked right at home in her studio. Anyone who came in would think he was part of an art project. Other kids drew or painted or worked clay, Ella made sculptures out of plastic toys.

She'd started when she was about 12, after Dad first moved out. Ella had been angry. Not angry at anyone in particular, but angry at the whole world and everything in it. Back then, she'd walked through life with the overwhelming feeling that her skin was made of fire and her thoughts were gasoline. She didn't need anything to fuel her rage, it propagated itself. Those were "perfectly normal emotions" Mom had said, though even at the time Ella hadn't known who she was trying to convince, herself or Dad.

Back then, Mom and Dad had argued about everything—where to put pictures of Jack in the house, whether Ella should carry Jack's old backpack, why Dad was drinking so much, and what to do about Ella's sudden fear of cars. Dad told Mom they all needed therapy. Mom told Dad they just needed time. Nobody asked Ella what she needed.

Then Mom and Dad sat her down and told her that Dad was moving out for a while.

"It's not your fault," Dad said.

"Sometimes people grow apart," Mom said.

"We love you very much," they both said. "Some things will change, but we want to keep your life as normal as possible."

And there was that word again, normal. Ella said nothing. The fire inside her flared so hot she knew that if she so much as opened her mouth she'd incinerate both of her parents, and the house, and maybe even the whole world.

She stood up, ignoring their attempts to explain, and went upstairs. Far away she heard her mother say, "Honey, we need to talk about this."

Dad said, "Let her go. She needs time to process."

Mom said, "You always think you know what . . ." which was the beginning of an argument, so Ella stopped listening.

She went to the one place where she knew no one would bother her—Jack's room. After Jack's accident Mom had closed the door and refused to open it again, no matter how much Dad had asked and argued and insisted she was being selfish and trying to forget her own son.

Ella, for her part, had often stood in the doorway and spoken into the empty room, telling Jack about her blue ribbon in the art fair, the mean thing Kristen had said, or the baby porcupine she'd found in the backyard. On those occasions, she'd never gone further than the doorway.

That day the doorway wasn't good enough. She opened the door softly, slipped inside, and closed it as gently as a breath. She couldn't slam or shout, she was trying to hold all the fire inside. It was like carrying an armful of dynamite through a match factory.

With the greatest care, she sat down on Jack's bed. Her hands sank into the green comforter. She looked around. Jack wasn't there. He hadn't heard any of her childhood confessions. He didn't even know that Mom and Dad refused to stop fighting.

Ella's angry gaze fell on Jack's mint condition action figures, standing in their dusty boxes on the bookshelf. Jack had once threatened to shave her head while she slept if she so much as touched them. But Jack wasn't there anymore. Jack was gone. Soon Dad would be gone. Ella stood up and walked toward the bookshelf.

She reached over her head for the action figure on the highest shelf. The box felt slippery and the plastic front shivered as she pulled it down between her sweaty hands. She peered through the cellophane window at the robot dinosaur trapped in his cardboard and plastic prison. He was anchored at the waist and throat with twist ties. Ella felt bad for him. Nobody to play with. Nobody to talk to. No one but her had so much as looked at him in almost six years. She imagined that she saw pleading in his little painted eyes.

Glancing back at the door, half-expecting Mom and Dad to burst in and ask her what the hell she was doing, she held the box under her arm and attempted to open the top, but a clear plastic sticker held it in place. Ella carefully slid her fingernail around the edge of the adhesive, probing for an imperfection. When she found it, she worked her nail underneath, peeling slowly so as not to tear the brightly colored artwork.

Except that, like every sticker everywhere, one tiny piece had an extra bit of adhesive that would rather destroy everything around it than let go when the time came. It clung to the slippery coating, tearing a miniscule gash right between the words "collectible" and "figurine."

Ella stared at the tiny imperfection she'd created. The box was ruined, which meant it wasn't mint condition anymore, which meant it was basically worthless. Trash. No more valuable or important than any dirty, broken toy forgotten in the bottom of the thrift store bin. She'd curled her fingers under the cover flap and pulled.

The whole top tore off, making a ripping sound punctuated with a pop as the sticker lost its grip. She reached inside, half expecting the smell of mint, and a little disappointed when only plastic and cardboard filled her nostrils.

Mint condition. Jack had said. Mint condition. Perfect. Not broken. Whole. Complete. Mint.

Ella snatched the action figure, still bound to his back-board, out of the box. She ripped the toy from its backing, leaving cardboard in tatters on the floor. When that was done, she set the dinosaur on the bookshelf and reached for another box.

She didn't notice she was crying until the taste of salt

trickled between her lips, and even then, she wasn't sure how long she'd been tasting it without noticing. Her face felt hot. She'd given herself a paper cut along the inner bend of her index finger. Blood oozed out of it. She pressed it to her lips to quench the flow and looked around at the destruction she had wrought.

Shards of cardboard boxes, torn apart at the seams, some ripped into pieces no bigger than a credit card. Random accessories strewn around her feet. One lodged in her sock when she tried to move. She plucked it free. It was a tiny plastic blaster. She placed it gently in Princess Leia's lap. The action figures were sitting neatly on the shelf at eye level. It might be her imagination. In fact, she was almost sure it was, but she thought they looked happier out here.

Nobody had ever questioned her about what happened that day, not even when she came downstairs with a trash bag full of torn cardboard and crackly cellophane. And nobody questioned her when she moved some of her art supplies into Jack's room a few days later.

It had been hers ever since, and she'd made it her own. Well, really, she'd filled the chinks in Jack's space with her own stuff. The action figures, now liberated, had been moved to the top shelf to make room for glass jars full of paintbrushes, and coffee cans filled with assorted doll arms, and little plastic bins full of Matchbox cars with one wheel or three wheels or none.

Watched over by those liberated toys, Ella had started turning discarded playthings into art. Making art out of trash wasn't a new idea. Artists like Leo Sewell and Elliott Hundley and even Tara Donovan had done it before her, and probably done it better. But Ella thought she might be the only one in the world who worked almost exclusively in toys.

Now she sat down in Jack's old chair at his old desk and sifted through a pile of sketches. She was looking for the drawing she'd done a few weeks ago when she and Liv had found a rotting duck carcass lying on the beach next to Dexter Lake.

Ella didn't believe in sketchbooks. Oh she had tried keeping them before. When you started doing art, well-meaning adults started buying you sketchbooks, but Ella always found them too restrictive. The pages were all the same size, texture, and dimensions. There were no weird folds or unidentified stains to work around. How was an artist supposed to create in such a sterile environment? Besides carrying a sketchbook was a pain. Better to keep a couple of pencils in her pockets and just draw on whatever was handy at the time.

Ella found the drawing she was looking for just as her phone buzzed. She unlocked the screen with her right hand, picking up a pencil with her left. It was Dad. Of course it was.

DAD: Hy El, skool tdy?

Ella rolled her eyes. Dad still typed like he had one of those antique cell phones with three letters to a button.

ELLA: Yes

DAD: Fn?

ELLA: Not really

The drawing of the dead duck wasn't nearly as interesting as she remembered. She squinted at it. Then crumpled it up and threw it in the general direction of the trash can. It missed, but that was okay, because there were plenty of other paper balls on the floor to keep it company. That was another advantage of not using sketchbooks; you didn't have to tear anything out. You could just throw it away if it wasn't working. Once, when Owen had been going through a paper mache phase, she'd given him piles of discarded sketches. He'd used them to create a two-foot tall tree and called it "Rebirth". Then he'd gotten bored with paper mache and moved on to pastels.

Her phone buzzed again. She looked down at it.

DAD: Comovr this weknd?

She sighed. It had been about two weeks since she'd been to Dad's apartment. She loved her dad, of course, but she didn't like where he lived. It always smelled like someone had been smoking something foul, and Dad was such a sad sack. But he didn't seem to know it. He was always just about to start a big job.

She glanced at Maximus Tron. Even without a head, he seemed to be looking right at her, as though waiting for her to answer her father.

ELLA: Yes

Then she queued up the Totorro *Come to Mexico* album on YouTube and got to work looking for the perfect sketch to inspire the piece that would win her the Congressional Art award. Or at least wipe the snarky smile off of Kristen Lund's stupid face.

CHAPTER ELEVEN

Exquisite Corpse

PhiTau had expected lights and colors. He'd been prepared for noise and voices. He thought there might be laughter, or even screams. But it was quiet in the dream. Dim and cool and hushed.

Awareness poured into his mind like a well-worn memory. He knew his role instinctively, as a dream plant knows to twist toward the moonlight. In the other dreams, AlphaBeta had been the tender and he'd just been an observer. Now, he was in charge.

At least, he was just as in charge as the dreamer. What he and his dreamer were about to do, what they were doing even as he settled into the dirt to wait, would be a collaborative act. A kind of conversation. She wouldn't know he was there, and yet, even half-buried like a seed in the ground, he could still see and hear and feel everything his new dreamer experienced.

She was here in the dream with him. Well, inside a

dream house across the yard. But she was in the same dreamspace at least. His new dreamer was a girl named Ella who had a dead brother who was both older and younger than her, and divorced parents who lived in different worlds, and a love of making trash into a different more organized kind of trash. He knew her as well as she knew herself, because he was both lying in the dirt outside, and tucked into the dreamspace in her mind. From both places at once, PhiTau watched and felt and tried not to let the sensation overwhelm him. He had a job to do.

The house is full of water from floor to ceiling. Ella can feel the weight of it pushing down on her. She holds her breath as she swims toward the kitchen door. A dish towel flutters in her wake. She reaches the door and grabs the handle. She knows that when she opens it, the water will rush down the steps and across the yard, but that's the only way to get outside. Someone is out there, waiting. Waiting for her.

PhiTau knew it was him outside, waiting, but also that Ella would not know that. She would see him in the form the dream had given him—a human form, well almost.

When she opens the door, she expects water to rush down the steps and across the yard. Instead it stays level with the doorframe, as though some sort of force field holds it in place. Ella blinks at her yard, turned dreamy and damp by the wall of water. She extends one hand into the empty air beyond.

Suddenly she is standing next to the pile of dirt left by

the septic tank workers, with no memory of how she got there. Ella looks down into the hole. Jack is lying there. She can only see his face and a bit of his hair. The rest is covered in dirt. As she watches, his eyes pop open. She should be afraid, but she isn't. Jack isn't scary. How could he be? He's her brother and she's missed him so long. PhiTau knew his lines. They flowed into his mind as though he'd magically learned to read and they were written on the insides of his eyelids. All he had to do was open his mouth and let them out.

"Ella Bella," Jack says. He smiles. "My legs fell asleep. Help me out."

Ella reaches down and grabs the first bit of him she can reach, an ear. She pulls him from the grave. Not all of him. Just his head.

She notices this with surprise but decides it would be rude to mention that most of him has gone missing. Anyway, it isn't gruesome. There's a divot at the base of his skull, and she can envision his neck popping into place just there, if only they could find the rest of him.

"Jack-Jack," Ella says, "I missed you so much."

PhiTau could feel her excitement, the sheer joy at seeing her brother's face again. Underneath that, a hint of confusion. She seemed to know that something wasn't quite right. PhiTau opened his mouth and let the next line out.

"You took so long to find me."

"I'm sorry." She looks down at his head, cradled in her arm like a baby doll. "Next time I'll be faster."

His head laughs. "Next time we play hide and seek, it's your turn to be it."

"It's hard to find you when you're so small," Ella says.

"You're the one who has grown," Jack answers.

"No, I haven't." Except even as she says it, she realizes she has. She's ten feet tall, all knees and elbows. The house, the yard, it all seems so small, too small. How will she ever fit back inside?

"Promise you won't go away again," she tells the head of her brother.

"I never left," he says.

Ella wakes in the dark. She has fallen asleep in Jack's room again. Her head is on the desk. The headless body of Maximus Tron lies just inches from her face. She picks up the action figure and looks at it by moonlight.

"You should have stayed buried," she whispers to the doll.

"You don't really mean that," it answers.

Ella stares at the plastic figure. She wonders how it can talk when it doesn't have a head. The house is filling up with water again. She can feel it lapping around her ankles. Why does that keep happening? It's like someone is afraid the house will burn down if it isn't flooded.

Ella stands up.

~

PhiTau flailed his arms and fell backward. None of the practice runs had been like this. It took him a moment to realize that the noise in his ears was SigmaSigma and UpsilonChi and a third tender drawn out of his garden by the noise.

They were all talking at once, asking what had happened. Where he'd gone. Why he'd fallen over. He began to roll onto his side, intending to get back to his feet. It was hard to remember where his feet were when his body and head had been separated for so long in the dream.

"Stop!"

PhiTau froze at the sound of all three tenders shouting at once.

"You'll squash it," SigmaSigma said. "Just roll to the left and then get up."

PhiTau did as he was told. His legs still seemed to know where they were even if he didn't. Sitting up, he looked to his right and saw a tiny green shoot protruding from the soil.

CHAPTER TWELVE

Pentimento

Ella and Owen were in the same English class. You had to take English all four years whether you liked it or not. Ella didn't. Once you got past A is for Apple, reading was a waste of time as far as she was concerned. YouTube had turned reading into antique technology. It was practically obsolete.

As for writing, that whole idea of pictures being worth a thousand words made writing equally unnecessary. It wasn't like she was going to grow up and write books for a living or something. But she'd ended up in English Composition because it was the only English class that fit with her schedule.

Mr. Hitchens had, of course, launched right into essay structure. Like they'd never heard that before.

"And conclude with a clear and lucid final paragraph that summarizes what came before without simply restating the premise."

He strode back and forth as he pontificated to the class. "Since I have hopes that at least a few of you will be attending college next year, your first assignment will be to write a college admissions essay."

Kent Chamberlain raised his hand and said, "I'm joining the Army."

Mr. Hitchens barely glanced at him. "You still have to do this assignment. I want each of you to write about something important to you, something that changed you as a person and made you who you are today."

Groans and mutters fluttered around the room. Even the kids who actually liked writing didn't look particularly thrilled about this prompt.

"Try to write about something unique to you. Something no one else could write. Think about what would make you stand out to an admissions committee."

Ella tried not to roll her eyes. A bunch of kids from a collection of equally backwater small towns didn't exactly have a wealth of unique experiences to pull from. Most of them had gone to school together since kindergarten. Two kids in this class had been in her preschool.

Riley Perkins raised her hand and waited until Mr. Hitchens said, "Yes, Riley."

"Can I write about how I won the State Gymnastics Competition last year even though I was only a junior?"

Ella fought the urge to throw a textbook at the airhead. Riley-freaking-Perkins couldn't go one day without talking about the damn gymnastics tournament even if you promised her five billion dollars and a venti chai with dairy-free whipped cream. It wasn't as though anyone in the world actually cared, but she'd kept the medal hanging in her locker for the whole second semester last year.

"That's a good question," Mr. Hitchens said, causing Riley to beam like a blonde lighthouse.

"Your essay needs to show growth, conflict, it should be about something that challenged you."

"I trained wicked hard. You have to really dedicate yourself to be a state champion," Riley said.

Ella blinked rapidly, wondering if anyone would notice if she punctured her eardrums with her pen right about now. Owen looked sidelong at her and smirked, like he knew what she was thinking.

"Well then, maybe write about your training regimen." Even Mr. Hitchens seemed about done with the Riley show. "I'll give you all 15 minutes to brainstorm ideas. Everyone find a blank page in your notebook and get to work."

High school, Ella realized, was full of blank pages and teachers asking you to fill them up. She had no idea what to write about. Her parents' divorce? Not exactly unique. Some of the kids in the room were on their second set of stepparents. Something that challenged her . . . she could write about the constant struggle to not run screaming from the room every time Riley Perkins opened her mouth.

"I should see pens moving," Mr Hitchens said. "Brainstorming is about just getting your ideas on paper.

Write down everything that comes to mind. Don't worry if it's good or not."

Ella started to draw. She inked a three-inch grid and then started coloring in boxes at random. Maybe she could write about the art contest. *I worked really hard and lost to a dog in a tutu . . .* that was not likely to land her a scholarship.

Jack.

She could write about Jack. Nobody else in the class had a brother who died. It had certainly challenged her. And it had caused plenty of conflict. Would she be who she was today without Jack's accident?

When Mr. Hitchens called "time" Ella had just two things on her paper—her brother's name, and a collection of randomly colored-in boxes.

"Now switch papers with the person next to you."

Ella hadn't expected that. She wished she'd written down more ideas as she handed the paper to Owen and took his in return.

"Read through your neighbor's list and circle one or two ideas that jump out at you."

Owen's list said: being held back, Irish twins, going vegetarian, realizing I was bi.

Ella looked up, surprised. "You're vegetarian?"

Owen shrugged. "Yeah, for a while now."

"I didn't know that."

The corner of Owen's mouth raised just a little, but his eyes were bright when he said, "I'm a mysterious guy."

"Wearing Batman boxers doesn't make you the Dark

Knight."

"I'll have you know I'm wearing the Iron Man ones today." He pulled at his waistband and looked down. "Yeah, definitely Iron Man."

Ella threw her pen at him.

"Ella and Owen. Have you picked your topics?" Mr. Hitchens said. He didn't wait for either of them to answer. "Switch your papers back and let's move on."

Ella looked down at the page. Owen had circled Jack's name and then colored in a few more boxes to form a pixelated heart. Apparently, he thought Jack was a good essay topic. Hopefully Mr. Hitchens would too.

~

Ella sat down at their usual lunch table across from Liv and Owen. She made a point of looking at Owen's tray. Salad, fruit, bread. How had she not noticed that he hadn't been eating meat? She knew she spent a lot of time in her own head, but it seemed like the kind of thing you should notice about a person you eat lunch with every day.

"So, the vegetarian thing? When did that happen?"

"Seriously?" Liv asked before Owen could get a word in.

"Since like July," Owen said.

"How did you not notice?" Liv said. "We haven't had meat in months. Months!"

"Why?" Ella asked. "I mean, have you tried bacon? Wait. We?"

Owen tried to grin while shoving salad into his mouth. It wasn't a good look.

Ella looked at Liv's plate. Peanut butter and jelly on wheat. An apple.

"Sometimes I wonder if you live in the same world as us," Liv said.

"She lives in Ella land," Owen said.

"Must be nice there." Liv tore into her sandwich like she was mad at it. Maybe she was. Ella would be pretty upset if she had to live in a world without bacon.

"So did you become a vegetarian so you'd have something to brag about in your college essay or what?" Ella asked.

"What?" Liv looked bewildered until Owen filled her in on English class.

Liv listened, and focused on completely the wrong point. "You guys haven't started your college essays yet?"

"I did," Owen said. "I wrote four whole words." He held up four fingers.

"What did you two do all summer?" Liv practically wailed.

"You know what I did," Owen said, bending his head over his plate.

"Made stuff," Ella said. "Most of us don't spend our summers doing schoolwork you know."

"That's not schoolwork. It's your future," Liv said to Owen's bent head. "Have you even picked out your first choice school?"

Owen's head shook.

"Yup. MECA," Ella said.

"That's great!" Liv said.

"All the way to Portland, huh?" Owen said. "That's not New York."

"Yeah, but it's cheaper," Ella said, knowing she wasn't fooling anyone. They knew she wasn't really going to New York. Why did Owen keep needling her about it?

"What about you?" she countered. "Where are you going?"

"Dunno. Maybe I won't go to college."

"Owen—" Liv started, but Owen interrupted her.

"Are you saying everyone needs to go to college?" he demanded.

She frowned. "No, obviously not."

"So maybe I won't."

Liv looked like she wanted to say more but she tore into her sandwich instead. It hadn't occurred to Ella that not going to college was an option. Jack had been planning to. But he never got there. So why should she? Yes, the idea of not going to college had a certain appeal. It wasn't like she was an academic genius anyway. Plus, you didn't need a degree to be an artist, right?

"Maybe I won't either," Ella said. "We can rent the vacant apartment next to my dad and just make art all day."

Owen looked up, the corner of his mouth twitching. "How would we pay the rent?"

"We'll be starving artists. We'll trade canvases for rent

and beg for paint in the streets."

"That's a really harmful stereotype," Liv said. "Artists should be paid for their work."

Ella rolled her eyes. "Okay, okay. We'll sell our art for a fair and equitable price and also grow a garden to feed Owen and I'll steal a pig. Then when you come visit us you can bring baked beans."

"Why baked beans?" Liv asked.

"I just assumed you were going to MIT or Harvard or something. They're in Boston, right? Isn't that where baked beans come from?"

"Cambridge actually," Liv said.

"Forget the beans," Owen said. "Why would you steal a pig?"

"Bacon," Ella said and took a big bite of her BLT.

CHAPTER THIRTEEN

Dream Grotesque

PhiTau lay on his side, cool dirt against his cheek. From this vantage point, the new shoot seemed to fill the whole world. He had never seen a plant so brilliantly green. At least, not outside a human dream. He felt an urge to cup his hands around it, to protect it from the sharp eyes of other tenders, from their breath, from their very thoughts.

"PhiTau, you did it," SigmaSigma said.

PhiTau heard, but the voice was far away. He was busy tracing his eyes across the delicate pattern of veins in the two verdant leaves.

"What did you do?" EpsilonChi asked.

"I met my dreamer," PhiTau said. "I tended a dream."

PhiTau sat up, as though waking from a dream himself. Which, he realized giddily, he was.

"Are you okay?" SigmaSigma asked.

PhiTau tore his eyes away from the plant. SigmaSigma and EpsilonChi hovered just outside the fence line.

PhiTau realized he knew what the fence was made of now. Toys. Little plastic toys, like the kind Ella used in her art. Some of what she knew, a bit of who she was, had seeped into his consciousness.

"How did you do it?" EpsilonChi said.

"I just sprinkled some dreamstuff."

"But AlphaBeta said wait until the ground goes dark," EpsilonChi protested.

PhiTau shrugged. "Maybe the first time it needs a little boost?" He didn't really know. He'd just tried something and it had worked.

EpsilonChi hurried away without so much as a thank you.

When he was gone, SigmaSigma asked, "What was it like?"

"It was amazing . . . overwhelming. The lights and colors are just the beginning. The practice runs . . . they weren't. I mean . . ." He tapered off, unsure what he was even trying to say.

Panic crept across SigmaSigma's face.

"I mean, it was like the practice runs, but not. AlphaBeta didn't tell us about the feelings. I could feel what she felt. See what she saw. I *was* her but also outside of her at the same time. There's this . . . this space in her mind and her whole consciousness just echoed through it."

SigmaSigma stared at him. His toes made little crunching sounds in the gravel path.

"I don't think I can do this," he said, so quietly that

PhiTau wasn't sure if he was supposed to have heard. He felt a little surge of sympathy. All of this was overwhelming. He knew it, and SigmaSigma seemed somehow more fragile than the rest of them. PhiTau got to his feet and walked closer to the fence line.

"Of course you can," he said, matching SigmaSigma's tone.

SigmaSigma looked up at him, brow furrowed. "But if you were overwhelmed, how will I do it? The training trips were almost too much for me. I thought this might be easier without the whole group but now . . ."

"It was a lot, but it wasn't bad. Really it was exciting. I'm just not explaining it well. You just have to do it. Then you'll understand."

SigmaSigma's head shook slowly, side-to-side, side-to-side. "I'm not like you PhiTau. I was happy as a harvester."

"You could be happy as a tender, too."

SigmaSigma turned away, looking back over the fields toward their former lives. His shoulders slumped. The fur on his cheeks quivered.

"Look," PhiTau said. "What if I went with you?"

SigmaSigma's wings shuddered against his back.

"You'd do that for me?"

"Of course. Why not? We could go now."

He stepped over the toy fence, walking toward SigmaSigma's little plot of land. Realizing his friend hadn't moved, and simultaneously realizing that this was the first time he'd ever had a friend, he stopped just outside SigmaSigma's garden.

"What are you waiting for?" PhiTau asked.

"Is this allowed?"

"I don't see why not. We did it with AlphaBeta. Besides," PhiTau shrugged, "nobody told us not to."

SigmaSigma rocked from foot to foot.

"Come on," PhiTau said. "It's only scary until you do it."

"I'm not sure I believe that," SigmaSigma said, but he crunched his way over to the fence.

PhiTau felt a rush of relief. Of course he wanted to help SigmaSigma, who was a good oneiroi, although timid. But he was also looking forward to returning to the dream. To feel that rush of knowledge, of certainty. To know that he wasn't just a random creature in a random field doing a random task. Besides, he was curious to see what SigmaSigma's dreamer was like.

Even so, he waited for SigmaSigma to step over the fence before entering the garden. Somehow it didn't seem right to enter another tender's garden without him.

From edge to edge and corner to corner, the soil was perfectly smooth. Between that and the straight edged fence line, it couldn't have looked more different from PhiTau's garden. He almost felt bad making footprints in it.

"Where did you plant your seed?"

SigmaSigma opened his fist to reveal a round black ball. It didn't have the tapered shape of PhiTau's seed. That was interesting. He'd assumed all of the seeds were the same.

"You haven't even planted it?" PhiTau said.

SigmaSigma grimaced and PhiTau realized he'd said the wrong thing.

"It's okay, go ahead and try it now."

SigmaSigma shuffled toward the center, leaving furrows in the soil. After kneeling and planting the seed, he sat back on his heels.

"Now what?"

"Now just sprinkle the dreamstuff like AlphaBeta showed us."

Following PhiTau's direction, SigmaSigma reached into his dream pouch. PhiTau drew closer so he'd be inside the circle when it flared.

~

PhiTau could taste the fear. He didn't share the dreamer's mind the way he had with Ella. He should have expected that. This wasn't really his dream. Even so, the fear was as thick as the clouds that filled the air. He heard a man cough.

No. Not clouds. Smoke.

PhiTau looked down at his body, but there was nothing to see. Just more smoke. He had no form at all. The dreamspace seemed to be ignoring him. He could watch and listen, but not participate. That was unusual. He felt a drop of disappointment. *But this is fine*, he told himself. He was only here for SigmaSigma anyway.

PhiTau looked around, trying to locate his friend in the smog. There. A girl sprawled on the floor, as though she'd collapsed while crawling across the carpet. Her legs were pale beneath her pajama shorts, her oversize tee shirt had bunched up around her waist. As far as PhiTau could tell, she looked to be about the same age as Ella, but she wasn't Ella. She had darker hair that fell like a veil over her face. This was the form the dream had given SigmaSigma. But where was the dreamer?

Another cough. PhiTau, despite having no form here, was able to look where he wished. He turned the head he did not have and saw the man feeling his way across the room. His eyes were bloodshot, straining wide. One hand held the collar of his shirt before his nose and mouth, the other flailed wildly in the smoke. The dreamer.

The man dropped to the floor, letting his collar drop too. It didn't seem to be doing him any good anyway. He began to feel his way across the floor.

PhiTau wished the smoke would clear just a little for the poor man. And clear it did, not much, but just enough for the dreamer to spot SigmaSigma in the form of a girl stretched out along the floor.

When the man's fingers fell on the girl's arm, PhiTau saw her twitch and wondered if that was SigmaSigma playing his role or reacting with real fear. PhiTau couldn't tell where SigmaSigma's anxiety ended and the dreamer's began. It was all one big cloud of smoke and terror.

The dreamer slung the girl's body over his shoulder and stumbled toward the exit. But fire flared in the doorway, blocking his path. Suddenly, the flames were everywhere, engulfing the whole world, casting demons in the smoke.

Everything happened at once after that. The girl disappeared. The man screamed. The dream shattered. Almost instantly, PhiTau found himself alone in utter darkness, the terror still pressing in all around him.

AlphaBeta had told them the dream dissolved without a tender. Was it clinging together because PhiTau was still here? But the dream was gone, fully dissolved, nothing left but a feeling. He was alone in utter darkness, his eyes open yet unseeing.

"John," a voice said. "John, you're having a bad dream."

Startled, PhiTau stumbled backward out of the dream and landed on his back in the dirt. SigmaSigma, pale-lipped, his fur sweat soaked and curling around his face, knelt over him looking down. "Where were you?"

PhiTau blinked rapidly. When he started to get up, SigmaSigma sat back on his heels, making space. PhiTau sat up slowly.

"Where were you?" SigmaSigma asked again.

"In the dream," PhiTau said. "I think."

SigmaSigma shivered. "Did you feel what it was like in there?"

"They won't all be like that," PhiTau said, but he wondered if he was telling the truth.

PhiTau returned to his own garden. He sat down, criss-crossing his legs beneath him. With knees on elbows and chin on fists, he sat and stared at the brilliant green shoot. Disturbing as SigmaSigma's dream had been, the part that PhiTau kept recalling was the very end. He'd been left in the dark alone and he'd heard a voice. A voice that seemed to be outside the dreamer.

Was it possible for him to stay with the dreamer after the dream was over? Could he hold himself in that secret space in her mind? Even bad dreams were worth it if he could find a way to stay there in the human world forever.

CHAPTER FOURTEEN

Still Life In Situ

Mom pulled the Jeep into the potholed, slushy mud pit in front of Dad's apartment complex. "I'm just going to the bank and the grocery store and then I'll be back this way. You call me if you need anything."

Ella unbuckled her seatbelt. "I put everything on the list."

She noticed Mom trying to catch her eye in the rearview mirror and bent to grab Jack's backpack from between her feet.

"You know what I mean," Mom said.

Once, and only once, when Ella was in eighth grade, she'd needed to be picked up early from her weekly visit with Dad. Ella had gone up to Dad's apartment to find the door unlocked. Being young and stupid, she'd pushed inside without thinking too much about it. She'd called hello, but gotten no answer. Thinking he must be in the bathroom or something, she'd dropped her bag by the door and headed for the fridge.

The apartment was old and narrow, basically just a long hallway with doors on either side. To reach the kitchen, she had to pass the living room. The living room door was standing open as usual, but the lights were on even though it was daylight outside, which was strange.

Through the open door, she spotted Dad, slumped so far sideways in his recliner that Ella held her breath. The air from her lungs could have toppled him over the arm of the chair.

"Dad?" she said. No answer. She smelled something sweet and sickening. Something that made her stomach roll. A step closer, and she saw the dark stain seeping into the rug. She ran from the room screaming, convinced her father was dead.

He wasn't dead. Just dead drunk. The neighbors heard her screaming and someone got her mom on the phone. An ambulance came. At the hospital, someone shoved a couple of dollars into Ella's hand and told her to get something out of the drink machine. When she came back her parents were arguing. That is: her mom was arguing and her dad just sat there, looking beaten. Ella found a bathroom to hide in until Mom came looking for her.

But that was almost four years ago. Dad said he wasn't drinking anymore and Ella was pretty sure that was mostly true. These days, he always watched for her out the window and came to the door to say hello. He went to meetings. He was doing much better.

Ella looked up at the second floor window and saw

him exactly where she expected him to be. He saw her looking and waved. Ella waved back.

"I'll see you this afternoon," Ella said to Mom.

"You're welcome," Mom said, just before Ella shut the door.

Ella picked her way across the so-called parking lot. When she reached the relatively solid footing of the porch step she turned. Mom's car hadn't moved. Ella made a heart with her hands. She mouthed "love you." Mom shook her head, but she was smiling when she did it. She started the car.

Climbing the stairs to the second floor, Ella felt a twinge of anxiety. She'd seen Dad in the window. That meant he was fine, but she still couldn't be certain what she'd walk into.

Dad hugged her right away. She squealed in protest but he ignored this. "I've been waiting forever," he said.

"I'm like five minutes late," Ella answered.

"Exactly." Dad released her. "Did you eat?"

"I ate." Ella followed him down the hall to the living room. She dropped Jack's backpack in front of what she thought of as the Jack wall of fame. Dad liked to claim they were family photos, but other members of the family only made the wall if they were standing next to Jack.

"What do you want to do today?" Dad said.

Ella shrugged. "I have a paper you can help me with."

"Um . . . I'm not much of a writer."

"It's research actually. I'm writing a paper about Jack, and I wanted to talk to you about it."

Dad's eyebrows jumped toward his hairline and Ella noticed they had further to go these days. Obviously her dad was old—he was her dad—but was he receding hairline old?

"Really?" Dad said, his tone excited but a teensy bit skeptical.

Unlike Mom, who seemed perfectly happy to pretend Jack had never existed, Dad loved talking about Jack. Ella usually didn't. She liked thinking about him, sometimes even talking out loud to him when no one else was around, but talking about him with someone else who had known him well made her feel uncomfortable in ways she couldn't explain and didn't like to think too hard about.

"Yeah."

"Well in that case." Dad sat in his recliner, his body pitched forward, elbows on his knees. "Did I ever tell you about the time Jack won the science fair with a homemade water cannon that broke two tiles in the gym? I helped him make it."

Ella flopped onto the couch. "Yes, I've heard that story like sixty billion times. I was thinking more about when I was little."

"You were so little," Dad said.

Ella squirmed inside but tried not to show it.

"I remember you were so mad at us the day of the wake. You said we'd lied."

Ella felt sweat break out all along her hairline. She remembered that too. She had expected Jack to be at the wake. Everyone had said he would be there. She hadn't realized they meant he'd be in a box. She'd thrown a fit in the middle of the funeral home. Angry, confused, sad. Anna's big brother had been there. He'd hugged her, or maybe she'd hugged him. Either way they'd hugged, and she'd pretended he was Jack. Sometimes she thought it was her first real memory.

She shook her head to bring her back to the present. "No, I mean before that. Like everyday life stuff. You and Jack were building me a playhouse. I remember that."

Dad smiled. "Jack drew up the plans himself. Wait. I think I have pictures somewhere." He jumped up and strode across the room to the ancient desktop computer on its rickety desk in the corner.

"You know they have these amazing inventions now called laptops," Ella said as she followed him. "So small. You can sit in your recliner and use them. They have wi-fi and everything."

Dad, engrossed in sorting through the frankly terrifying number of desktop icons to find the folder of pictures, ignored her. He clicked through a rabbit trail of nested folders. Ella watched over his shoulder. Dad's files were surprisingly well organized for a man who still used a wired mouse like it was the year 2000.

"Here!"

He pulled up a photo of Jack, standing on the second step of a three-step ladder so he could work on the roof of the nearly constructed playhouse. The roof he'd never finished. For a moment Jack's unlived life loomed behind her, threatening to push her into the dark.

"Did I ask for that?" Ella asked, to shove the thought away. "The playhouse. Or was it his idea?"

"You'd been watching some cartoon I think, and there was a commercial for a playhouse. I knew we could build you one more cheaply than they were selling those silly plastic things for. Plus, it was a good project for Jack. He was smart. Too smart for his own good sometimes."

Dad went off on a tangent about the time Jack lit the lawn on fire with a magnifying glass because he'd read in a book that the lens would concentrate heat and wanted to test the theory, but Ella was only half-listening. She was clicking through the pictures. Most of them were of Jack sawing a board, hammering a nail, leaning over a sheet of paper that must have listed measurements or something. Ella saw herself in the background of one, sitting patiently on a blanket with all her friends: Baby Sarah, Legs the Frog-man, Barbie, and Maximus Tron, the latest addition to the group.

"Did I ever go anywhere without those dolls?"

Dad returned from whatever cloud of memory he'd been on. "What? Oh, almost never. I guess that's what happens when you live outside of town and your sibling is so much older than you. Not many kids your own age to play with."

"Yeah," Ella said. Looking at the tiny towheaded version of herself, conspiring with the dolls as though they could hear her, made her feel lonely.

She flipped to the next photo. "Mom's not in any of these."

"Who do you think took all of them? I am not a photographer, I can tell you that. Every picture I take comes out crooked, blurry, or looking suspiciously like my thumb."

He laughed. Ella laughed. But she thought about how strange it was that her mother had taken all of these photos. Presumably she had planned to look back at them someday, and now the only picture of Jack in their whole house was his junior year school photo, neatly framed beside the photo of Uncle Steve who'd died even before Jack. They were in the hall, the one leading to Ella's room and studio, where Mom never went.

Ella leaned one arm on the desk and took control of the mouse. She flipped quickly through several pictures. Something caught her eye. Actually, she was flipping so quickly that she stopped one photo after the one that caught her eye. She clicked the back button.

"What the he-heck?"

Dad grinned. "Oh you were playing "Savers of the Universe" I think you called it. I'm pretty sure it was based on some Japanese TV show Jack used to watch. You'd both run around the yard and pretend to be robots or something. There may have been aliens involved. Or a giant duck maybe? Unless that was a different game."

On the screen, tiny five-year-old Ella wore a pink and blue princess dress and sparkly silver shoes. Her arms akimbo, her stance wide, she looked like she was probably thrilled with whatever was going on. You couldn't tell for certain, because her entire face was hidden by a plastic robot mask. "Maximus Tron," she said.

"Oh, yeah, he was Jack's favorite toy when he was about the age you are there." Dad's eyes went all misty again.

"I still have him, the toy I mean," Ella said. She realized her voice was sharp, almost defensive. She tried to smooth it out with minimal success. "Jack gave him to me and I still have him."

She felt strangely guilty. Would Dad be mad if he knew that she'd buried the toy that Jack had loved so much? That she'd broken it all those years ago?

"Can you send me this picture?"

"Uh, sure," Dad said. He reached for the mouse, and stopped. "So, do I just attach it to an email or . . ."

"Here, let me do it."

She nudged Dad out of his seat. He was hopeless with technology.

~

Ella is inside the playhouse that Jack and Daddy are building for her. She's tiny, not a little girl, but a one-eighth scale version of her 17-year-old self. When she tilts her head back, she can see stars and a bit of the moon through the hole where the roof isn't quite finished yet.

PhiTau was not one-eighth scale. He towered over her, wearing the shape of Ella's Legs the Frog-man toy stretched to larger than human size. The giant frog had a hard hat perched between his bulbous eyes. He carried a clipboard. PhiTau worried that Ella would be afraid of him. He didn't want that, but she seemed unsurprised by his presence.

When he opened his mouth to shout his first lines, the words came out garbled. He got the impression that he was speaking in frog language. He could tell that Ella didn't understand what he'd said either, but this too didn't seem to bother her.

Something blots out the light. Ella stares upward. She can see the outline of Maximus Tron's helmet silhouetted against the moon. He slides a piece of the roof on. The hole narrows. Ella hears what sounds like a giant hammer pounding a giant nail a hundred feet overhead.

". . . most done here."

Ella brings her attention back to Legs the Frog-man foreman, who has both of his eyes swiveled toward her. "What?" she asks.

"I know we're a bit behind schedule, but projects like this . . . well, it's hard to find help a hundred feet tall and willing to swing a hammer."

"I'm sure," Ella says, trying to be polite.

And then Maximus Tron must slide the last piece onto the roof, because the room goes black.

PhiTau felt Ella's anxiety ratchet up as the light disappeared. Humans didn't like to be in darkness. And the darkness was nearly absolute. PhiTau couldn't see his clipboard anymore, he wasn't even sure he was holding it.

From another room Ella hears Baby Sarah wail.

Once again, PhiTau got the sense that Ella knew something was wrong here. She didn't think the playhouse had more than one room. But the sound had to come from somewhere.

He rode along in her mind as she moved toward the noise, grateful that there was no furniture to trip her.

As she inches forward, she wonders what happened to Legs. *He must have gone home*, she thinks, *since the job is over*. But how would he fit on the shelf in her bedroom now that he was at least eight feet tall?

Eventually, she spies a yellow light, which gets brighter as she approaches. Soon it's an open door. It leads into the room where Baby Sarah is lying in an oversize version of the little pink crib Ella had when they were both much younger. Ella bends over the crib, intending to pick Sarah up, but shock freezes her in place.

It hit PhiTau like a slap.

The baby isn't Sarah at all. It's Ella, little six-year-old Ella staring up at her future teenage self. For a brief, terrifying moment, Ella wonders *if that's me in the crib, then who am I?* The baby who is really a child who is really Ella is still wailing and the wail becomes the sound of Ella's alarm.

CHAPTER FIFTEEN

Eidetic Dreamer

AlphaAlpha approached Lord Morpheus. The Dream Lord sat, as he so often did, in a half-lotus position on the round blue cushion, which rested on the smooth wooden floor, the easier for Lord Morpheus to reach the piles of dreamstuff which mounded up on his left and right and were constantly replenished by the harvesters.

No matter how many times he saw the Lord at work, AlphaAlpha couldn't help but marvel at the deftness of his fingers. At the way the light fell upon his dark hair and soft blue garments. His body remained nearly still as his fingers wove shapes in the air.

Currently he seemed to be making a pink and green tiger shark wearing a false mustache. AlphaAlpha noted this with pride. Few oneiroi had learned enough of the human world to put names to the Lord's designs. No one had seen as many of Lord Morpheus' creations as he had. Sometimes, Lord Morpheus even spoke over his work, naming them before they went out into the world. Few were trusted to enter this room and hear the Lord himself speak, but AlphaAlpha had been the Lord's assistant for a long time, longer than any other oneiroi had existed.

Except that somewhere in the depths of his consciousness, he remembered, or thought he remembered, the single-named oneiroi who had come before: Alpha, Beta, Gamma, giants of an old world. Now long dissolved, and long may they shine. Only AlphaAlpha and his kind remained. He hoped the news he bore would not drive him to share their fate.

As he watched, the tiger shark swam through the air toward the far wall. It popped through without so much as a sound. On the other side, AlphaAlpha knew, gatherers waited to collect the dream creations and deliver them to the tenders.

"Yes, AlphaAlpha?" Lord Morpheus said without looking up.

"Excuse me, Lord Morpheus."

"Go on." He reached to the left to gather a handful of the raw dreamstuff.

AlphaAlpha watched as his fingers began to move. "My Lord, you recall how you asked me to monitor the greenhouses? To see that the records are kept in good order."

"To avoid a repetition of the Eric incident. Yes, AlphaAlpha, I recall."

"And you asked me to alert you if anything seemed outside the ordinary."

Lord Morpheus' green eye looked up but his fingers continued to move. "Speak, AlphaAlpha."

"There is an . . . anomaly."

"What sort of anomaly?"

"One of the plants appears to be flourishing." He realized this didn't sound like much of a problem. "I mean flourishing well outside normal bounds. Excessive flourishing."

The blue eye drifted over to peer at him. "Interesting."

Suddenly, Lord Morpheus surged to his feet, the half-finished whatever it was he'd been working on fell to the floor and disappeared in a puff of sand. AlphaAlpha felt a pang of guilt, he hated to see broken dreams.

"Let us see this *excessive flourishing*," Morpheus said. He enunciated the last two words, making AlphaAlpha cringe inwardly.

"It may be nothing, Lord," he said, as he followed Morpheus out of the workshop and into the fields of Dream.

"Oh, I doubt very much that it is nothing. You wouldn't come to me with nothing."

AlphaAlpha wondered if there was a threat curled up between those words. He wouldn't dare ask, or even hint that he had noticed any such thing, in case it turned out to exist.

"But what it is remains to be seen," Morpheus finished.

They passed a group of three harvesters delivering their wheelbarrows of dreamstuff. The Lord did not acknowledge them, but they all paused in their work to avert their eyes. AlphaAlpha nodded, this was as it should be. Not like that upstart youngling, PhiTau, his name was, who the Lord in all his wisdom, had chosen to elevate to the role of tender. The one whose work was so affecting his dreamer's growth. AlphaAlpha would never doubt the Lord's judgement, but privately, he did wonder at the logic of that appointment.

When they arrived at the greenhouse, nothing looked out of place. That was to be expected. The greenhouse, like all buildings in the Dreaming, was no more than a facade marking the portal from one space to another. Every plant in it could have been uprooted and used to build a bonfire hot enough to melt the world, and the outside would still look like a quaint glass greenhouse, its walls misty with condensation.

Morpheus merely raised his hand and the door swung open for him. They passed into the damp, perfumed air. AlphaAlpha took a deep breath, as was his habit. Nothing else in the Dreaming had any real scent to it. Only the plants inside the greenhouse gave off an intoxicating aroma. It was enough to make some of the younger oneiroi giddy on the few occasions they were allowed inside. AlphaAlpha had grown less foolish after a lifetime of service, but he still relished the opportunity to experience such sweetness.

He trotted to catch up. Lord Morpheus was already moving between the rows of plants. As he passed, leaves reached out to brush his sleeves, his hands, his face. They never did that for AlphaAlpha. At best he could sometimes coax a flower to face him.

Morpheus seemed to sense where the trouble was, if trouble was even the right word, without being told. The greenhouses had recently grown by some unknown exponent. In the past, plants were only germinated if the Lord felt a need to inspect a human's dream history more closely. These days, every living human over a certain age had their own plant. It had something to do with a human named Eric. AlphaAlpha had never gotten the whole story, but the Lord had been exceedingly wroth over it. It was just a mercy that humans didn't live very long, or the greenhouses would have been almost unmanageable. As it was, it had taken AlphaAlpha longer than it probably should have to notice the problem with this particular plant.

No such problem of perception challenged Lord Morpheus. He passed by hundreds of trees and shrubs, flowers, and vines without so much as a glance, and stopped directly in front of the one wild sunflower that had driven AlphaAlpha to raise the alarm.

It was, admittedly, an impressive sight. AlphaAlpha had never seen a sunflower plant grow an arm's length taller than the Lord, nor put out such an array of flowers. There must be at least a dozen currently in bloom, each one a different pattern and hue.

Morpheus made a sound in the back of his throat, halfway between a grunt and a laugh. Then he plucked a bit of raw dreamstuff from thin air. His fingers worked, forming a small three-legged stool. When he pulled his hands apart the stool stretched until it stood hip height. He sat down on it, facing the sunflower plant.

"My Lord—?" AlphaAlpha began.

"Shh," said Morpheus. "This is just getting interesting."

AlphaAlpha looked from Morpheus, who sat elbow on knee and chin in hand, to the sunflower plant which was growing almost imperceptibly.

~

While the other tenders smoothed the soil in their gardens or walked the fence line out of restlessness or boredom, PhiTau just sat on the ground, watching his plant. He wanted to see if he could actually notice it growing.

Already it was knee-high with several leaves. He thought the tight bundle of green at the top might even be the very beginning of a bud. Peeking at the gardens to his left and right, he confirmed that, yes, his plant was growing faster than everyone else's. He didn't know why. Maybe he just wanted it more. Maybe it was something to do with Ella. She was an artist, which meant, as far as PhiTau understood the term, that her mind was more colorful than other people's. Maybe she was making their plant more beautiful somehow. It certainly couldn't be him. There was nothing special about him.

Someone said his name. PhiTau looked up to find AlphaBeta standing just outside the fence, watching him.

PhiTau hadn't realized how engrossed he'd been. He hadn't even heard AlphaBeta's footsteps on the crackling path.

"Yes?" PhiTau said. He was surprised to see AlphaBeta again so soon. He must be checking up on their progress.

"How are you, PhiTau?"

"My plant is doing well."

"So I see," AlphaBeta said. There was no approval in his voice. In fact, if anything, he seemed a little strained.

"It might be about to flower," PhiTau added. "No one else has flowers yet."

"There's no need for comparisons, PhiTau. Every relationship grows in its own time. Would you come here please?" He shifted his weight, making the gravel crunch underfoot.

PhiTau cast one more look at the plant before climbing to his feet. He walked a wide arc around it, to avoid disturbing it in any way. At the fence line he stopped, and looked back over his shoulder. The leaves were broader now, he was sure of it.

"PhiTau, it has come to my attention that you've been," a pause, "helping other tenders with their work," AlphaBeta said, his voice low so the others couldn't hear from their gardens. A good plan since EpsilonChi was definitely looking in their direction.

"Was that wrong?" PhiTau asked.

"Not, wrong, exactly, but . . ." AlphaBeta paused. "Your plant really is doing quite well."

PhiTau grinned. "I take very good care of it."

"So you and your dreamer are getting along?"

"Ella? She's wonderful. She's an artist, you know. And her dreams . . . they're so . . . I bet she barely needs me. They'd almost run on their own."

"No, PhiTau, the dreams need a tender or they won't bloom. You are a, do you know the word conduit?"

"Is that like a river?"

AlphaBeta looked at him sharply. "Yes, the dreams are like a river and you are the banks. Without you they'd spill out everywhere. The dreamer couldn't bear them alone."

PhiTau nodded, but his eyes were on the plant.

AlphaBeta sighed, "You have a knack for this PhiTau, you truly do. And I understand your urge to help others to whom this work comes less easily . . . but save your energy for your own dreams, please."

"Yes, AlphaBeta," he said. Although he couldn't see what difference it made. He hadn't done anything except stand around inside SigmaSigma's dream. He hadn't even been given a role to play.

Besides, he knew AlphaBeta was right. PhiTau would need to focus on Ella, maybe even figure out how he could stay with her even when she was awake. He thought about asking AlphaBeta if this was possible, but a teacher who got annoyed at him for helping another student probably wouldn't want to help him do anything else outside the curriculum. He'd just have to figure it out on his own.

"Very good," AlphaBeta said. His eyes drifted over PhiTau's shoulder, and PhiTau knew he was looking at the plant. A bright bubble of pride rose in PhiTau's hearts. Even AlphaBeta could see how perfect his plant was.

When AlphaBeta walked off toward SigmaSigma's much less impressive garden, PhiTau went back to his post. Before he sat down, he stopped to measure the plant against his leg. It didn't seem to have grown while he was gone, but he knew big things were coming. He could feel it.

CHAPTER SIXTEEN

Grim Intimism

It was Sunday which meant that Mom would spend most of the morning on the couch with a book and a cup of tea. Mom always called Sunday a day of rest, even though Ella had never seen her set foot in a church except for Jack's funeral and cousin Melodie's wedding two years ago. Whatever the reason, it meant that Ella could spend the morning in her studio with no fear of being called away to do the chores she'd been ignoring all week.

Most Sundays, Ella managed a solid two hours of creativity before Mom got tired of resting and dragged her off to pluck every blade of grass from the front flower bed or match every pair of socks in the house or some other equally mind-numbing task. Apparently the secular Sabbath only lasted until about noon.

She stood between Jack's desk and the tall stool she often used as a pedestal for works in progress. Her head tilted to one side, half-listening to Versus the Ghost as they played through her laptop speakers, and regarding the Shopkins shopping bag sculpture she hadn't quite finished over the summer. She was trying to power through the finishing touches but she couldn't find her flow. Her brain kept running in the background, trying to remember more details about the day that Jack gave her Maximus Tron.

She'd only been a little kid and it hadn't seemed that important at the time. Really, she wasn't sure why it was important now. It wasn't like remembering what color shirt he was wearing would change anything.

It was that stupid essay, that was it. Maybe if she just wrote the damn thing it would stop rattling around in her brain. She sat down at Jack's desk, opened a document and began to type.

My brother died when I was six years old. A shaft of metal from the undercarriage of an 18-wheeler stabbed through his face when the car he was driving crashed into it. Nobody told me that's what happened. I found the news story myself. His best friend Anna was in the car with him. She also died. I could have been there too. I wanted to be. All that morning I had begged and pleaded to go along, but it was a trip for big kids. Jack was 11 years older than me. That's the same as the number of years he's been gone. Which means, I've lived without him just as long as he lived without me.

Ella sat back and reread the words she'd typed. Her

fingers felt numb. She flexed and closed them a few times. She'd never thought of it that way before, that Jack had lived more of his life without her than he had with her. It made her feel like she barely knew him at all.

She snapped the computer shut and went downstairs.

As expected, Mom was on the couch with a cup of tea in one hand and a book in the other. Ella stood in the doorway and watched as Mom balanced the cup on her knee so she could turn the page. She went on reading even though she must have known Ella was there.

Ella huffed a big sigh and made her way across the room as noisily as possible. Mom ignored this. Ella flopped down in the armchair hard enough to make the frame creak. Mom hated when she flopped on the furniture. Mom ignored this too. Ella crossed her legs, then uncrossed them and tucked one foot under the opposite thigh. She pulled her phone out of the pocket of her sweatshirt, stared at it for a moment without even unlocking the screen, and then put it away again.

"Mom," she said.

"Yes, Ella?" Mom said in a tone that told Ella she'd heard every bit of Ella's attempts to get her attention and had been waiting for a more grown-up approach before entertaining any of them. A mom can convey a lot in two words.

"Do we have any pictures of Jack from when he was a kid?"

The mug paused halfway to Mom's lips.

"Why do you ask?"

"It's for . . . for a school project." Parents couldn't resist school projects. You could tell a parent that you needed access to their bank account information and a bar of uranium, and they'd get them for you if it was for a school project.

"What kind of school project?"

"Just an essay thing."

"You need photos for an essay?" That was Mom's skeptical voice.

Ella tried to keep from squirming. Mom paid attention to things like that. "I'm not illustrating it or anything. They're for inspiration."

"Inspiration?"

"I'm writing an essay about Jack."

"Oh, Ella." Mom closed her book. "Isn't there something more pleasant you could write about?"

"More pleasant?" Ella sat up. "What does pleasant have to do with anything?"

"Well, it's Sunday and the sun is shining and I'm about to find out whether Claudio wins the heart of Eleanor . . ."

Ella rolled her eyes. "Is it a romance?"

"Yes."

"Spoiler alert: He does."

"Yes, but the point is how will he do it?"

"Life isn't a romance novel, Mom."

"Yes. I know that. It's most of the reason I enjoy reading them." Her tone was stiff. She looked down at the book in her hand. Her eyes blinked rapidly.

Ella rolled her eyes again. "Well, I'm sorry my life isn't more pleasant. I didn't ask for a dead brother."

She'd gone too far. She knew it before Mom reacted, which was almost instantly.

First she said "Ella!" In a tone sharp enough to draw blood. Then the tea mug hit the side table so hard it sloshed. "Is that any way to talk?"

She swiped a tissue from the box and dabbed at the table. The fussiness of the gesture fueled Ella's anger. She knew she should just shut up like always. She knew there was no point in talking to Mom about this. Mom would rather pretend Jack had never existed. She cared more about tea on the stupid table than she did about her own dead son. But the anger was there and it was hot and loud and insistent. It spilled out of Ella's mouth before she could stop it.

"Why don't you ever want to talk about him? Didn't you love him? Did you even like him? Doesn't it bother you that he's dead?"

Ella realized she was standing and wondered when that had happened. Just for a moment, before Mom got angry, she looked like she might collapse on the floor sobbing. Ella almost wished she would. At least then she'd know for certain that Mom really did miss Jack, that Ella wasn't alone in her grief. But the moment passed, and Mom's face went blank.

"How dare you? Of course I . . . I don't . . . you have no idea." Her fury tangled up the words before she could spit them out. "Go up to your room. I don't want to speak to you right now."

That last part was so cold Ella expected the words to condense in the air and fall in shards between them.

Ella threw herself toward the door. She couldn't even look at her mother right now. Couldn't bear to see that expression on her face. She pounded up the stairs as fast as she could and bolted into her studio. Slamming the door behind her, she threw herself on Jack's old bedspread and pulled the pillow over her head. She wanted to scream, but she thought that if she did she might not be able to stop. If she opened her mouth now every atom of breath in her body would spill out in one furious rush, she'd scream until her face turned red, then blue and then she passed out. They'd find her cold body days later, curled on its side, empty of breath. Cause of death: asphyxiation.

Instead, she breathed the musty smell of bedding that hadn't been slept in, or even washed, for eleven years. As she got her breath under control she felt something begin to creep up her back, not a bug, despite the unaired bedding. It was a sense of shame.

Mom really had looked sad. But Ella needed more than a flash of emotion. She wanted something in between Dad's near-obsessive reliving of Jack's greatest hits and Mom's complete silence. There had to be something in between. Otherwise, what hope did Ella have?

The air was turning solid around her. She needed a distraction. Not that stupid essay. Forget that. She'd throw together an outline at some point maybe, but not now. She sat up and spotted Maximus Tron spilled sideways on the desk. That was an idea.

It didn't take long to find English dubbed reruns of *Savers of the Universe* online. She brought her laptop back to the bed and curled up against the wall with the laptop on the bedspread beside her.

"Maximus Tron, you have been called," said the voiceover. "Will you be a Saver of the Universe?"

With four whole seasons of *Savers of the Universe* to watch, Ella avoided Mom for the rest of the day. It wasn't very difficult. Mom didn't seem eager to run into her either. They mutually avoided each other with great success. Ella stayed in her studio or her bedroom, ate snack bars from her backpack when she got hungry, and only used the upstairs bathroom. Mom presumably finished her book, did all the chores without demanding help, and happily pretended she had no living children at all until bedtime.

~

The thing in PhiTau's hands made him want to throw up. He was standing in Ella's kitchen wearing the body of a man and holding a plate heaped high with meat. Apparently humans ingested this stuff. He thought their noses must be different somehow, because even in the dream, he found the smell of animal flesh nauseating.

In her room on the second floor, Ella wakes up happy. She jumps out of bed and heads downstairs for breakfast.

Someone is cooking bacon. She can smell it. Passing through the hall she notices something strange about the pictures hanging there. One is missing. She stops to look.

Jack's photo is gone. The frame is gone. Someone rearranged all the photos. Uncle Steve's is off to the side, and right in the middle, between the portrait of cousin Melodie in her wedding dress and the snapshot of Ella and Liv at Girl Scout camp is a big photo of Mom and Dad and Ella all standing together and smiling. She can't remember when it was taken.

Did Mom somehow change the photos around while Ella slept? That seems like a lot of effort to go through for an argument. Besides, how had Ella not heard her doing it? The photos hang right outside her bedroom door. And even further besides, why would Mom choose a photo that includes Dad?

Her anger and confusion mixed with the odor of charred flesh and made PhiTau's stomach roll. He tightened his grip on the plate. It was time for his first line.

Ella goes downstairs, ready to shout, and stops. She hears a voice, a man's voice, low and rumbly. It's coming from the kitchen. Ella runs toward the sound.

PhiTau heard her footsteps and knew that was his cue.

Mom is sitting at the kitchen table, a plate of eggs steaming in front of her. She looks up and smiles, not at Ella but at Dad, who has just come around the corner with a platter of bacon in his hand.

"Dad?"

"Good morning, Ella. You're just in time for bacon."

The plate looks like it holds an entire pig. Slabs of bacon pile at least a foot high and drip grease over the edges.

"What are you doing here?"

"Cooking breakfast for my two favorite ladies."

Ella looks at Mom for explanation, but gets nothing. Mom just sits there, smiling.

"Sit. Eat," Dad says.

Ella stays where she is. Something isn't right here. As far as she knows, Dad hasn't set foot in this house in years.

"So you two are, what? Back together?"

"What are you talking about, sweetie?" Mom says. Her smile is creeping Ella out. It's too bright. Too rigid. She's only ever seen a smile like that on a Barbie doll. The light is wrong too, like someone turned up the saturation on the Instagram filter of their lives.

Dad sets the plate of bacon down in the middle of the table. Ella thinks it must have grown in the time it took her to be disturbed by Mom's smile. Pretty soon, she thinks, she'll see a snout and two beady little eyes looking out of that pile and she'll have to run screaming from the room. Which, honestly, pretty much describes what she wants to do anyway.

Bending, Dad kisses Mom on the cheek and then sits down. "Come on, the bacon is getting cold," he says.

"Are you drunk?" Ella asks. "Am I drunk?" She's never actually been drunk, and she doesn't remember drinking, but it seems like a more reasonable explanation than anything else she can come up with. Maybe she has some sort of fever.

Mom and Dad laugh, like she's said something truly witty.

Deep inside Ella's mind, PhiTau cringed. He didn't want to be laughing. The situation wasn't funny. He could feel Ella's emotions all tangled up with his own—fear, confusion, disgust.

"Really, Ella, you should eat," Mom says. "You're looking so thin."

"Let's put some meat on those bones," Dad says. And something about the way he says it turns Ella's stomach.

She finds herself sitting down, without meaning to, without wanting to. She looks across the table at her parents, who look so . . . so . . . happy. What the hell is going on here?

Dad reaches across the table to tip a huge fork-full of bacon onto her plate. That's when she sees it. The eyes, looking out from under the pile of glistening meat. She'd known they would be there. She'd known.

She doesn't want to look, but she can't turn away. It's worse, so much worse than she expected. Because the eyes looking out are blue, and the mouth held open with an apple is human, and the head beneath the bacon is Jack's.

She scrambles backward, screaming . . .

~

PhiTau held on while Ella screamed. The sound plunged into his belly and twisted. He wanted to do something to comfort her. As the dream fell apart around him, as the fork disintegrated between his fingers and the room melted into darkness, he tried to hold his ground.

Last time, he'd managed to stay through her alarm, but then a blinding light had pushed him out of her mind and back to the Dreaming. Now, he crouched low toward the quickly dissolving floor, hoping that whatever force pulled the dream apart would somehow miss him. Of course it didn't work. The floorboards popped out of existence one by one.

He closed his eyes and forced himself to focus on her breath, catching in her throat, on the scrambling sounds of her hand across the bedroom carpet. These were terror sounds, nightmare noises, but he clung to them, because he wanted to stay in the real world. And, he realized, he wanted to help her. He wanted it more than he had ever wanted anything before.

He hadn't even known it was possible to want so deeply, to want with a pain in your belly and a fist around your hearts.

Even as he thought this, the sounds faded. He risked opening his eyes, hoping Ella had fully wakened from the dream and he was still with her. But no, the green plant filled his vision.

PhiTau muttered one of the swear words he'd picked up from Ella, but it did no good. Maybe they only worked if someone else could overhear your vocal rebellion.

His hands shook. Poor Ella. PhiTau wanted to protect this tiny vulnerable human. But what could he do? He was only a tender. He couldn't interfere with her dreams. That would be blasphemy. If he could just find a way to stay in her mind. That wouldn't be interfering with the dream, it would be more like extending it. A good thing, surely. It would give them time to work through what was scaring her.

For the first time, PhiTau looked at the plant and hated it. The delicate green leaves, the straining bud, seemed to mock him. How could something so beautiful come from a dream so ugly? And if the point of dreams was to help humans work through problems, as AlphaBeta said, why did they always end before anything was resolved?

He couldn't bear this. He plunged his hand into the sack at his waist, pulled out a heaping handful of dreamstuff, and threw it up into the air. It rained down on his shoulders, catching in his fur.

One piece drifted into his eye. He blinked it away and found himself in darkness. He blinked several more times, but the darkness remained. In fact, it made no difference whether his eyes were open or closed. Either way, the darkness was absolute.

He strained his senses for something, anything. A sound, a sight, a scent. Nothing. Nothing. Nothing.

But, perhaps something. A sensation like a trickle of water stirring the fur on his foot. He reached for it, hungry for anything real, but there was nothing. It tickled the opposite foot. Again he reached. Again, his hands came away dry.

And then a sound that might have been the chuckle of running water, far away. PhiTau strained his ears to hear it. He even stood up, as though movement would bring the sound closer to him.

Light bloomed. He was back in his garden, if he had ever really left. He swiped at his head and shoulders, suddenly anxious that no dreamstuff be left tangled in his fur.

"What are you doing, PhiTau?" called a voice to his left. He recognized it as EpsilonChi's.

PhiTau blinked, trying to bring the world back into focus. "Nothing. It was just a dream."

"Are you okay?"

"Fine."

"How did you make your plant do that?"

"Do what?" PhiTau looked down. The bud had burst, revealing narrow crimson petals around a dark and textured center.

"I don't know," PhiTau said. "I wish I did."

He lowered himself back down to the ground, slowly, and discovered that the flower was now almost level with his eyes. The plant had grown again.

CHAPTER SEVENTEEN

Tricks of Perspective

Ella moved like a zombie through most of the next day. She hadn't ever really gone back to sleep after the terrible dream with Jack and the bacon. During math class, she filled a notebook page with stars instead of notes, and when the teacher handed out a quiz, she just filled in random numbers. That would probably be a problem later, but she couldn't think about it now.

When she had been little, and she was overtired, Dad had told her that there must be some sleepy seeds left in her eyes. That, he said, was why people rub their eyes when they first wake up, to get the seeds out. Ella had scrubbed her face every morning for weeks after hearing that. The last thing she wanted was sleep seeds sprouting in the corners of her eyes. She'd end up stuck lying on her back so the plants could grow up toward the sun. Maybe that's what the sandman secretly wanted, to keep people asleep forever. She shook her head like it would help clear her thoughts. She wasn't making sense and she knew it.

"You two look like a couple of zombies," Liv said when she sat down across from Ella and Owen at the lunch table.

Ella blinked at Owen, and realized he also looked like he hadn't slept very well. Or possibly like he'd fallen asleep at his desk and had woken up just in time for lunch. There were dark circles under his eyes, and his hair was even wilder than usual.

"How are you not tired?" Owen yawned in Liv's general direction. "You stayed up half the night reading. I saw the light under your door."

"Practice." Liv grinned. "You two though, you're going to start rumors if you both walk around looking like you've been up all night."

"Don't start that again," Ella said, too tired to even make grossed out noises. It wasn't just last night. She didn't think she'd been sleeping well for the last few. It was the dreams.

"You had a bad dream?" Liv asked.

"How did you know?" Ella said, genuinely confused.

"You just said, dreams."

"I did?"

"You did," Owen said.

"Yeah, weird dreams." Ella set her elbow on the table and leaned her cheek against her hand. "And I had a fight with Mom."

"Oh no," Liv said. "Is that why you barely texted me yesterday?"

"Yeah." Ella drew patterns in her mashed potatoes with her fork.

"What was the fight about?" Liv asked.

"Can we help?" Owen said.

Ella looked from one to the other. She suddenly felt weepy. "I love you guys."

Owen reached across the space between them and patted her hair in the same way he might pet an overexcited golden retriever. "Shh, El, you're talking crazy. Go to sleep now."

Ella collapsed against his shoulder and pretended to snore. A crash startled her upright. She looked around. Everyone at the next table was staring at Kristen Lund, who had apparently just slammed her tray down in front of her. She turned her back to them, but even Ella could see annoyance in the set of her shoulders.

Ella couldn't help it. She started to giggle. Owen put his arm around her face, pulling her into a soft cavern of Old Spice and coffee, but she could feel him laughing too.

~

Ella got to the house before Mom, as usual. That meant she could nap, hopefully without any weird dreams. She really needed sleep. Besides, it would be way easier to avoid Mom if she was unconscious. It wouldn't even seem rude.

When Ella tried to lie down, something angular and hard stabbed her in the back. She felt around and found

Maximus Tron wrapped up in the blankets. After some rummaging she was able to extract him from his blanket cave. She didn't even remember bringing him to bed with her when she'd finally crawled in around dawn.

"Had a nice sleep, did you?" she asked the doll.

She held it overhead. There were still little bits of dirt caught in the crevasses of the plastic. One speck rained down and landed in her eye. She blinked and lowered him against her chest.

"Well, now it's my turn. You stay up and keep watch for nightmares."

Maybe it was because she was so tired or maybe it was Maximus Tron watching out for her, but Ella managed to sleep with no dreams at all.

She only woke up when Mom called up the stairs, "Ella, dinner." By the tone of her voice, it wasn't the first time she'd called either.

Ella jumped out of bed, startled. For a moment she thought it was the middle of the night and then she thought it was early morning, and then something hit her foot. She looked down at Maximus Tron, sprawled on the floor near her toe.

"Sorry," she said. "Coming!" she shouted to Mom.

She grabbed Maximus Tron and propped him against her pillow. Maybe she could reconstruct a head for him.

"I'm eating without you," Mom shouted. Ella smelled garlic bread. Her stomach rumbled. She made it to the top of the stairs before she remembered that she and Mom were fighting. They didn't have dinner together every night. It was more like every third night with fend-for-yourself leftover meals in between. Was this a ploy to get them to stop avoiding each other, or was it just dinner?

She came down the stairs slowly, one hand in the pocket of her hoodie. Part of her wished she'd brought Maximus Tron down with her. But that was stupid. He was just plastic. Plus, he was too big to fit in her pocket, and she didn't want to explain him to Mom.

"I made spaghetti," Mom said.

"Cool," said Ella.

Mom smiled. Ella had a flashback to her dream the night before, when Mom's smile had been so stiff and doll-like. She shuddered.

"Are you cold?" Mom asked.

"No." Ella slipped into a chair. Not the same chair from her dream. A different chair. It wasn't the one Ella usually sat in. She reached across and pulled the place setting over in front of her. Mom's eyebrows furrowed, but she portioned out the pasta without comment.

They chewed in silence. Finally, Mom broke it by asking how school was.

"Fine," Ella said.

"You like your teachers this year?"

She shrugged. "I don't like Mr. Hitchens."

"He's the English teacher?"

"Yeah." Ella waited for the follow-up question about her essay. It didn't come. She felt relieved, and then angry.

It's not that she wanted to fight. She hated fighting.

But it was just like Mom to pretend everything was fine when it clearly wasn't. They'd practically screamed at each other just yesterday and now they were sitting there chomping pasta like it was date night at the Olive Garden.

"He's making us write college admissions essays," Ella said.

She saw Mom's cheek twitch at the word essay.

"The outline is due tomorrow," Ella added.

"What about art class? How's Ms. Beaudry?" Mom said.

Ella almost laughed at the clumsiness of Mom's attempt to change the subject. Instead she said, "We're seriously not going to talk about it?" She was proud of the way that her voice didn't change at all.

Mom also kept her voice level. "I'd rather not if it's all the same to you."

Ella slammed her fork on the table. "It's not all the same to me. You just expect me to pretend he never existed. Well, he did exist. I remember him!"

"We all remember in our own way, Ella."

Ella snorted and pushed her plate away. She'd completely lost her appetite.

Mom set her fork down gently, too gently. "You're not the only one who misses him."

She grimaced after she said the words, as though voicing them somehow hurt her. This was the closest Ella had ever heard her come to actually talking about Jack. She knew she should say something kind, something that would keep the conversation going, but she was angry again. Why should she be the adult here? Mom should be the adult. Mom should comfort her. Not the other way around.

"Could have fooled me," Ella muttered.

Mom rubbed her face with her hands. Her expression was complicated. Ella couldn't read it. "Maybe you need someone to talk to."

"You mean like a therapist?"

"Maybe."

Ella blinked. Now Mom of all people wanted her to go to therapy? Where was this when she was six and she'd told her parents that Jack had talked to her in the night? No, it wasn't a dream, he was speaking to her from the other side, she knew it. Dad had immediately suggested therapy. But Mom had gone to a "shrink" after her own brother died, and she claimed it hadn't done her any good. She said they'd just give Ella some medication that turned her into a zombie. They'd fought. Of course they had. They'd gone through the whole thing again after Mom and Dad separated, like they weren't the ones who needed therapy. Now Ella had no interest in spilling her guts to some stranger who wouldn't understand anyway. No one understood.

Ella got up and left the table without asking to be excused. But she did take her plate to the sink because she knew Mom would call her back if she didn't, and then there would be another argument.

I'm trying to talk to you. Ella thought loudly in her mother's direction, but Mom didn't seem to notice. She just watched as Ella walked over to the sink, set her plate in it, and then turned and left the room. *I don't want to talk to a stranger. I want to talk to you.*

She couldn't say the words out loud. She couldn't bear to be rejected again. The anger would boil over, a bubbling lava that would spill out of her and burn the floor, and the dirt, and the granite bedrock until it fell right into the molten center of the Earth, overheated everything, and killed the entire planet.

Carefully, so as not to overflow, she carried herself up the stairs and into the studio, where she closed the door behind her.

~

Something is after them. Ella runs through a dark forest with Maximus Tron. Even though they're all wearing their Savers of the Universe helmets, Ella knows that Legs the Frog-man, Barbie, and Baby Sarah are behind her. And something is coming. Something big.

Trees snap at her face, her arms, her legs. "Over there!" Legs shouts. He points one webbed finger at a tiny house, the playhouse, nestled in the trees.

"It won't find us in there," Barbie says.

PhiTau, wearing a human-size form of Maximus Tron, didn't know what it was. But he thought it probably would be able to find a group of talking toys hiding in a playhouse. He swung in that direction anyway. That's what he was supposed to do.

One after another they duck inside. Ella feels the terror recede. The playhouse is dark and secret. It's still there, but not quite as overwhelming. If they stay inside, they'll be safe.

PhiTau went over to the window and pretended to look out. The dream was dissolving out there. No point in keeping it together when the dreamer couldn't see outside.

Ella looks around in confusion. The room is getting smaller. No, Ella realizes, she's getting bigger. She looks around. All her friends, who were about her height a moment ago, now look like toys. They stare up at her with frightened eyes.

Only Maximus Tron keeps watch out the window. Finally, he turns to look at her. At least, his helmet turns in her direction. She isn't sure whether he has a face under there or what it would look like if he did. The cartoon never showed. Even so, the hollow darkness of his eyes seems to stare right through her.

"You have to stop this," Maximus Tron says, as though she'd meant to grow to freakish size and lift the roof off the place, as though it was all her fault.

"I can't," Ella says. "I can't help it." Tears sting her eyes.

Her shoulders press into the eaves now. She fights the urge to stretch out her arms. They're so cramped, but if she moves the whole thing will collapse and they'll be exposed.

PhiTau's hearts were breaking. He didn't want to make this any worse for Ella. He turned his eyes away, careful not to move his head. She wouldn't know that he was looking at the wall when he said his next line.

"You have to stop growing," Maximus Tron says.

But Ella just gets bigger.

~

Ejected, once again, from Ella's mind, PhiTau sat in his divot in the dirt and contemplated his plant. It was in full bloom, with multiple flowers in different hues. He was just wondering if scary dreams made darker flowers than happy ones, when he noticed movement out of the corner of his eye. It turned out to be SigmaSigma standing up and walking toward the edge of his garden. At first PhiTau thought nothing of it. All of the tenders walked around their gardens now and then, just for a change of pace. It was better than harvesting of course, but tending could be boring in the time when the dreamer was awake. PhiTau wondered idly if he would ever be given additional dreamers to tend. AlphaBeta had said something that made him think he would eventually. He wondered how he would ever have enough room in his heart and mind for another dreamer. Ella seemed all-encompassing to him now.

The crunch of gravel pulled PhiTau out of his reverie. SigmaSigma was walking down the path away from his plot. PhiTau stood up and called to him.

"SigmaSigma, where are you going?"

The other oneiroi hesitated. PhiTau thought he might

not turn around at all. And then he did. "I'm leaving," SigmaSigma said.

PhiTau hurried to the edge of his garden. He felt uneven plastic against his shins. "What do you mean leaving? You can't just leave. Your dreamer needs you."

SigmaSigma shook his head. "The dreams, they're so loud . . . and confusing. And the colors . . ."

"Yes," PhiTau said happily. He loved the colors. Even when Ella was having a bad dream, as she had the last few nights, he loved the colors.

". . . they're terrifying." SigmaSigma surged back toward PhiTau, feet crunching on the gravel. When they were close enough to touch he looked around as though he thought someone might be listening.

Apparently satisfied, he dropped his voice and said, "Did you ever stop to wonder what happened to the tenders before us?"

PhiTau's eyebrows knitted together. "They must have gotten new assignments, right?"

SigmaSigma leaned closer. "Maybe, or maybe that's just what they want you to think. Maybe they couldn't handle the dreams and . . ."

"And what?"

"I don't know. Maybe their heads exploded."

"That doesn't make sense."

PhiTau would have chuckled except that SigmaSigma looked so serious. "That's how it feels to me," SigmaSigma said.

PhiTau stared at him, speechless. He'd known that

tending didn't come as easily to SigmaSigma but he hadn't suspected his friend was so unhappy.

SigmaSigma must have read the confusion on PhiTau's face because he said, "Look, PhiTau, I'm not like you. I wasn't made for this. I'm going to tell AlphaBeta that I quit."

"Are we even allowed to quit? Lord Morpheus chose us."

"I don't know, but I'm going to try. I can't do this anymore."

He turned and walked away. PhiTau stood watching him go, listening to his feet crunch on the gravel. He noticed that SigmaSigma's shoulders looked more hunched than ever. His head hung down. His feet dragged with each step. PhiTau wished he could think of something to say, but no words came to him. Instead, he hopped over his fence and ran after his friend.

The gravel announced his presence so SigmaSigma turned just in time for PhiTau to catch him in a hug.

"What are you doing?" SigmaSigma cried. His arms and torso had gone stiff. PhiTau squeezed and let go.

"Saying goodbye. I'll miss you, SigmaSigma."

The troubled face smoothed a little. "You're a good tender, PhiTau."

PhiTau cracked his toes in embarrassment.

A voice called SigmaSigma's name. Both PhiTau and SigmaSigma looked up. They saw AlphaBeta walking toward them and SigmaSigma froze. He stayed that way as AlphaBeta approached. The look on their teacher's face was not one to inspire confidence. He looked . . . angry.

PhiTau suddenly felt afraid, but he might as well have been invisible. AlphaBeta had eyes for only one oneiroi.

"Why are you out of your garden, SigmaSigma?" AlphaBeta asked.

"I want to return to the fields."

AlphaBeta shook his head slowly. PhiTau wasn't sure what that meant. Apparently, neither was SigmaSigma because he added, "I was a good harvester."

"And I told you, you will be a good tender."

SigmaSigma was looking at the ground when he said, "I don't think so."

Suddenly, AlphaBeta turned all of his attention to PhiTau. "Go back to your garden, tender," he said.

PhiTau went.

He'd almost made it to the fence when he gave into temptation and glanced over his shoulder. AlphaBeta was standing in the same spot, head lowered, hands clasped in front of him. He was alone. SigmaSigma had disappeared.

CHAPTER EIGHTEEN

Criticism

When Ella went out her front door the next morning she found both Liv and Owen standing outside next to the still-running car. This was unusual. Ella stopped on the porch and looked at them, surprised.

Liv had backed the car around so the trunk was facing the house. She stood inside the open driver's side door holding the keys in one hand. The other rested on the hood of the car. Owen hovered near the trunk. His arms held a bundle wrapped in white tissue paper. Both were smiling, but while Liv's grin was amused, Owen's was a little anxious in the corners.

"Uh, hey," Ella said. "What's going on?"

"Owen made you a thing," said Liv.

"I made you a thing," Owen echoed.

Ella walked down the stairs. "What kind of a thing?"

"Just open it," Liv said.

Owen thrust the gift in Ella's direction. A breeze

stirred his hair, and the tissue paper, making a sound like dry leaves shuddering. Ella picked her way across the half-frozen mud in the driveway.

She took the package from Owen. It hardly weighed anything. She might have been holding nothing but a pile of tissue paper, except that she felt a rigid edge in there somewhere. She set it on the trunk of the car. Liv drew closer. Ella looked from one to the other again. They were both watching her. For a moment, she worried that she was dreaming. *But if I was dreaming I wouldn't notice I was dreaming. So I can't be dreaming, right?*

Still she hesitated.

"Open it already," Liv said. "I want to see it before w're late for school."

Ella glanced at Owen, who half-smiled.

Folding back the tissue paper revealed a delicate ring strung with gold thread. Ella picked it up with both hands, lifting it high so it caught the light. Glass beads, feathers, and other trinkets glittered in the web and hung down beneath the circle.

"It's a dream catcher!" Liv said.

"It's a dream catcher," Owen echoed.

Ella looked at him through the web. A blue bead covered one of his eyes.

"Because you said you were having bad dreams," Owen added.

She pressed her lips together. A warm feeling welled up in her chest. She blinked at Owen. And then at Liv, who was grinning like a proud mama.

"You made this?" Ella said.

Owen tugged at his ear. "Is it okay?"

"Owen, it's beautiful." Ella felt tears welling in her eyes. Mom may not want to talk to her, but Owen and Liv actually listened.

"It was my idea," Liv said.

"Eh," said Owen.

"Okay, it was partly my idea. And I donated the beads."

Ella laid the dream catcher gently on the trunk of the car so she could throw one arm around each of them. They squirmed in an awkward triangle hug.

"Hey, hey. Enough of that," Liv said. "We're going to be late."

Ella squeezed harder, giving herself another second to get the tears under control before they could get a look at her face.

When she finally let go, Liv said, "Run and put it away. Quick."

Ella ran.

~

Mr. Hitchens couldn't be like every other teacher in the whole school and just scribble a few notes in the margin of your paper. Oh no. He had to have a one-on-one conversation with each and every student so that you knew exactly how terrible a writer he really thought you were. He set a chair next to his desk. It was turned toward the wall to give the illusion of privacy. The student sat there like a condemned prisoner hearing his charges read. Meanwhile, the rest of the class was supposed to work on their reading assignments and pretend they weren't eavesdropping on your little critique session.

Ella went up to the chair actually feeling kind of okay about her essay outline. She'd spent way longer on it than she'd spent on all her other homework combined. She'd even double checked her spelling and stuff. It had seemed disrespectful to Jack to do anything less.

She sat down in the chair next to his desk, which put her back to the room. She glanced down at her paper on his desk. There wasn't too much red. That was a good sign.

"Ella, you did pretty well with grammar and spelling here. I can tell you actually used spell-check."

"I did, yeah."

"Yes," he corrected her.

"I did, yes," she said, not rolling her eyes at all.

"The structure you've laid out makes sense too."

Ella felt pretty good about that. Maybe this whole critique thing wouldn't be so bad.

"My real concern is the subject. It might not be exactly what admissions officers are looking for."

Speechless, Ella blinked at him. She hadn't expected this.

Mr. Hitchens must have seen her confusion because he added, "You were only six years old."

Ella's good mood spilled all over the floor. "You

asked for something that challenged me, something that made me who I am."

"Yes, but I meant you as a nearly adult going off to college, not as a preschooler." He said this calmly, as though he wasn't dismissing everything she was.

All she could think to say was, "I was in first grade."

"Even so."

Ella felt like he'd punched her in the gut. It made her nauseous and angry. "Oh sorry, I didn't know my dead brother was a childish topic. My mistake."

Without stopping to think, she snatched the paper off his desk and ripped it in half. It made a sound like the destruction of worlds. Certainly the destruction of any world in which Ella wasn't getting sent to the principal's office. She felt the whole class look up. Whispers bunted around the room. Nobody was even trying to pretend they weren't listening. Ella felt her face go red.

Mr. Hitchens stared at her. "Now that was childish," he said.

Ella's stomach heaved. Her face was hot but her hands had gone cold. She could feel 18 pairs of eyes boring into the back of her skull. If she didn't get out of here soon they'd punch right through and out her forehead. She imagined all of her rage bursting through the holes to spatter the whiteboard with caustic red sludge.

The chair squeaked against the floor as she stood up. She would not cry, not in front of her whole class and this arrogant ass of a teacher. She would not cry, but if she stayed here one second longer she wouldn't have any choice.

Bursting into the hall felt like a prison break. Ella looked left and right, unsure of where to go now. She didn't have a plan. She just needed to get out.

She still felt like crying or screaming or both. *Hurry up*, she told herself. Mr. Hitchins might come after her any second. Tears stung her eyes and she wasn't sure how long she could hold them back.

She forced herself to walk away from the door, holding back from running because if she started she was sure she'd run down the hall and past the office, across the parking lot full of hand-me-down student cars, and over the crumbling country roads to her house.

Her feet wanted to take her to the art room, but that wasn't a good idea either. Ms. Beaudry probably had a class. She could go to the girls bathroom, but someone else might be in there and she didn't want to be that girl crying on the bathroom floor. Word would get around. The halls were empty, quiet. Maybe she could just stay out here until the bell.

Behind her, a door opened. She heard footsteps on the linoleum. Mr. Hitchins was coming after her. Her whole body tensed.

"Ella, wait."

It wasn't her teacher. It was Owen. Ella turned. His face looked like worry.

"He sent you after me?" Ella said.

"Not exactly."

He stopped next to her in time to catch her sideways

look. "I was coming to check on you and he told me to sit down. So I told him to go to hell and I left."

"You actually told him to go to hell?"

Owen chewed at his bottom lip. "Yup."

Ella shook her head. "You're getting detention you know."

Owen shrugged. "At least we can suffer together." He put his arm around her shoulder and towed her in the direction of the stairwell. "What did he say to you? I didn't hear the whole thing."

"I wrote about Jack."

Owen nodded, "I figured."

"He said no college wants to hear what happened to me in preschool."

"Ass," Owen said.

Ella smiled. Owen understood.

They drifted to a stop beside the door that led to the outbuildings. The school had added them decades ago as an allegedly temporary solution to overcrowding. Ella had taken a sign language class out there once. The trailers, because that's all they were really, were cold in the winter and hot by the end of the school year. But it still made her wistful to think that this was the last year students would have to suffer in them. They'd probably be demolished once the new school was built—broken down into their component parts and dumped in a landfill. By the time this year's freshman were seniors, no one would remember where the outbuildings had stood.

"I feel like everyone wants me to just forget he ever

existed."

"Well, that's not going to happen. But, . . "

"But what?"

"Maybe there are some people who don't deserve to know about Jack. Like . . . like how there are some people who just don't get art. Maybe there are some people who just don't get the Jack thing."

"It's not a thing, Owen." She half-expected the outbuildings to burst into flames from the intensity of her stare. She'd thought Owen understood, at least partially, but he was just as clueless as the rest of them.

"He's my brother. What would you do if Liv dropped dead tomorrow?"

"Honestly, I have no idea. And that's what I mean. People who have never been there don't get it. Maybe they can't get it."

Ella hugged her arms across her chest.

"Why not? It's not that hard. My brother's dead. I'll never be normal. How hard is that?"

Owen shook his head. He looked like he was about to speak, but the PA system clicked on before he could. "Ella Pratt and Owen Butler, report to the office. Ella Pratt and Owen Butler."

~

Ella didn't really care about getting detention. It wasn't like she did anything after school anyway. She'd just use the time to finish up her homework and then maybe sketch something if she got really bored. Detention would have been no big deal at all, except that the school insisted parents had to sign detention slips. Ella suspected it was a way to shame students into behaving. She couldn't just forge one of her parents' signatures either. First, because she had terrible handwriting. Second, because the school also sent out helpful emails to let parents know that there was something to be signed. Dad wouldn't ever notice, but Mom was obsessed with keeping her inbox clean.

Ella considered just leaving the slip on the kitchen table and hiding upstairs until Mom went to work again. Except that wouldn't work at all. Mom would call her down and give her a lecture about facing up to your mistakes. Ella had heard that one before and didn't look forward to an encore.

So, she waited downstairs until Mom came home from work. She passed the time by putting away the dishes and sweeping the whole downstairs. Maybe Mom would be less annoyed if she saw that Ella was helping out around the house. While she worked, she rehearsed how she'd break the news. They were still technically fighting, so Mom probably wasn't going to be understanding about this. Ella just hoped she'd get a chance to tell her side of the story before Mom flew off the handle.

When Ella heard the Jeep pull into the driveway she rushed to dump the dustpan and stow the cleaning stuff back in the closet. She was already halfway to the front door when she thought maybe she should have held on to the broom so Mom would have visual confirmation that Ella had done chores. But it was too late to go get it now. The door was opening.

"Hi Mom, how was work?" Ella tried to keep her voice light and casual.

Mom set her bag down inside the door. "Fine."

She looked at Ella with raised eyebrows, like she expected more.

"Any big meetings today or anything?"

"Nooo," Mom said. "Just a regular day. Are you feeling alright?"

"I can't ask my mom about her day?"

Mom headed for the kitchen. "You can," she said over her shoulder. "You just usually don't."

"Maybe I should."

"Uh-huh. What happened at school today?"

Ella hesitated. Was that an, *I know what happened at school today because I already checked my email?* Or was it an, *I have no idea what happened at school today and I'm just playing along with your awkward question game?* Ella hovered in the dining room. It was easier if she didn't have to look at Mom while she talked.

"Owen got detention."

"Oh no, what did he do?"

Ella could hear Mom rooting around in the refrigerator. "He told Mr. Hitchens to go to hell."

"The English teacher?"

"Yeah."

"Why?"

"He was kind of defending me."

Mom poked her head around the doorway. "Why did he feel the need to defend you?"

"Mr. Hitchens said my essay was childish and . . ." she pulled the yellow detention slip out of her sweatshirt pocket.

Mom glanced down at the detention slip then back up at Ella's face. She just stared at her daughter for a long moment. "And he gave you detention because he didn't like your essay?"

"Not exactly . . ."

"What exactly?" Mom planted herself in the doorway, arms folded.

"I . . ." Now that she had to tell someone about it, it did sound childish. "I left the room without permission." She left out the part about tearing the paper in half because it kind of embarrassed her. Besides she didn't think just tearing the paper would have earned her detention. Probably.

"Because he didn't like your essay," Mom said, her voice flat.

Ella felt her face flush. "Well, he didn't have to be such a jerk about it."

Mom sighed and pressed her fingertips against her forehead. "Was this the essay about Jack?"

Ella nodded.

"Ella," Mom took a deep breath. Here came the shouting. But no, her next words were equally flat. "He's the teacher. You're the student. That means you show him respect whether he likes the topic you've chosen or not."

Partly relieved that Mom hadn't blown a gasket and partly annoyed that of course Mom was blaming her for everything, Ella said, "What if he doesn't respect me?"

Mom looked tired. "Ella, you can't just storm out of the room every time someone says something you don't like. You have to learn to talk things through like an adult. I'm sure if you'd explained to Mr. Hitchens why you'd chosen that topic—"

"Nobody listens when I talk," Ella interrupted.

"Ella . . ." Mom began, but Ella turned on her heel and walked away.

The detention slip fluttered to the floor behind her. She hardly noticed. Mom would sign it or she wouldn't. Ella didn't care. All the way up the stairs and down the hall and even after she'd made it to her room and shut the door, Ella expected Mom to call her back. Her ears strained, ready to hear her name. In the safety of her room she stopped and listened. Downstairs, only silence.

CHAPTER NINETEEN

Redream

AlphaAlpha went looking for Lord Morpheus in the greenhouse. He was easy to find. All you had to do was follow the reach of the plants and the faces of the flowers from the front door to the aisle where Morpheus sat on his stool, watching the sunflower grow.

Every plant and flower in this section reached toward him as far as their branches, leaves, or tendrils would let them. One enterprising vine had crept its way across the other plants and come within a breath of Lord Morpheus' shoulder. He paid them no notice. All of his attention was for the sunflower.

Well, all attention that he could spare from dream making. The Dream Lord's hands were rarely idle. Dunes of processed dreamstuff mounded near his feet, nearly touching the bottom rungs of the stool. AlphaAlpha made a mental note to send someone to sweep it up. He wouldn't want to waste even a crumb of the Lord's prestigious creative abilities.

AlphaAlpha stopped at a respectful distance. The plants could be unpredictable when Lord Morpheus was around. One of AlphaAlpha's assistants still nursed itching welts he'd gained after one of the pricklier shrubs took offense to the way he'd blocked its view of Lord Morpheus.

Really, the sooner Lord Morpheus lost interest in the Ella-human's sunflower the better. Still, AlphaAlpha didn't relish the news he now brought. Lord Morpheus would be . . . displeased.

"My Lord," he said. Morpheus did not turn his head, but the slowing of his fingers at work over some new dream told AlphaAlpha he was listening. "We have a problem with one of the new tenders."

"I know, AlphaAlpha," Morpheus said in a voice of theatrical patience. "That is why I'm sitting on this stool in this hothouse rather than reclining in the comfort of my workshop."

"Excuse me, my Lord. I mean, another problem with another tender."

This did convince the Dream Lord to turn his head in AlphaAlpha's direction. "What kind of problem?"

Despite the glint of red in Morpheus' green eye, AlphaAlpha held his ground. He had been the Dream Lord's right hand for the entirety of his life, and was accustomed to the Lord's mercurial moods.

"He has quit."

The blue eye, which had been watching the sunflower

while Morpheus' attention was divided, paused its vigil to stare at AlphaAlpha. Leaves rustled. AlphaAlpha tensed. If Lord Morpheus grew agitated here, the plants would not wait for orders.

"He cannot quit."

"No, my Lord."

"I made him."

"Indeed, my Lord."

"Why would he even want to do that? I chose him, me, the Lord of the Dreaming. I stretched out my hand and plucked him from obscurity, gave him a noble purpose and plot of land to call his own. And he wants to," Lord Morpheus paused, as though examining the word before he spoke it, "quit?"

"It would seem, my Lord, that he does not believe himself to be a very good tender. He wishes to return to the harvest."

Lord Morpheus stretched out his legs and his stool disappeared in a shower of dream dust. He hung in the air for a moment, and then situated his feet beneath him. AlphaAlpha watched with a prickle of anxiety. It appeared that Lord Morpheus was too agitated to bother with the charade of walking. That did not bode well for young SigmaSigma.

AlphaAlpha would never have admitted it to anyone, but he did feel a certain amount of pity, even kinship with the young oneiroi. They were both echo names. That didn't mean they had anything real in common, of course. Alpha was much higher than Sigma, but it was a point of empathy at least.

When the Lord had returned to his large round cushion in the center of his workshop, AlphaAlpha went to collect SigmaSigma. He was standing near the Horn Gate, flanked by the two oneiroi AlphaAlpha had tasked to guard him. They fidgeted as he approached. They weren't used to idleness, and just standing around waiting for him to collect their charge was like planting a prickly plant in their belly and telling them not to scream.

If it came to that, SigmaSigma looked like he could start shouting at any moment. His face was pale and his tongue flicked nervously over his lips. It seemed the reality of his situation had sunk in. Poor thing.

"You two, go and sweep the greenhouse. Bring a cart and shovel. You." He pointed at SigmaSigma who flinched. "With me."

AlphaAlpha made no attempt to adjust his stride for the shorter, bow-limbed SigmaSigma. It would do the young one good to work off some of that nervous energy before he entered the presence of Lord Morpheus. But the barn soon loomed ahead of them, a squatting ogre in the gloaming.

AlphaAlpha pulled the barn door open and ushered SigmaSigma inside. He took his time shutting the door, buying SigmaSigma a few extra moments to collect himself. Then he led the young oneiroi to the shaft of light that sliced the air in front of Lord Morpheus' seat.

The Lord of the Dreaming sat in a half-lotus position, his back perfectly straight, his six-fingered hands moving with regal grace over his work. As they watched, he drew his hands apart, stretching a sword between them. It had a curved blade and a red leather hand grip. He tossed it into the air, and AlphaAlpha knew he was performing for the young tender's benefit. The sword flashed as it spun, once, twice, a languid cartwheel. When it reached the apex of the throw it exploded in a shower of processed dreamstuff.

SigmaSigma made a small sound in the back of his throat.

"Lord Morpheus, I present SigmaSigma, Journeyman Tender."

AlphaAlpha stepped out of the light. The shadows seemed deeper in the barn today, as they often did when Lord Morpheus was annoyed.

Lord Morpheus rose, allowing his legs to unfold beneath him until he hovered just above his cushion. SigmaSigma stared. He seemed to be trying to make himself as small as possible.

"Ah, yes, SigmaSigma," Lord Morpheus said, his tone flat. "I hear you have some sort of complaint."

He drifted closer, his feet still not touching the ground. Both eyes, the green and the blue, trained on the quivering creature. SigmaSigma's wings rustled like dry leaves.

"No, my Lord . . . I mean, not exactly, my Lord. I want to go back to the fields, my Lord."

"Back to the fields?" Lord Morpheus finally allowed his feet to touch the ground. He paced slowly around SigmaSigma and stopped behind him, close enough that

SigmaSigma might have felt the Lord's breath on his neck, if he had decided to breathe, that is.

"You would rather work the fields than tend a dreamer?" he said to the back of SigmaSigma's head.

"Yes, Lord."

Morpheus clasped his hands behind his back and continued his circuit. He stopped where SigmaSigma could just see his face without having to turn. Then he leaned forward, until their faces were almost touching. SigmaSigma's head seemed to retract into his shoulders.

"Why?" Morpheus asked.

"I-I think I could better serve you as a harvester, Lord Morpheus. Sir."

Morpheus leaned back. "Oh, you think so? Do you hear that, AlphaAlpha? This oneiroi thinks."

"So he says, my Lord."

"Do you know what I think, tender?" The tone was soft, hiding the sharp edge AlphaAlpha knew was there.

SigmaSigma's head shook in tiny anxious jerks.

"I know that I chose you for a reason. Though at this moment I admit I can't recall why. But I am the Lord of the Dreaming, your all-knowing creator. Yes?"

When no answer came, he prompted, "Well?"

This time the head nodded, emphatically.

Lord Morpheus reached out and put what he possibly thought was a comforting hand on the oneiroi's shoulder. SigmaSigma flinched.

"Consider my reputation," Morpheus said. "If I sent you out in the fields, people would talk. They'd say the

Lord Morpheus must be losing his touch. He made a mistake. He chose SigmaSigma for a new and important mission. But where is SigmaSigma now? Back in the fields with us."

SigmaSigma's words tumbled out in a rush. "I won't tell anyone, my Lord. You could assign me to a different field, and different crew. I won't tell. I won't say a word."

Lord Morpheus' eyebrows quirked upward. "A vow of silence."

"Yes, Lord. I could be silent. I'm good at silence."

Morpheus turned his back on SigmaSigma, who sagged.

"AlphaAlpha, bring me a handful of raw dreamstuff," Morpheus demanded.

AlphaAlpha hurried to do as he was told. Lord Morpheus could have plucked the dreamstuff from the air, but he was putting on a show and AlphaAlpha would play his role as instructed.

He gathered up a wispy handful from the pile beside the round blue cushion and brought it back to where Lord Morpheus stood. Morpheus took it from him and turned to face SigmaSigma. His task done, AlphaAlpha started to retreat, but Morpheus said, "Stay."

He stopped where he was, at Morpheus' right hand.

"I will give you a choice, SigmaSigma," Morpheus said. "It is yours to make and yours alone. You may either return to your garden and do the task I chose for you, keeping your voice and your name. Or you may surrender both name and voice to return to the fields as a harvester.

Which do you choose?"

"I surrender my name."

"Think carefully."

"I won't say anything."

Lord Morpheus looked at the dreamstuff in his hand. "You're sure?"

"Yes, Lord. Thank you, Lord."

"Open your mouth, little no-name. Wider."

Lord Morpheus gathered the dreamstuff into a ball and inserted it into SigmaSigma's open mouth. "Close."

SigmaSigma closed his mouth as best he could. AlphaAlpha wasn't positive what was about to happen, but he had an idea and he wished he didn't.

"AlphaAlpha, go find the list of unowned names. Our young friend will need a new one."

"Yes, Lord." AlphaAlpha hurried toward the corner stacked with creates full of paperwork. The Dreaming generated a surprising amount of paperwork lately. Lord Morpheus' voice followed him to the edge of the room.

"Now, as such a devoted harvester, I'm sure you know that long exposure to the dreamstuff wears you thin after a while. We've all seen the poor stub-fingered elders working the fields, haven't we?" His voice was kind, as though he were explaining the facts of dreaming to a new-made oneiroi. "Go ahead and chew that, but don't swallow. You wouldn't like what happens if you swallow. As I was saying, it's not just exposure to raw dreamstuff that does it of course, it's the friction of raw dreamstuff against your fur, your nails, your skin, your teeth. Keep chewing. Good. Where was I? Oh yes . . ."

AlphaAlpha found the list and hurried back toward the center of the room where Lord Morpheus was in mid-speech.

". . . it's not just friction that wears on you. It's also heat. Heat isn't good for processed dreamstuff. It tends to melt in unpleasant ways. Now I'm sure you understand that you . . . do you have a name for me AlphaAlpha?"

"PhiZeta."

"You, PhiZeta, are made of dreamstuff. You were formed by me with these hands." He spread all twelve fingers for inspection by the oneiroi who was no longer SigmaSigma. "And when raw dreamstuff rubs against warm processed dreamstuff, well, the processed stuff doesn't have a chance. It just can't stand the heat." He smiled as though he expected them to laugh. When no one did, he added, "Open your mouth."

PhiZeta did as he was told. Delicately, Lord Morpheus reached two fingers into the open mouth. The oneiroi was trembling so much, AlphaAlpha worried that he would accidentally bite Morpheus, and the consequences of that were nearly unthinkable. Morpheus pulled the sopping clump of raw dreamstuff from the mouth. Dream dust clung to the sodden mass and spilled from the ragged lips. AlphaAlpha didn't want to see what the stuff had done, but he couldn't look away. PhiZeta's teeth were worn down to flat stubs, barely taller than his gum line. Beyond the button teeth, PhiZeta's mouth was empty. His tongue had disappeared.

PhiZeta made a panicked noise low in his throat.

Lord Morpheus ignored this and turned to AlphaAlpha. "Now, you may return him to the fields."

"Yes, Lord." AlphaAlpha took PhiZeta's arm, ready to tow him away, but Morpheus placed his hand once again on the young oneiroi's shoulder. "Enjoy the harvest."

AlphaAlpha waited until they were outside before he let himself shiver. Those last words from Lord Morpheus had been sincere. He really did think that he'd done PhiZeta a favor.

CHAPTER TWENTY

Kitsch and Kin

The next morning, Ella slept late on purpose. She waited until she heard the Jeep pull out before she got out of bed. Another chat with Mom was the last thing she wanted right now. A flash of light in the corner of her eye turned out to be the dream catcher Owen had made for her. She'd hung it from the end of her curtain rod, where it twisted gently in an invisible air current. It must have worked, because Ella couldn't remember a single dream from the night before. She might as well have been in a coma.

She hustled to get ready so she'd have time for breakfast before Liv and Owen showed up. If she skipped a shower, she should have plenty of time.

Downstairs, Mom had left a laundry basket on the dining room table. That's where she always left stuff she wanted Ella to take upstairs. On her way to the kitchen, Ella noticed a piece of paper on top of the neatly folded laundry. It was yellow.

Good, at least she'd signed the damn detention slip. Except there was an envelope too. It had her name on it. Ella picked it up and stared at it.

It wasn't sealed. She reached inside and found a flash drive. There was no note, nothing. Ella weighed it in the palm of her hand. Who even used flash drives anymore? She could have just sent an email. There was no reason to bring hardware into the equation.

Ella stuffed the flash drive and the signed detention slip into her pocket. Then she picked up the laundry basket. She'd get into trouble if she left it here.

Upstairs, she dropped it just inside the door of her room, and then went into the studio. While her laptop turned on, she pulled the flash drive out of her pocket and tried to imagine what might be on it. Emancipation papers? A PowerPoint presentation about what a disappointment Ella was as a daughter? Letters of apology to every teacher Ella had this year?

As soon as the computer powered on, Ella plugged in the drive. It took her a minute to figure out how to access the contents. She couldn't remember the last time she'd used an external drive with this computer.

The folders were labeled 1 through 17. Ella clicked on 1. It was full of pictures. The first showed Mom in a hospital bed looking exhausted but ecstatic, a white and blue bundle on her chest. Ella swallowed hard. She backed out of that file and picked the one marked 17.

Even in a thumbnail, she recognized the first file. It was the same picture of Jack that hung in the hall outside her room. Tears blurred her vision as she tried to back out of the folder again. Seventeen folders for seventeen years of Jack's life. A whole life on a drive smaller than a keychain. And Mom had given it to her.

Outside, a car horn beeped. Liv and Owen were here. Time for school. But Ella couldn't move. She just slumped in her chair, staring at her brother's face gone fuzzy with tears.

The horn beeped again. Ella jumped up, slammed the laptop shut, and ran out of the room.

~

Most days when they got to school, Liv would immediately rush off. She always had to bother some teacher about the finer points of comma placement, or why she only got a 99 on the last test. Meanwhile, Ella and Owen would take their time dropping stuff in their locker and meandering over to homeroom.

Today was different. They'd barely passed the office when Liv announced, "I have to pee. Come on, Ella."

She grabbed Ella's arm and tugged her toward the bathroom. Ella didn't understand why this needed to be a two-woman operation. She glanced at Owen, who shrugged.

"I'll meet up with you guys in homeroom," he said.

When the bathroom door had swung shut behind them, Ella turned to Liv. "What's up? You need a tampon or something?"

"No, I wanted to talk to you without Owen around."

Liv bent to peek under the stalls and see if any were occupied. Ella clicked her tongue at her friend. "That's why God invented texting you know. Super-secret conversations. No possibility of being overheard."

Apparently satisfied that they were alone, Liv straightened up. "I know, I just thought you might take it wrong in a text."

Ella felt the muscles in her neck tense. "Take what wrong?"

"Look, El, Owen can't afford to get into trouble."

Was Liv seriously going to yell at her because Owen got a detention? As if that made any kind of sense.

"Why not?"

Liv blushed. "You know he doesn't have the best grades, and . . ."

"Owen's a big boy, Liv, he can take care of himself. Besides, I didn't ask him to follow me."

"I know. That's not what I'm saying. It's just, sometimes Owen gets over-excited and that's not good."

Ella stared at Liv, completely at a loss. What was she trying to say? Was she jealous that Ella and Owen seemed to be getting closer this year? Annoyed that Owen had been the one to comfort Ella not her? As if Liv would ever risk her perfect record by storming out of a class. And she wasn't there anyway.

"It's not my fault you're not in any of our classes," Ella said.

Liv threw up her hands. "What does that have to do

with anything?"

"What does any of this have to do with anything?" Ella turned away, but she could still see Liv in the mirror.

She watched as Liv opened her mouth. Closed it. Took a breath. "I'm just saying, take it easy, okay?" Liv said.

"Yeah, sure, whatever." Ella turned and slammed through the bathroom door so hard it bounced against the water fountain. Stupid bathroom door. Stupid school. Stupid Liv getting her all annoyed. What in the hell was she even talking about back there?

Ella skipped her locker and went straight to homeroom. Owen's eyebrows jumped when he saw her burst in. She tried to dial it back a little bit, but the confrontation with Liv had shaken her. They used to be best friends. BFF's. Soul sisters. Now Ella couldn't even understand what Liv was upset about. It was stupid and she hated it.

She dropped into her seat without saying anything to Owen. For the first time, she was grateful for assigned seating in homeroom. That meant she could sit with her back to Owen. Who knew, maybe he'd asked Liv to say all that stuff.

"What's up?" Owen asked.

"Nothing."

She felt a nudge on her foot. His toe against her heel. "Really, though?"

"Ask your sister." Ella pulled up her hood and settled back in her chair, legs stretched out in front and well out of nudging range.

Liv showed up right on cue and took her seat behind Owen. Ella could hear them whispering back there.

That was fine. She didn't want to talk to them anyway.

~

Ms. Beaudry stopped at Ella's table and looked down at Ella's drawing. Ella didn't have to look up to know her teacher was standing there with one hand on her cheek, her head tilted slightly to the left. Ella picked up a pink colored pencil and began to fill in part of the design. Ms. Beaudry made a soft noise in the back of her throat. Ella sat back on her stool. She set the pencil down gently.

"It's a lovely concept, Ella. It really is."

Ella heard the "but" coming. She was not disappointed.

"But." Ms. Beaudry paused as though uncertain how to phrase what she was about to say. "I wonder where is Ella in this?"

Ella looked down at the drawing. She'd planned a three-foot sculpture depicting a family of ducks made of soda bottles and other plastic trash.

"It's a commentary about the impact of plastic on aquatic life," Ella said. She knew she sounded defensive. She was defensive. She'd been debating over which sketch to finalize for weeks. It was this or the school of salmon made of tinsel and wrapping paper. Both were a little off-brand for her, but she'd thought maybe it was time to branch out from toys.

"I see that . . ." Ms. Beaudry said. She paused. Ella waited. They both looked at the drawing. All around them, the other students continued to sketch with an intensity that implied they were absolutely not listening even a little and were 100 percent focused on not paying any attention to this conversation.

"It's an important message," Ms. Beaudry said. She sighed and clasped her hands together. "But it's not exactly new, is it?"

Ella sagged. She'd known that this was derivative. She'd said so at the very beginning. It wasn't as though changing it from fish to ducks made such a huge difference. She was just tired of people not understanding her work.

"An artist has a responsibility, Ella. You have a point of view that no one else in the world has because it belongs only to you. That means you have something to say, and only you can say it. If you don't, the world will be a little poorer." Ms. Beaudry touched the corner of the drawing with one finger. "This is someone else's story. Where's yours?"

Ella looked up into Ms. Beaudry's face for the first time in this conversation. The teacher wore a soft smile. She looked into Ella's eyes as though trying to read her soul.

Ella dropped her eyes to the page. Slowly, she turned the sheet over.

"Well done," Ms. Beaudry said softly. She moved on to the next table.

Left alone with her blank page, Ella rummaged through her pencil box and found a black marker. She stared at the white expanse of paper.

Ms. Beaudry was wrong. Nobody wanted to hear her story. Nobody wanted to talk about her dead brother, or her refusal to take Driver's Ed, or the fact that every school day brought her one day closer to the end of senior year and the yawning black hole that was her future. Sometimes she didn't even blame them. Ella didn't want to talk about it either.

Everyone was happier pretending it hadn't happened, that Jack had never existed. Ella felt like an immigrant trying to hold on to her native language, while all around her, everyone insisted on speaking only English. They'd read about that in history class.

It made her angry. That's how she felt. Angry. And nobody understood. How did you sculpt anger? How could you draw it?

She hefted the black marker as though it were a knife, then slashed the page, once, twice, leaving thick black wounds. That wasn't right. They were just marks. Stupid paper, all two-dimensional.

Ella dropped the marker. She snatched the sheet of paper and crumpled it into a ball. The other kid at her table, Kathrine or Kit or whatever her name was, inched away, as though anger were an infectious disease. Across the room, Owen caught her eye and raised one dark eyebrow. She looked down at the crumpled sheet, trying to ignore him. He was probably wondering if she was going to throw another fit and storm out again.

Her fingers picked apart the wrinkles. Her hand smoothed the page. Now the black lines looked jagged. The thick paper held damage, refusing to return to its original shape. That was fine with Ella. She'd work with what she had. What could be more authentic than a sketch drawn off the top of her head? Ms. Beaudry couldn't object to that.

The lines looked like part of a skirt, fluttering in the wind. Ella added legs, a head, hair. She hardly knew what she was drawing until she'd drawn it, but each line fell easily after the other, until she was staring down at a picture of a little girl standing tall at the crest of a hill, as though waiting for someone. She clutched a Maximus Tron toy against her chest. Her fierce expression stared straight out at Ella. Ella clenched her teeth.

The artist part of her, which was very nearly all of her, had already plunged on ahead, thinking about how to sew a dress for the girl out of old Barbie clothes and stiffen it with wire so it seemed to flutter in the breeze the way the astronauts had made the flag for the moon landing.

She'd have to be careful with perspective. She wanted to make it larger than life-size, but still recognizably a little girl, not a grown-up. Someone you had to look up at even if you looked down on her for being young, and female, and playing with toys.

Could she shape a whole human figure out of plastic? She'd never tried. Usually her sculptures were abstracts or three-dimensional mosaics that formed a recognizable image only if you stepped back far enough and maybe squinted a little. This was different. But stores had mannequins right? It couldn't be that hard.

By the time Ms. Beaudry came around again, Ella had filled her paper with drawings, sketches and notes. It was a crumpled messy disaster of a sketch. Ms. Beaudry looked down at it and smiled.

"I knew you had something to say."

Ella set her jaw. It was true. She did. And Ella was going to say it, whether anyone wanted to hear it or not.

CHAPTER TWENTY-ONE

Rational Absurdism

When Ella reported to detention after school, a few other kids were already slumped around the room, but Owen hadn't showed up yet. She snagged a seat near the middle with empty seats on either side. Owen had been fine at lunch, and Liv had stopped ranting about whatever had gotten under her skin this morning, so there was no reason why he shouldn't want to sit next to her. But she was glad she didn't have to be the one to make that call.

Ms. Alley was the teacher in charge, which sucked, because she was one of those super young teachers that tended to only stick around for a year or two before they got fed up and moved on to a school with a bigger budget and fewer problem students. She was the type who would try to enforce rules that made no sense with whatever authority she thought she had.

A more experienced teacher would have glanced around the room, marked down who was there, and left them to their own devices until it was time for the activity bus. Not Ms. Alley. She stood at the front of the room, all five-feet-two and 120 pounds of her, and took attendance, calling out their names one-by-one like this was actually a class.

Owen slipped in just after she'd said his name. Ella smiled when he slumped into the seat next to her.

"Are you Owen Butler?"

"That's me."

"You're late."

"Sorry, I was working on an art project."

Ms. Alley sniffed in a way that made her nostrils go round like a pig's. Ella swallowed down a giggle. She'd never had Ms. Alley but she was obviously the kind of teacher who would try to make her explain the joke.

"I expect everyone to stay busy and quiet during the next 75 minutes. You should all have homework to keep you occupied. If you don't, or if you finish early, there are free reading books at the back of the classroom. Unless you're getting a book, I expect you stay in your seats and stay focused. If you need help, raise your hand. I will come to your desk."

Ugh. Ella hadn't even been all that upset about detention, but that little speech made her want to graffiti the walls out of spite. It stayed peaceful for about two minutes, while students got settled for an hour plus of purgatory.

Then Ms. Alley approached Owen's desk.

"Owen, you should be working on homework, not

doodles." She spoke out loud, making no effort to not disturb the other students. Apparently, it was more important to make an example out of Owen than to let students actually get anything done.

"This is homework. It's for art."

"Is that really the best use of your time when you have a teacher here able to help you with more demanding work?"

Owen's eyebrow furrowed. "Yes."

Ms. Alley seemed nonplussed, apparently that wasn't the answer she had expected. Fortunately for her at that moment Mitch Trasker announced, "I have to piss, where's the bathroom pass?"

Ms. Alley forgot all about Owen to focus on that train wreck.

Ella rolled her eyes at Owen. He shrugged. He was always way more chill than her.

Across the room, Ms. Alley had gotten pulled into an argument with Mitch. Always a bad move. Mitch was one of those guys who argued with people just to see what happened. Plus, at six-two, he towered over her.

"I am a grown man. You can't tell me I can't go to the bathroom."

"If you were a grown man, you would have planned ahead and gone to the bathroom before you came in here."

"I didn't know I had to piss at the time."

"Mitchel! Choose a better word."

Mitch sat up straight. "You don't call me Mitchel. Only my mom calls me Mitchel."

Ms. Alley put one hand on her hip. "Would you like to explain to your mom why a grown man like you got two detentions in two days?"

Mitch rolled his eyes and sat back down. Ms. Alley relaxed. Ella knew that was a bad move. Ms. Alley thought she'd won, but more likely Mitch was just regrouping.

Some freshman in the front of the room raised his hand like this was actually some sort of study hall. Ms. Alley looked positively delighted to explain semicolons to him. Ella stopped listening and tried to refocus on her planning sheet. This sculpture was going to be complicated. She needed a materials list and budget and possibly some sort of schedule or she'd never get it done in time. Ella was deep in the art planning zone when Ms. Alley's voice snapped her back to reality.

"Owen Butler. Put the cards away."

Owen blinked. He looked tired. Maybe he was just sick of this argument. "I need them for my art project."

"I believe I told you to work on something more substantial. You can play games on your own time."

Owen muttered something under his breath.

Ms. Alley's face flushed. Her nostrils flared again. She looked even more like a pig now, Ella thought. A skinny, angry pig in a blue pencil skirt.

Mitch took advantage of the distraction to stand up and amble toward the back of the room.

"What did you say?" Ms. Alley demanded.

"Nothing," Owen said. He started packing up his art

supplies.

"You said something."

A shriek from the back of the room snapped Ms. Alley's head around. It was followed by what sounded like someone trying to fill a metal bucket with a narrow hose.

"Mitchel!" Ms. Alley squealed.

Ella spun in her seat to see Mitchel standing in front of the metal trash bin with his back to the room. It took her a moment to realize what he was doing. Forbidden a trip to the bathroom, Mitchel had found a more accessible receptacle.

Some students were screaming, others were laughing. Someone whipped out a cell phone and pointed it in Mitch's direction.

"Mitchel, you stop that at once," Ms. Alley said. She waved her hands in the air, trapped between the desire to discipline him and the reality of what she might see if she stepped too close.

"Can't stop midstream." Mitch's voice bounced off the wall.

Ella felt frozen in place. She looked over at Owen, who was bent over his drawing again. He didn't seem bothered by the chaos behind him.

"Everyone sit down this instant!" The rage in Ms. Alley's voice sent kids scuttling for their seats. No one wanted to be in the blast radius when she came down on Mitch.

"You," she pointed one quivering finger at Mitch,

"don't move." Ms. Alley picked up the classroom phone. Probably to call the resource officer.

Mitch grinned and sauntered out of the room. Ella watched him go. She disagreed with his tactics, sure, but there was something impressive about someone who could just stir up rage like that and not seem bothered by it at all.

Ms. Alley slammed down the phone and returned her attention to the class. "No one is to post that on the internet. Do you hear me? I will personally call the parents of anyone who so much as discusses it online."

Ella pretended to be absorbed in her work so Ms. Alley wouldn't see her eyes roll. Empty threats like that were exactly why kids like Mitch found her such an easy target. But at least all the commotion had eaten up a good chunk of detention. Plus, Ms. Alley was too flustered to bother Owen anymore.

Ella didn't know what Ms. Alley's problem was. Maybe it was that Owen had drawn attention to himself by coming in late, because Ella was sitting right next to him, also drawing. At least Owen's work actually looked like work. He'd sectioned off his paper into rectangles and was sketching out the major arcana of a tarot deck in a neat grid. His goal was to design and paint an entire deck of tarot cards, each suit in a different artistic style.

Later, when Ella and Owen were walking down the hall, Owen said, "So that's detention, huh? Overbearing staff and piss-poor entertainment. Two stars. Would not recommend."

"Agreed," Ella said. "But at least Mitch distracted Ms. Alley. What was her deal with you?"

Owen shrugged. "Dunno. I guess she thinks problem students like us need extra guidance." He threw an arm over Ella's shoulder. "Surely she could have beaten the creativity right out of me with enough detention periods."

"Not likely," Ella said.

"You're the one who should be relieved. If she'd given me another detention you would have had to shave your head, or write a strongly worded letter or something."

"Um, why?"

"Protesting my unfair treatment! You were working on your art project and she didn't say anything to you."

"That's because mine looks like a hot mess. She couldn't tell if it was art or calculus. I am relieved though. I don't need any more trouble."

"Your mom still mad?"

"Yeah, her too."

Owen stopped with his hand on the front door. Ella could see the activity bus through the window and, off to the right, Liv's car.

"Liv didn't get on your case about me getting detention, did she?"

Ella clenched her fists inside her hoodie pocket. She hadn't really meant to tell Owen about that. "She might have brought it up."

"I didn't tell her to," Owen said.

Of course he hadn't. She should have known he hadn't. It wasn't like him and she knew it. But it was nice to hear him say it.

"It's okay." Ella reached past him to open the door.

He sidestepped, so her hand brushed his torso instead of the door handle. She jerked it back, surprised.

"No," Owen said. "It's not."

He stormed through the door and toward the car. Ella ran after him. "Owen, wait!"

But he didn't wait. He strode to the passenger door, wrenched it open, and threw himself into the seat beside Liv.

"Listen, I got detention because I mouthed off to Mr. Hitchens. I knew what I was doing. It wasn't Ella's fault."

Ella froze on the sidewalk. She did not want to be drawn into this. Did not want to see Liv's face.

"She shouldn't have—" Liv began.

"No," Owen interrupted. "You may be smarter than me, but last time I checked, I was the older sibling here. You need to stop treating me like a kid."

"Really? I need to stop treating you like a kid? You think we should all behave like adults here? Is that what you want Owen?"

"Yes."

"Oh well, I appreciate your honesty," the words twisted with such sarcasm that Ella almost lost her balance.

"Don't make this about something it's not," Owen snapped back. "Get in the car, El."

"No, I'll just . . ." Ella began, not at all sure what else she could do, but certain she didn't want to plunge into the wave of anger that was building inside that car.

"Get in the car," Liv said.

Owen, his door still gaping wide, leaned forward and put his head in his hands. He muttered something that sounded like, "I have a headache."

Liv opened her door and stepped out. She looked over the top of the car at Ella. Her voice was much gentler than it had been a moment ago. "Come on El, get in the car. We all need to get home."

Ella hugged her arms across her body. "I didn't mean to say anything."

"It's fine. Just let's go, okay?" Her smile was thin and brittle at the edges, but at least she wasn't shouting. Ella nodded and got into the car.

Liv slipped them past the bus and across the driveway. People shouldn't drive when they were angry. Road rage caused accidents.

The road in front of the school was weirdly busy for the time of day. There must be some sort of sportball game or practice or something. Liv drummed her fingers on the steering wheel. Ella closed her eyes and tried to breathe deeply. She was safe. Liv was a good driver. But Liv was also mad. But she wouldn't let emotion get the better of her. But it's harder to focus when you're mad, and driving requires a lot of focus.

When the car surged onto the road, Ella squealed. She couldn't help it. Her eyes were closed tight and she clutched her seatbelt in both hands.

"Olivia," Owen said, his voice soft.

The car seemed to slow down a little. Out of the sparkling darkness behind her eyelids, Ella heard Liv say, "Sorry, Ella. I just needed to get us on the road. It's okay now."

"Okay," Ella echoed, but she kept her eyes closed until they got to her house.

~

Later that night, Ella was watching a YouTube video from @trash_art when she got a text.

LIV: Sorry about the drive home.

She felt the knot in her stomach uncoil a bit as she texted back.

ELLA: I didn't mean to cause trouble. Is O still mad?

LIV: Nah. Over it. #siblinglove

ELLA: Cool.

She set the phone down gently. She was glad Liv and Owen weren't fighting, glad not to be in the middle of it. At the same time, she couldn't help but remember their argument. How they seemed to be talking about two things at once. Even their fights had this secret subtext that Ella couldn't hope to understand. It made her feel . . .

cold, somehow.

That night, Ella went to bed early. She hoped Owen's dream catcher would give her another night of restful sleep.

It didn't.

CHAPTER TWENTY-TWO

Vanishing Point

Over the next few weeks, every waking moment that Ella wasn't in school she spent working on her assemblage. She was going to make a work of art so commanding, so startling, that the judges would have to award her first place. She started the work at home, partly because Ms. Beaudry didn't have the space for a piece as big as she was envisioning, and partly because she wasn't entirely sure what she was doing, and didn't really want an audience for her bumbling. Maybe she just needed some new materials.

She texted Liv.

ELLA: Can you bring me to the Salvation Army Store? I want to dig through the toy bins.

LIV: I'm kind of busy today.

ELLA: Please. Mom won't.

LIV: You know this wouldn't happen if you could drive.

Ella stared at the phone in disbelief. Had she really just read that? Had Liv really typed it? Ella threw the phone down on the desk so hard it bounced. She might have cracked the screen. She didn't care. How could Liv be such a bitch? She knew why Ella wouldn't drive. She was one of only like five people in the whole world who did. So why did she have to be like that?

Ella paced up and down the room. Nobody cared about her. They were all so busy with their own lives that they didn't give a shit about her or her art. She stalked toward the row of small sculptures she'd worked on all summer. What good were they? Wastes of time. Childish toys in infantile patterns. Trash. Part of her wanted to tear them apart and throw them in the garbage where they belonged.

Behind her, the phone vibrated.

She ignored it, imagining plastic parts snapping under her hands. The useless pieces falling in shards around her feet like angry snow. She went so far as to pick up the mallet she sometimes used for dissecting stubborn toys.

She raised the hammer. *Yes*, said a voice in the back of her head. She paused. It had sounded so real. Almost like another person inside her, one who relished destruction for its own sake. She lowered the mallet. Was that who she was? A destroyer of art?

Trash, the voice argued, and this time it sounded more like her own voice in full self-doubt mode. She wasn't falling for that.

"No," she said to the empty room. And then felt stupid. She laid the mallet gently on the desk and reached for her phone instead. She was going downstairs. Maybe even outside. It was cold outside. Maybe it would freeze her aimless rage.

The text message light was blinking. She had three messages.

LIV: I'm sorry. That was mean.

LIV: I shouldn't have said it.

LIV: I'm just busy today. Another day. I promise.

Ella stared at the messages. She knew about "another day" she knew about "we'll do it tomorrow." Oh, yes.

She knew all about having the tea party tomorrow and finishing the playhouse later, and going to the beach when you're older, and I promise, I promise, I'll play with you another day. She knew all about that. And she knew it was bullshit.

Later was a gentle way of saying never.

Her anger cooled so quickly she imagined steam spilling out of her ears and nose. It left her frozen inside, numb. She realized she'd stood looking at the phone so long that the screen had dimmed. She tapped it with her thumb.

ELLA: No worries. Another day.

Forget it. She would work with what she had. Might as well use up all these toys. Who knew? It might be the last sculpture she'd ever make. She queued up Totorro on YouTube and went back to work.

~

The Dreaming seemed even more barren without SigmaSigma. It wasn't as though they'd actually spoken all that often, but SigmaSigma had always been there. PhiTau was used to knowing that a slight turn of his head would show him the closest thing he had to a friend in this world. Except now SigmaSigma's garden was empty. The tiny sprout he once tended was withering. PhiTau wondered if a new tender would be assigned to it.

SigmaSigma had put the idea in his head that something bad must have happened to the tenders before them. Ella was 17 years old and SigmaSigma's dreamer had been even older than that. They couldn't have gone all this time without a tender, could they? Where had those former tenders gone?

PhiTau shook his head. He didn't want to think about this anymore. He wanted to see Ella. With shaking fingers, PhiTau sprinkled the dreamstuff onto the patch of tilled dirt. Then he tightened the satchel around his waist and stepped into Ella's dream.

~

The Savers of the Universe are running down a dirt road in the dark. Trees loom high on either side, their branches enmeshed with the night sky. No stars, no moon. The light comes from everywhere and nowhere. It's just enough for Ella to see Maximus Tron running at the front. Behind her is Baby Sarah, Barbie, and Legs the Frog-man.

Wearing the Frog-man shape made running difficult for PhiTau. His limbs moved in long and messy arcs that threatened to tumble him toward the dirt at any moment. It didn't help that Ella's fear was pushing them forward, making him move too quickly.

Behind them swoops something terrible. As wide as the sky and as dark as the night, it rushes toward them without talons or eyes. But Ella knows, and PhiTau knows with her, that when it reaches them it will shred them like so many moth-eaten ragdolls.

And so they run, but Ella's feet are stiff and somehow cold. They feel like blocks of ice. She stumbles. The icy feeling radiates up her legs. She staggers to a halt in the middle of the road. Maximus Tron runs on ahead, oblivious. The others slow, hesitate. Maximus Tron disappears into the dark. Ella feels the loss of him, like a cavity in her heart.

"It's coming," Barbie says, dancing from one stiff toe to the other.

"Run, Ella," says Baby Sarah, eyes blinking in her massive head.

Ella tries, but her legs are frozen in place. She feels the cold rising to her groin, her hips, her belly. She can't move.

"I can't," Ella says.

PhiTau knew his line was coming. He couldn't say it. He wouldn't say it. Damn the rules and damn Morpheus and damn the whole damn dreaming. He wouldn't say it and he certainly wouldn't do it.

He compressed the lips of Legs the Frog-man so no sound could escape. He would not speak, no matter what.

The dark thing sweeps closer. It's casting shadows in the shadow. They shimmer just there, on the edge of vision. Barbie and Baby Sarah pull at Ella's ice-cold hands.

PhiTau felt the frogman's throat distend. It was filling up with sound, filling up with the words he should have said already.

The other Savers look at him, questions in their eyes, but Ella does not turn. She can't. The darkness is here. Here and now.

PhiTau felt his own terror tangle up with Ella's. He opened his mouth to scream and the words spilled out. Two words. Two tiny, terrible words.

"Leave her."

And then, "We'll come back for her later."

The Savers flee. The darkness dives. PhiTau's screams mingle with Ella's between the worlds. And in the darkness behind the shadows, a sound that sounds like "yes."

~

Liv made an extra effort to be nice to her for a few days after their fight by text. It almost felt like they were back to normal, although Ella still felt the coldness deep in her belly. She knew that Liv was trying, but trying wasn't the same as being. And that was fine. They were growing up, right? That's what everyone kept telling her. Lives would change, paths would split. Friends today might not be friends tomorrow.

Ella didn't let it bother her. She kept her head down. Did her work. Made small talk with Liv and Owen. It helped that Owen hadn't been talky lately either. He and Liv had their own issues to work out, sibling bond or not. The last thing Ella wanted was to be in the middle of that.

Well, that was a lie. All Ella had ever wanted was to stand in the circle of Liv and Owen's sibling love. She wanted it more than almost anything in the world. It was the next best thing to having her own brother back. But if life had taught Ella one thing, it was that you didn't always get what you want. All you could do was make art, and hope the music in your earbuds would drive away the dreams.

CHAPTER TWENTY-THREE

Vanitas Presumed

Ms. Beaudry had asked Ella to bring her sculpture into school. She needed to see "evidence of progress." It wasn't the first time Ella regretted the scale of this thing. Wouldn't it have been just as effective at two feet tall as it was at six? It wasn't even finished and already it wouldn't fit in Liv's car, certainly not with Ella and Liv and Owen all in there as well.

So Ella got up early to ride in with Mom and the sculpture. It just about fit in the cargo area if they tilted it so the shoulders of the girl rested against the top of the rear seats. Good thing Ella hadn't put the head on yet or they would have needed Dad's truck, and she certainly wasn't about to ride in that death trap. It didn't even have back seats.

Owen and Liv had offered to help her carry it to the art room, but they weren't at the doors when Mom pulled up in front of the school.

"Where are they?" Mom asked.

"I'm not sure. They said they'd be here."

Ella texted Owen. No answer.

After five minutes, Mom said, "I can't wait anymore. I'm going to be late to work. Do you want me to help you carry it down?"

Ella sighed. She eyed the patches of ice on the sidewalk that hadn't quite melted under their sprinkling of salt. She didn't want to carry it alone, but she also didn't want to make Mom late.

"We can just get it out of the car and you can go."

"Are you sure?"

She checked her phone. Still no answer. If they were on their way, Owen would have his phone handy. They must be running late.

"Yeah."

They wrestled the stiff form out of the car and set it on a dry patch of sidewalk. Buses were starting to come in. Kids glanced at it as they streamed past. Ella tried not to imagine what they were thinking. A nude, headless girl turns heads even if she is only made of My Little Ponies and Calico Critters. Ella wished that she'd finished sewing the dress before she'd brought the assemblage to school. It seemed indecent somehow to leave her standing naked in the snow.

Mom waved and pulled away. After the Jeep had gone, Ella looked at her phone one more time. Still no answer. Maybe they were ignoring her. She sighed.

The sculpture wasn't that heavy, just awkward. Maybe

she could carry it herself?

She put her arms around its waist and lifted. Yeah, this was doable. Probably. Now if everyone would just stop staring. Hadn't they ever seen an art project before? She'd barely made it through the front door when she heard Kristen Lund's nasal voice rise over the cacophony of student shouts and slamming lockers. "What. Is. That?"

Ella pretended she hadn't heard.

Kristen stepped in front of her and Ella almost rammed her in the shins with the base of the assemblage. Kristen would not be ignored. Of course not.

"I said, what is that?"

"It's my art project." Ella set it down carefully, leaving her arms loose around it to deflect the moving bodies in the hall. "It's not done yet."

"I can see that," Kristen stood with one hand on her hip, her head cocked at an obnoxious angle. "Why are you carrying it by yourself?"

Ella shrugged.

"You and Owen fighting?"

Ella didn't need to put up with this. She needed to get her assemblage to Ms. Beaudry's room before the bell. She lifted it again.

Kristen clicked her tongue. "You take the shoulders. Those are shoulders, right? I'll grab the base."

She started to lift before Ella had agreed. Attempting to shift her grip without dropping the thing, Ella said, "You want to help me?"

"When I beat you in the contest, I don't want it to be

because your sculpture hit the floor and it turned back into a toy box."

She walked backward as she talked, forcing Ella to go along or lose her grip. Kristen bumped and elbowed her way down the hall, making room for them to pass in the rush of students. Ella, holding up her end, wondered why Kristen was really helping. Maybe she was going to try a new tack: make friends with Ella to get to Owen. Probably wouldn't work considering Owen hadn't even shown up. Ella itched to check her phone again. Where were they?

"Alright, you sit over here, don't you?" Kristen said, already moving toward Ella's corner.

Before Ella could answer, Ms. Beaudry strolled over. "Hello girls, what have you brought me?"

"It's my art project," Ella said.

"It is big, isn't it? Can you just nudge it into the corner a bit so nobody knocks it over?"

They did as they were told. Then Kristen stood up and dusted her hands together. "You're going to build a head for it, right?"

"Yeah, of course."

Kristen pursed her lips and nodded. Overhead, the first bell rang.

"You girls had better run off to homeroom," Ms. Beaudry said. "I'll see you in class later."

Ella trailed Kristen out of the room. "Thanks," she said.

"No worries," Kristen smirked and took off around the

corner. Ella didn't have much mental space to overanalyze Kristen's motives, because Liv and Owen still hadn't answered her texts.

And they weren't in homeroom when Ella got there. Where were they? Ella tried to calm herself down. Liv was probably ambushing some teacher over a homework problem she hadn't been able to solve on her own. That made sense.

Owen was harder to rationalize. He was always in homeroom five minutes before the bell, sipping from his travel mug and ignoring the airheads who chattered to each other in the back row. Today the airheads were there, but Owen wasn't. Maybe he was in the art room. Ella had just come from there, but she'd had to run upstairs to her locker first. Maybe she'd missed him on the way by. Did she have time to go back and check before the second bell?

The bell rang. That would be a no then. Ella went to her seat.

"Hey Ella, where's your girlfriend?" Trent asked her.

"Shut up, Trent."

"I'm just saying, you should maybe put some clothes on her."

Pig, Ella thought. She imagined a giant, snorting pig squeezed into Trent's Abercrombie and Fitch shirt. He'd probably smell better, because Ella had never met a pig who thought it was necessary to literally bathe in body spray.

All through announcements she kept expecting Liv

and Owen to burst through the door all flustered. Owen had slept in and Liv hadn't been able to leave until he'd made his coffee. Or Liv had been putting the last finishing touches on a math assignment and lost track of time. Or the power had gone out and their phones had died. Or Liv's car had refused to start. Or Liv's car had started but there was a deer in the road and Liv had to swerve to avoid it and now they were both bleeding out in a ditch somewhere.

Someone dropped a book with a thump. Ella almost screamed. One of the airheads from the back of the room giggled. Ella wondered if they were giggling at her. But no, they weren't even looking at her. She should just go to Chemistry. Everything would be fine.

All the way down the hall, and at her locker and while she climbed the stairs she kept looking over her shoulder. Part of her expected Owen and Liv to show up any minute. Part of her was afraid they never would.

Someone touched her elbow. Ella spun, ready to shout at Liv. It had to be Liv. But no, it was the girl who sat across the aisle from her in Chemistry. She had the locker next to Ella's. Kayla, no, Kara, that was it.

"You okay, Ella?"

"What? Yeah. What's up?"

"You were just standing there staring down the hall for like five minutes. Are you sick or something?"

Ella shook her head, trying to clear it. "No, just, just thinking."

Kara didn't look convinced. "Right, yeah. I think class

is about to start."

"Right." Ella looked down the hall one last time. Still no Owen.

Ella made it to Chemistry on autopilot and dropped into her seat. The other kids chattered around her. The words might as well have been in Japanese. Ella's eyes flicked from the clock to the door and back. She expected Owen to stroll in any minute. She believed he'd never appear.

She stared at the clock, eyes narrowed. Somehow, she'd slipped sideways through a crack in the world and ended up in a place where time ran at one-tenth speed. Every breath seemed to take forever. Every exhale was so long that she feared she'd forget how to breath in again when the time came.

Something terrible had happened. Liv and Owen were dead, gone away from her, slipped through a different crack into a world where she could not follow. They were dead and gone and she'd never see them again, just two shiny wooden boxes that she wasn't allowed to touch topped with flowers that had no smell. They'd left her behind to face the world alone.

But no. They were out there somewhere. They had to be. *I should go look for them,* she thought. And she very nearly did so. She placed both her hands flat on the lab bench, ready to stand up and run from the room, unable to bear another moment of frozen indecision. Except that just as her hands pressed against the cool flat surface, a figure appeared in the doorway.

Owen. Smiling.

Ella collapsed back on her stool. She'd been so silly. Of course he was fine. Nothing bad had happened. They'd just been running late. Maybe they'd stopped to get coffee. Except Owen never bought coffee in the morning. He always made it at home. And he wasn't carrying his travel mug.

That's when Ella knew that she'd been at least partially right. Something was wrong. Something bad had happened. Owen without a coffee cup was like Kristen without an attitude. It just didn't happen. Ella tugged her sleeves down to cover her palms.

All her senses strained in Owen's direction. Mrs. Finch would ask him where he'd been, and he'd have to tell her and then Ella would know. *Knowing is better than not knowing*, she told herself.

But Mrs. Finch only glared at Owen and said, "Mr. Butler, after class."

Owen nodded and moved toward his seat. As he passed, he grinned at Ella. He must have known she'd been worried. It was probably all over her face. She tried to smile back, but was pretty sure she looked like she was about to cry.

Chemistry class went on forever. Ella drew spiky shapes in her notebook and colored them in so hard that her pen wore through the paper to the page beneath. Her head ached. She tried to tell herself that everything was fine. Owen was here and smiling which meant Liv had to be okay too. Owen wouldn't be grinning if something had happened to his sister. *Everything is fine. Nothing is wrong.* She chanted it over and over until the words lost all meaning. *Everything is fine, nothing is wrong, everything fine, nothing wrong, nothing is fine is wrong, everything is wrong is wrong.*

Finally, finally the bell rang. Ella was on her feet before the echoes had died away. She snatched up her notebook and practically vaulted over the lab bench behind her to get to Owen.

"Where were you?" she asked, and her voice sounded immature and whiny even to her own ears.

"Just running late," Owen said. Then he blinked and Ella knew he was lying. "Did you get your assemblage moved okay without us?"

Ella opened her mouth to demand an explanation, but Mrs. Finch came up behind them and said, "Mr. Butler, nice of you to join us today. Do you have a note?"

Owen produced a folded piece of paper from his back pocket and handed it to Mrs. Finch. Ella craned her neck to look at it. It was from the office, not from Owen's parents. That's all she had time to see before Mrs. Finch tilted the note away from her.

"Ms. Pratt. Don't you have class?"

"Not really."

"Go on, El. I'll see you at lunch," Owen said.

Ella really didn't have class, just study hall. It wasn't like it mattered if she missed it, but Mrs. Finch clearly wasn't going to let Ella hang around here.

She went straight down to the art room. Ms. Beaudry

could call Mr. Kent and let him know where she was. Ms. Beaudry was nice like that. Ella had Creative Writing homework she hadn't finished for third period, but she didn't care. Mr. Hitchens hated her anyway and there was no way she'd be able to focus on schoolwork until she'd had a chance to actually talk to Owen and figure out what was going on.

A bunch of sophomores, with a couple of juniors and seniors mixed in, gathered in Ms. Beaudry's classroom. These were the kids who took Art because they thought it was an easy elective, not because they loved it. Ms. Beaudry wouldn't mind if Ella worked on her sculpture while they learned about pointillism or whatever.

"Hello, Ella. It's good to see you again so soon," said Ms. Beaudry. "Where are you supposed to be?"

"Study hall with Mr. Kent."

Ms. Beaudry nodded and went to the phone without another word. Ella could have hugged her. That woman was the greatest teacher in the world. At least one person was still acting like themselves today.

Ella pulled her tub of supplies from the cubby on the wall and went to her sculpture. Two girls were sitting at the next table. Ella recognized one as a fellow senior. She looked vaguely familiar. Maybe she did track with Liv?

". . . heard they just slipped off the road." One girl was saying. "It was slippy this morning."

"Oh my God, is her car okay? My parents would kill me if I so much as scratched my car. A tiny little rock cracked my windshield last week and I thought my dad was going to have a conniption."

"I think they busted a headlight that's all. They were lucky though, Olivia said . . ."

Were they talking about Liv? Ella stopped rummaging through plastic bits to hear what the senior girl was saying.

". . . that if the snow hadn't been so deep they would have hit a tree for sure."

Ella couldn't move. Couldn't breathe. Owen and Liv had been in a car accident and Owen had lied to her about it. He'd lied right to her face. They'd almost died and he hadn't told her.

Why would he do that?

She felt hot and cold at the same time. Her breath gasped in jagged little shards that stabbed her throat. She was going to throw up, or scream, or both.

At the front of the room, Ms. Beaudry clapped her hands for attention. Ella fled toward the door.

Fortunately, there was a bathroom right across the hall from the art room. Even more fortunately, it was empty, because class had already started and the only classrooms down this wing were art, band, and the weight room.

Ella sunk to the floor, hyperventilating. Her vision narrowed to a point. She couldn't even see the tiles between her sneakers. She closed her eyes tight and tried to breathe.

They're fine, she told herself. *You saw Owen. He was fine. Not even scratched.*

But what about Liv? He lied about the car accident.

Maybe he lied about Liv too. Maybe she's dying. Maybe she's already dead.

That's stupid. If she were dead, Owen wouldn't be in class grinning his stupid grin and lying to your face about it. He'd be curled up in his bedroom closet in a nest made of stuffed animals.

Maybe that was true. Or, maybe, he was in shock. A delayed reaction to trauma. Delusional. Maybe . . . maybe . . . maybe.

I have to find out.

Ella rubbed her eyes. That actually made sense. She'd go find Liv. She'd go and see her, sitting right in the front of the classroom taking copious notes, and then Ella would know that everything was fine. She was worrying for nothing.

Having a plan made her feel better. She managed to get to her feet.

Looking in the mirror was a bad idea. Her eyes were red, her face blotchy, but her lips were somehow pale. She looked like she had the plague. Which was fine, right? Later on she could tell Ms. Beaudry she'd felt sick and nobody would think anything of her disappearance from the art room.

Right.

Now what class was Liv in right now? Ella tried to think. She and Liv had compared class schedules at the beginning of the year and discovered that they shared the same lunch period every day. So was today an A day or a B day? A, because she'd just left the art room. No, B, because she was supposed to be in study hall with Mr. Kent. Okay so that meant that Liv was in . . . had to be Honors History, right? Or Calculus. It might be Calculus. No History. Yes. Definitely. Probably.

Anyway, the history room was closer. She'd just run by there. Check that Liv was okay, and then be back in Ms. Beaudry's room before anyone noticed she was gone. Ella took a deep breath and pushed through the bathroom door into the hallway. She thought she glimpsed Ms. Beaudry through the narrow window set in the art room door. Was she looking this way?

No. It was fine. Fine. Ms. Beaudry was chill. She wouldn't get Ella into trouble, not without talking to her first. And Ella could say she'd felt sick and went to the office to call her mom. It would work if she was quick.

She was already at the end of the hall. The double doors to the cafeteria were wide open and she could hear the lunch ladies wheeling the carts of trays across the floor. She crossed the doorway quickly. Up the ramp, past the stage door. She had to walk past the glass window that looked out of the main office. There was always the possibility that the vice principal would be hanging out in there, just waiting to see who might walk by, but nobody stopped her.

Almost there, she told herself. Past the bathrooms and the stairway and then the history room was the third door on the right. All she had to do was get to the door and she'd be able to see Liv was just fine. Not lying in a casket or bleeding in a ditch. No metal rod thrust through her brain. She was alive and she was fine. She had to be. Ella just had to see for herself.

She stopped just outside. Her heart was pounding. What if she looked through the window and Liv wasn't there? What if her seat was empty? But it wouldn't be. Everything was fine. She wanted to believe it, but she had to know for certain. She peeked through the window.

Liv was not in the classroom.

CHAPTER TWENTY-FOUR

Fantastic Realism

Ella thought about running down the hall and out the front door and just not stopping until she got home. She could run up the stairs and into her room and hide in her closet until everything stopped being awful. But home was a long way away, and her legs suddenly felt weak.

She wavered in the hallway. Should she keep looking for Liv, try to make it all the way to her calculus class on the other side of the building? Or should she find Owen, demand to know what was going on? He was the only one who had the answers. Except that he'd probably just lie to her again. Liv had disappeared. Owen was a liar. And the hallway had gotten really dark. Ella strained to look through the window again.

The door popped open. Ella nearly screamed. She fell back a step. Her heart jumped into her throat. She couldn't swallow it back down. She was going to drop dead right here, suffocated by her own heart, with no idea what had happened to Liv.

Someone was talking to her. She tried to focus, but the beating of her heart was so loud. She thought she might throw up. "Liv," she said. "Where's Liv?"

She thought she heard Liv's voice say, "I'm here, Ella. I'm right here." But that couldn't be right because Liv was gone, crashed, dead. Liv was gone and Owen had lied about it.

"It's okay. Just breathe. It's okay." The voice that sounded like Liv's kept talking as an arm encircled Ella's shoulder. "Let's get you to the bathroom."

Ella realized she was shaking. Her vision had cleared a little, so she could see her feet moving over the maroon and gray linoleum. The voice kept telling her to breathe, and she kept trying. But what was the point when she was dying? Liv was dead and Ella was dying and there was nothing she could do about any of it.

She clenched and unclenched her hands. They felt like they were barely connected to her arms. Like they'd been detached and while she wasn't looking, removed at the wrist and replaced with molded plastic, finger-shaped but unfeeling.

"You're having a panic attack," said the voice that sounded like Liv. Someone guided Ella to sit on a cold toilet seat. She didn't fight it. It was a relief not to have to support her body on plastic legs that refused to bend properly.

Someone took her hands and squeezed them. "Ella, tell me what you see." The voice was firm. It really did sound like Liv. Ella tried to focus.

"I see . . ." Her throat constricted. "I see a face."

"Good. What else do you see?"

Ella's eyes dropped, exhausted. "Pants," she said.

"What else?" The voice refused to leave her alone. It was going to keep asking questions forever.

"Shoes."

"And what do you hear?"

"Questions."

"Good."

Ella realized her back was damp with cold sweat. And her face, her face was wet. Had she been crying?

"What else do you hear, Ella?"

"My heartbeat."

The questions went on, pulling her back to reality bit by bit. Eventually, Ella sat exhausted in the handicapped stall of the downstairs girls bathroom. Her hands curled in her lap, her head bowed. A headache throbbed between her eyes.

Liv was crouched in front of her, holding her hands.

"You had me worried sick. Are you okay?"

"I had you worried?" Ella barked a dry laugh. Her throat was so dry. She wanted to ask what the hell had happened to her and Owen today. Why were they late, and where had Liv been when she'd looked through the window? But she was so tired.

"Do you think you can make it to the office?"

"Don't tell Mom," Ella muttered.

"We can't just not tell her. She has to come pick you

up." Liv put her arm around Ella and helped her stand.

"Don't tell her about panic." Ella tried to assemble enough brain cells to formulate a thought. "Say I threw up."

"Did you?"

"I wanted to."

Liv chuckled. "Fair enough."

~

PhiTau somehow knew Ella needed him. It was as though she'd called his name from across the field. Except, of course, she didn't know his name and never would. He was just her tender, invisible and unnoticed. The thought made him both angry and sad, but he reached into the pouch at his hip and pulled out a handful of dreamstuff.

He gazed unseeing at the glittering handful. It was probably a good thing she didn't know he existed. PhiTau hadn't forgiven himself for the part he played in her last dream. If she'd known who he was, she would probably be mad at him.

PhiTau sprinkled the dreamstuff and stepped into the circle.

Normally, PhiTau shared Ella's consciousness during a dream, but also had his own role to play. This time was different. This time he was inside her head, looking through her eyes, and feeling the residual emotion of her panic attack. He was as close to her as he had ever been, fully ensconced within her mind. He knew everything she knew, that she'd thought Liv was dead and that Liv wasn't, that there'd been an accident. That Ella might, possibly, have overreacted a bit.

Their eyes were half-closed, but through the cage of their lashes he could see the receptionist sitting at her desk, a phone in her hand. He could feel Liv's shoulder under their ear, her hand in theirs. He knew it was Liv because Ella knew, and he was both angry and relieved because Ella was. Her emotions were a storm, building, building, but not quite ready to break.

Something was wrong with this dream. It felt like a room with the door left open. The breeze of another world was drifting through. It was Ella's world, PhiTau realized, the human world not just influencing but actually overlapping the dream.

The room expanded, like lungs before a scream. The receptionist's desk was sliding away from them. "Your mom's on her way," the receptionist said, her voice echoing across the distance.

The sound reverberated in Ella's mind. No one else reacted, but Ella twitched.

Liv squeezed Ella's hand.

PhiTau felt the scream building in their chest.

PhiTau said, "It's okay. I'm here." He knew he was just a voice in Ella's head, but some of the turmoil inside her eased when he spoke. "Everyone is safe," he told her.

A buzzing filled Ella's mind, like feedback from a microphone. Was that his fault? He waited. Ella wavered between worlds. He wished they could stay this way forever—still, quiet, together.

But all too soon the dream wavered. Ella blinked and PhiTau found himself back in his garden plot.

~

Mom bought the stomachache thing without any problem. It helped that Ella was pale and shaky. Besides, she wasn't the kind of kid who lied to her parents all the time. It was just that she didn't really know how today had gone so far off the rails and she couldn't face anyone else's questions about it until she'd figured at least some of it out for herself. Maybe tomorrow things would make more sense.

Her phone buzzed as she walked down the hall past Jack's photo. She pulled it out of her pocket.

LIV: You okay

ELLA: Fine, are you?

Ella didn't realize she'd turned into her studio instead of her bedroom until she bumped into Jack's desk. She looked up just in time to see Maximus Tron totter near the edge. She lunged for him with her free hand, snatching him before he tumbled toward the ground.

"That must have given you flashbacks," she said to the action figure. He'd lost his head 11 years ago due to Ella's clumsiness.

She looked around the room. It felt sort of empty without the partially formed girl standing in the middle. It was almost a relief. If the assemblage were still here, she would have felt compelled to work on it. As it was, she could go back to her room and put off doing homework until bedtime.

She carried Maximus Tron back across the hall with her and sat down on the bed. Her phone buzzed again.

LIV: Fine? Why wouldn't I be

Ella didn't have the energy to answer that. She dropped the phone on her bedspread and just sat, rubbing the jagged spot where the head had broken off all those years ago. It was probably somewhere in the dirt pile. She'd put it in the shoebox when she'd buried him. Could she find it? Probably not. It was such a tiny piece of plastic.

Maybe she could dig through the random heads bin and find something that would fit him. But she was so tired. Besides, if she did that, would he really be Maximus Tron anymore? Wasn't a person mostly what went on inside their head? A different head would make you essentially a different person, wouldn't it?

Another buzz. Ella ignored it. She'd deal with Liv, and everything else, in the morning.

CHAPTER TWENTY-FIVE

Artifice Unveiled

Liv showed up at Ella's locker the next morning. Ella swung the door closed, and there she was.

"Hey," Liv said. Her tone was cautious. Owen hovered behind her, both hands wrapped around his coffee mug. They were going to try apologizing.

"Hey," Ella echoed. She adjusted the weight of books in her arm and turned to walk away. Ella wasn't sure she was ready to hear an apology. She certainly wasn't ready to forgive anyone.

"Look El, I'm sorry we didn't tell you about the accident."

Ella stopped. "You didn't just not tell me," she spoke without turning to face Liv. That made it easier. "You flat-out lied to me."

"We were trying to protect you," Liv said.

"We didn't want you to freak out," Owen added.

Anger spun Ella around. Her heart was burning in her

chest.

"You didn't want me to freak out? You could have died."

Liv held out both her palms. "It was a really minor thing, El. If you weren't in first period with Owen you would never have even known it happened."

"And that's supposed to make me feel better? We could have lied to you and you wouldn't have known. That's your defense?"

"She didn't mean—" Owen began.

But Liv interrupted him. "You're not the only one with problems."

"I didn't say I was. What does that have to do with anything?"

"I'm just saying, life is hard for other people too sometimes," Olivia said.

Ella thought she saw tears glitter in Liv's eyes and she felt bad. She didn't want Liv to be upset with her. She didn't want Liv to be upset at all. Ella took a step toward her friend.

"What do you mean? What's going on?"

The corner of Olivia's mouth twitched and she looked like she wanted to say something. Something important. Ella waited.

"Liv," Owen said, his voice soft. Liv glanced at him and when she turned back to Ella her face had gone smooth.

"I just mean that I know this was a hard situation for you. And we're sorry."

Ella's temper flared again. *Holy shit*, they were lying to her right now. They'd come to apologize and yet they were still keeping secrets. Meanwhile, Olivia just stood there with her big green eyes acting like she was so much better and more understanding than Ella was. Even if it was true, that didn't mean she needed to rub it in Ella's face.

"You know what, you're right. I wasn't looking at this from your point of view. It must be so hard to deal with a damaged little loser like me every day. I mean, I don't even know how to drive—"

Owen and Olivia both tried to interrupt her at once, but she just talked louder. People were staring. She didn't care.

"Here you are with your perfect grades and your perfect future and your parents who are still married and your brother who isn't dead, and who comes along to mess everything up but sad sack Ella. Better lie to her so she doesn't make a scene."

"Woah," Owen said. He actually took a step backward, as though staggered by the force of Ella's reaction.

Liv's eyes widened and then narrowed. Her face flushed. "You, you . . . child." She looked like she'd wanted to say something else but changed her mind at the last minute.

Owen touched his sister's arm. He tried to say something to her but she pulled away from him.

"Grow up, Ella. Just grow the fuck up. We're dealing with some real shit. And we're dealing with it now. Not in the past, not in my imagination, here and now. And a real friend would care about someone other than herself for five minutes."

Liv's face had gone all red and there were tears glittering in her eyes, but her mouth was a hard line.

Ella felt her heart constrict. She didn't want to be fighting right now. She didn't want Liv to be angry. She just wanted everything to stay as it had always been. She wanted to stay in school with Liv and Owen forever and be best friends and never have to change, never have to grow up, never have to figure out what real shit Liv was talking about. She'd seen enough real shit already. She didn't need anymore.

Liv stormed off.

"Liv, wait!" Owen cast an unreadable glance in Ella's direction and then shouldered a kid aside so he could follow his sister.

Ella realized then that everyone was either staring at her or very deliberately looking anywhere but at her. Her hands started to shake. She could feel the tremor travel from her heart down her arms. *Oh no, not now.* Her stomach heaved and she ran for the bathroom.

She made it about two steps through the bathroom door when the floor started to tilt. She grabbed for the wall to steady herself. It wasn't hard. The walls were closing in, making her vision dark around the edges.

"Whoa, are you hung over or something?" she heard a voice say just before her knees hit the floor.

Hands grabbed at her arms, but Ella barely felt them.

The darkness swallowed her.

~

Jack leans over her, his head silhouetted against the blue sky. "Hey, wake up sleepy head. We're supposed to be having a tea party."

Ella sits up. They're in the middle of a green field with nothing but grass in all directions. Ella has never seen this place before, but she likes it. It was smart of Jack to bring them here where it's safe.

They are sitting on a pink and white gingham cloth set with a full assortment of tea things, the kind that might have graced a southern lady's table in the 50s. It includes a graceful teapot and a double-decker plate crammed with delicate pastries. She and Jack are not alone. Legs the Frog-man grins at her as only a frogman can grin. Barbie, dressed in her most stylish sundress and floppy pink hat, adjusts her sunglasses, while Baby Sarah eyes the sweets as though deciding which five to devour first. This is so nice, all her friends together again, well, almost all of them. Where is Maximus Tron?

Floating in the sky far above the tea party, PhiTau heard Ella think of him, or at least, of the form this dream had given him. He waited for his cue.

Ella remembers that Maximus Tron is dead. They had a funeral for him and everything. How stupid of her to expect that he could come to a tea party when he was really six feet under.

"Are you going to pour the tea or shall I?" Jack says, in his best fancy British accent.

Ella giggles. "I'll do it."

She sits up on her knees and reaches for the teapot with both hands. It's big and she doesn't want to spill. The ground quivers under her. At first it is gentle. It might just be the beating of her heart in the stillness of the summer day. The unnatural stillness. As though the world is waiting for something, or hoping something will pass it by. The tremor shudders closer. Cups rattle on their saucers.

High above, PhiTau clenched his teeth behind his helmet. He'd hoped this would be a good dream for once, she deserved one, but he could feel Ella's anxiety mounting with every tremor. Something really was coming.

Ella looks at Jack who is on his feet, head cocked, listening. Her friends jump up, too. Ella notices that Legs is even taller than Jack.

"They're coming," Sarah says. She shoves a jam-filled cookie in her mouth. Powdered sugar spills down her yellow dress.

"Who's coming?" Ella says. She's standing next to Jack at the top of the grassy knoll. Her friends gather tense beside her.

"The giants," Jack says.

"We could plant a beanstalk," Legs says.

"No time," Jack answers. "We'll have to fight."

"I don't want to fight," Ella says.

In the distance a dark line approaches, trampling the grass, sending up plumes of dusk to block out the glorious golden sun and bottomless sky.

"I don't want to fight," Ella repeats. But it doesn't matter because the giants are coming. They don't need darkness to block out the sun. They do that all on their own. Tall, hideous deformed beasts. A solid mass of brown and gray. They could be one creature, one massive writhing darkness for all that Ella can see. They shout at the Savers of the Universe, at the sky, and at each other. It is their voices as much as their footsteps that shake the ground and make Ella sway.

PhiTau wanted to scream. He wanted to swoop down and save her from this place. Why was everything so awful? Why couldn't Ella have just one good dream? He should be down there with her.

She crouches in the grass. "I don't want to fight."

The others gather around her. "I don't want to fight," she tells their shadows.

From here, they too look as tall as giants. Ella is suddenly even more afraid.

PhiTau knew it was time for him to make his appearance, he spread his armored wings and dove toward Ella. It was where he wanted to be anyway.

A flash of color, a sound like the whistle of a firework. Maximus Tron falls like a comet from the sky. His red and yellow wings glow with the heat of his re-entry. Although Ella had never seen him fly before, she knows that it is him.

A boom, bigger than the rumble of the giant's feet, bigger than their thunderous voices, as Maximus Tron collides with the ground.

The landing didn't hurt, but PhiTau wished it had. If Ella had to be in pain, why shouldn't he?

Ella flings herself forward, dodging through legs and running to him even before she hears him say, "Ella, help me up."

She reaches down into the crater, grabs his hand and pulls. He's on his feet and bending to look into her face.

"What's the matter?" he asks.

"The giants are coming," she says.

Maximus Tron shakes his head. "You don't have to be afraid of them. You're much bigger than they are."

"I'm not," Ella says.

PhiTau reached up to remove his helmet. He knew the face beneath would be Jack's. At least that would comfort her a little.

"How did you get there?" Ella says. She turns to look for Jack among her gathered friends, but they are gone, and night is falling.

"Would I lie to you, Ella Bella?"

"You said you would build me a playhouse. You said we would have a tea party. You said you would come back."

Her words felt like prickly dream plants lodging their thorns beneath PhiTau's fingernails, but he managed not to show it when he delivered the next line.

"And here I am. Now put this on." He proffers the

helmet.

"I don't want to fight."

PhiTau bit his lip. He didn't want to say the next words. But they spilled out of him anyway. "You have to. The giants are coming."

Ella takes the helmet from his hands and puts it on her head. As the plastic closes around her face, she thinks, *How can I be bigger than giants?*

Somehow, Jack seems to have heard her, because he answers the thought out loud. "You are as big as you want to be. Always."

PhiTau felt her disbelief. Those platitudes weren't enough for her. She was terrified, tiny. And she didn't know she was in a dream. She didn't know she'd wake up safe. As far as Ella knew, she was really marching off to fight giants. He wanted to wrap her in his arms and fly away with her. He wanted to push her out of the dream and back to her world where there were no giants. He couldn't bear it anymore. He had to do something.

Just as she started to turn away he grabbed her arm and spun her toward him. "Don't be afraid," he whispered. "This is only a dream."

The dream shattered.

~

Ella thought the giants had found her. She could hear their huge voices, booming and echoing. One was talking about calling someone's mother. The other was saying, "She just fell over. I tried to grab her . . ."

Ella opened her eyes, and closed them again almost immediately. The fluorescent lights were too bright. They made her eyeballs hum. Tentatively, she moved one hand and realized she was lying on a cool tile floor. Lying down was good. Sitting up seemed like it was way outside her capabilities at the moment. In fact, she might never sit up again. She might live the rest of her life on this tile floor, just staring at the bright spots behind her eyelids.

A cool hand touched her cheek. Ella opened her eyes more cautiously this time. Someone was leaning over her, blocking the light.

"She's awake," a voice said.

Sadly, the voice was right. Ella was awake and she was laying on the floor of the upstairs girls bathroom at school. *Eww.*

She started to sit up. An arm encircled her shoulders. "Take it easy," a different voice said. Ella recognized it. Kristen, again. What was she doing here? And why was she being so nice lately?

"There she is," said the first voice. Ella tried to focus on the face. She felt so tired, like she'd stayed up all night working on an assemblage. The face was familiar, Mrs. Bartlett, the computer teacher. Ella had taken her class sophomore year because it turned out that Intro to Coding counted as a math credit.

"I sent someone to the office to call your mom," Mrs. Bartlett said. "Do you think you can stand up now?"

"I'm fine," Ella said. She tried to get her legs

underneath her. Kristen was surprisingly helpful. She let Ella lean on her and didn't even smirk about it.

Even after Ella made it to her feet, Kristen kept hold of her arm. Ella felt absurdly grateful for the touch. If she hadn't been so tired she might have thrown her arms around Kristen's neck and cried. As it was, she just cried. Small, quiet tears leaked out the corners of her eyes.

"Shh, no need for that," Mrs. Bartlett said. "We're just going to take a little stroll down to the office and wait for your mom."

Ella felt her hand close compulsively around Kristen's arm. "I don't want anyone to see me."

"Don't worry," Kristen said. "The bell rang. Everyone is pretty much in class."

"Okay."

The office might as well have been in China. Just walking down the stairs made Ella so tired they had to pause on the landing. She leaned heavily on Kristen's arm and felt bad about it.

Kristin escorted her the whole way. She even made sure Ella was settled into a chair before she turned to go.

"Thank you," Ella said.

Kristen shrugged.

"Really though," Ella said. "Why did you help me? You hate me."

Kristen rolled her eyes. "I don't hate you. Just because I don't like your art and I think your boyfriend is cute doesn't mean I hate you."

"He's not my boyfriend," Ella muttered because it was

the only part of that statement she'd understood. She was her art. How could anyone dislike it without disliking her? It was all too confusing and her brain felt like someone had just stuck it in a blender and pressed puree. She put the whole thing away to think about later.

"Besides," Kristen said, "you literally collapsed in front of me. What was I supposed to do, kick you and run away?"

Ella found herself chuckling. She was too tired to think straight.

Kristen smirked and twiddled her fingers. "I'll see you in art class," she said. Then she walked out of the office.

CHAPTER TWENTY-SIX

Secession

Never interfere with the dream. AlphaBeta had told them over and over in a dozen different ways. Hold the dream together, say your lines, but never, never interfere with the dream.

PhiTau stood with his eyes squeezed shut as though he could undo his sin by force of will. Lord Morpheus would find out. AlphaBeta would come for him. Whatever had happened to SigmaSigma would be a stroll in the moonlight compared to how PhiTau would be punished. And he deserved it, whatever it was. He had told the dreamer she was dreaming. PhiTau felt the consequences creeping closer every moment that he stood here.

Panic washed over him. His eyes popped open. He needed to escape, he needed to run. But there was nowhere to go. The world belonged to Lord Morpheus. He knew where PhiTau's garden grew. He had crafted every speck of dirt in it, and the seed that grew from it. He had shaped PhiTau with his own hands, and now he would unmake him.

PhiTau looked around wildly. His body refused to accept the truth. It wanted to run. To flee from the wrath he knew was rushing toward him even now. His roving eyes caught a glimmer of white in the distance. His hearts dropped. Were they coming for him already?

No. That wasn't an angry mob. It was the Ivory Gate. AlphaBeta had told them never to go there because it led to a world Morpheus did not rule. Perhaps PhiTau could find a new life there, or any life at all. Surely, when Morpheus caught up to him, non-being would be the only reasonable option.

He hesitated. It would mean leaving Ella. He didn't want to abandon her, didn't want to leave her alone. But what else could he do? A dead oneiroi was no use to anyone. He hesitated. Maybe it didn't have to be this way. Maybe he could just explain to Morpheus. . .

PhiTau recalled the way the blue eye had stared right through him. At the time it had been exhilarating, to stand before the Lord, to be seen and selected by him. But now PhiTau felt the truth in that gaze. He was no different than the dirt beneath Lord Morpheus' feet.

There would be no explaining. There would be only destruction. He had to run. And so he did. He fled his beautiful little garden as fast as his bent legs would carry him.

There was no time to inspect the Ivory Gate, no time for more than a passing thought about why it had been crafted out of hundreds of notched rectangles, or why the smaller ones were black while the larger ones were white.

Running full-tilt, he tried to glimpse something of the world beyond, but it was like the Horn Gate. Looking through it revealed only more fields. The only way out was through.

The gate flashed by. The light changed. PhiTau skidded to a stop. He knew this place. He'd seen it dozens of times in Ella's dreams.

~

PhiTau stood in the upstairs bathroom of Ella's high school. This must be the real world. He clasped his hands together as though trying to catch the moment between his leathery palms.

Instead, he caught his own reflection in the bathroom mirror. He was himself. At least, he assumed so. PhiTau had never actually seen his own reflection. But he had seen other oneiroi and he looked more or less like them— broad mouth, round eyes, hair pretty much everywhere. Yes, he was still him, but he was in Ella's world.

The bathroom door swung inward. PhiTau felt an instant of panic before it hit him in the face. He caught the curved handle to hold it open, using the door as a shield to block him from the human who was no doubt just on the other side.

PhiTau stood as still as he could, barely breathing, clutching the door handle. He could not be seen. Between his lessons and his adventures with Ella, he knew enough about the real world to know that he looked like a cross between an ape and a bat. His appearance would send humans screaming if he was lucky.

He tried to listen for footsteps, but couldn't hear them over the sound of his hearts trying to escape from his chest. Carefully turning his head, he tried to peek through the crack between the door and the wall, but there was nothing to see. He waited for any sound, any movement. Nothing. The human must have left.

PhiTau released the door. It swung shut, leaving him standing alone in an empty bathroom. He had to get out of here. Someone else could come in at any moment, and he couldn't hide forever.

There were only two ways out of the room. One was the door, which led to the hall through which hundreds of humans walked several times a day. The other was a long, narrow window set high in the wall. He scuttled across the room and into the bathroom stall closest to the window. This felt safer. He just wished the walls went all the way to the floor. He stepped up on the ceramic seat, and looked over the top of the stall toward the window.

He could probably have squeezed through, but outside was pitch black. That didn't seem right. He thought it should be light out.

For a moment, he wished he knew how to return to the Dreaming. Yes, Morpheus was probably searching for him. Yes, he deserved the cruelest punishment the Dream Lord could devise. But right now, he'd take the certain danger of the dreaming over the uncertain danger of the real world. Not that it mattered now. He didn't know how to go back. The only thing he could do was make a safe place for himself in this world.

He crouched on the toilet cover, his toes cracking with anxiety. Was there a safe place for him? He tried to remember the good parts of Ella's dreams. Where had Ella felt safe? In her studio. Yes, but he didn't know how to get there. He'd gotten the impression that it was far away from the school. She always needed someone to carry her back and forth. Where else?

The art room. Of course. The art room was the safest place in the whole school. It was ruled by a woman who loved everyone and encouraged them to be themselves. Certainly, if he could get to the art room he would be safe.

PhiTau clenched and unclenched his hands. He took a deep breath, and held it as he listened. No voices to be heard. No footsteps. He needed to move quickly before the bell dispelled the human children from their rooms. A peek over the stall door reassured him that the coast was clear. He slipped out, scrambled across the room, and stopped at the bathroom door.

Slowly, cautiously, he eased the door open just wide enough that he could press his eye to the crack and look down the hall. No humans. No anything, just floor and ceiling and lockers. Oh and more doors. Every one with a window in it that could betray him to the humans in the next room. He pressed his toes flat to keep them from cracking.

"You chose this," he reminded himself. Then he pushed through the door and into the hall. His hearts danced in his chest, terrified and elated. He was in the real world. He was walking the halls of a human high school. He tried to keep as close to the floor as possible to avoid being seen.

The art room was downstairs. Where exactly, he wasn't sure, but he'd just have to find it, and keep very quiet, and not be seen. Was this what he'd meant when he'd hoped for an adventure?

Keeping low while also looking in all directions to spot any passing human before they spotted him was difficult, but PhiTau managed it. He got almost to the end of the hall before he heard a door open behind him. He threw himself to the ground, wrapping his wings around his body for what little camouflage they afforded, and rolled toward a closed door recessed between two banks of lockers. His body made a soft thump as it hit the door. PhiTau hoped no one had heard. A voice inside the room was talking but he couldn't make out the words. PhiTau peeked around the locker to determine whether he'd been seen.

From his vantage on the floor, he could see a pair of bare feet walking away from him. They hadn't seen him then. Good.

He waited for the feet to turn and disappear, expecting at any moment that someone would try to open the door he was lying in front of and send him rolling across the tile floor under the gaze of a herd of adolescent humans.

That didn't happen.

The feet went their own way and PhiTau crawled on all fours toward the stairwell. When he reached it, he huddled for a moment. The light was dimmer here, and he felt less exposed. How could humans think with those bright lights humming overhead all the time?

He shuffled sideways, trying to keep both the door and the top of the stairwell in sight. If only his breath would stop echoing in his ears he might be able to hear if anyone was coming. He reached the railing and looked over. Stairs going down, a landing, then another set of stairs. No one on them.

He held his breath. Once he was on the stairs there would be nowhere to hide until he reached the bottom. Better to do it as fast as he could and get it over with. He ran. Almost lost his footing, but kept going. On the landing. Now the second flight. A voice came from the hallway, loud and accusing.

PhiTau crept to the inner door and peeked around the frame. Diagonally from where he hid, a classroom door stood open. The voice was coming from there. A teacher, it must be a teacher was saying ". . . us to our harm, the instruments of darkness tell us truth, win us with honest trifles, to betray's, in deepest consequence."

The words meant nothing to PhiTau, he hardly heard them. What mattered was that he couldn't see the teacher or the students. Which meant, he hoped, that they could not see him. He leaned out a little further to see what else was there. To his right a door, its narrow window blank with darkness. To his left, more lockers. More doors. He'd have to pass the open door classroom.

Sneaking and creeping, stumbling and fearful, PhiTau reached the end of that hallway. There the space widened, the axis of a wheel with four spokes. He crouched low and pressed against the end of a bank of lockers, trying to make himself as small as possible. To his left, a downsloping hallway, with voices echoing up it. Many voices. To his right, a set of six doors, all leading to the darkness outside. Ahead, a wider hall, with a big window looking into it from another room.

From this angle, he could only see the glint of glass. He couldn't tell if anyone was behind it. He didn't want to go outside, and he certainly didn't want to go toward the cacophony of voices. That left the window hall. If he stayed low to the ground and close to the wall, he could sneak by. Someone would have to stand right up against the glass and look straight down to spot him.

One, two, go . . . he scrambled. Across the open space under the window. He'd done it, but his celebration was short-lived. The voices were even louder. PhiTau's legs began to shake. He'd come so far, and every step seemed to be taking him closer to the unknown.

He clasped his hands as though he could hold himself together that way. He was at another intersection, with only left and right to choose from this time. Even before he looked he knew that there were humans, dozens, maybe hundreds, approaching from all sides.

Any second, eyes would fall on him. Someone would

scream. Someone else would rush toward him with strong, straight human arms raised to attack. Other humans would come running. They would pin him to the floor under the weight of dozens of angry bodies.

His terror fantasy had only gotten this far when a wave of humans turned the corner. They were packed wall to wall, all shouting voices and rushing feet, their faces barely discernible one from the other. He braced for screams. But no. The wave just broke around him, human bodies streaming past as though he were a stone in a river.

He looked down at his hands. They appeared to still be there. Not faded at all. He opened and closed them. Yes, he was definitely all there. But nobody could see him.

CHAPTER TWENTY-SEVEN

Oblivion

For a long moment, PhiTau just stood in the doorway of the art room, awed by the colors. A drawing pinned to the wall held him enraptured for far too long. Looking at it, he felt his hearts expand until they filled his whole chest with no room to pump. The sight of those blobs of paint made him feel like . . . like . . . well, they made him feel everything. His vision misted, and he reached up to touch one eye only to find that it was damp. Was he crying? He hadn't known that oneiroi could cry. He'd thought that was something that only humans did. Humans. Ella. He was in her world now. Blinking rapidly, he tore his gaze away from the painting.

Ella would come back here soon. She came here every day. All he had to do was wait. Even if she couldn't see him, there must be a way that he could help her. At least he would feel better knowing she was near.

He tried not to worry about the fact that it was

nighttime and Ella would be without a tender for the first time in her life. There was nothing he could do about that now. He'd just have to find a more direct way to help. Besides a new tender would certainly be assigned as soon as AlphaBeta noticed what had happened. He tried not to think about the fact that nobody had come to claim SigmaSigma's garden.

From his perch on Ella's stool on the left side of the room under the darkened window, PhiTau saw Ms. Beaudry enter the art room. He wasn't surprised to see her. This was her space, in the same way that Ella's garden was PhiTau's. He watched her walk across the room. It was only when she stopped directly in front of him that he began to worry.

When she spoke he nearly fell off the stool.

"And what are you doing here?"

"I . . . you can see me?"

"Of course I can see you. Do you think I'm blind?"

"No . . . I . . ." PhiTau blinked. He didn't know what to say. A thought bubbled to the surface of his mind. It filled the empty space in his head and spilled out of his mouth. "You're not Ms. Beaudry."

"Is that what you call this thing?" said the woman who was not Ms. Beaudry, looking down at herself. "Ugh."

She shrugged, and the shrug changed her. With the lift of a shoulder she grew taller. With its drop, her body slimmed, her hair grew and darkened. Her clothing dissolved the way a dream collapses as the dreamer's mind abandons it. Soon she stood, nude, and smiling a tiny, dangerous smile.

A human would have been utterly entranced by the perfection of the form before it. But PhiTau was not human. What he noticed, even before the shock of the transformation wore off, was her eyes. One blue like the staring dream-eye of Morpheus, the other blackness within blackness, as though the pupil had exploded and consumed the iris. Both eyes pinned him to his seat.

Except that the seat was shifting too. Everything was shifting. The stool, the tables, the vibrant colors on the walls muted, faded, until PhiTau was standing in featureless gray mist with this creature who was likely not a woman and certainly not an oneiroi. Which only left one option. PhiTau shuddered.

"You're a dream thing," the creature said.

"My name is PhiTau." His toes cracked. The sense that he was standing on nothing crept over PhiTau and he fought the urge to look down.

The creature stalked gracefully around him. PhiTau turned to watch her. The idea that she might stand behind him, out of sight, raised the fur on the back of his neck.

"Morpheus is sending spies now?"

"No. Lord Morpheus didn't send me. I . . . I ran away."

She stopped. Her smile went broad and bright. "A defector. How delightful. And where were you running away to?"

"I don't know. AlphaBeta, my teacher, told me that if I passed through the Ivory Gate, I would leave Lord Morpheus' realm. I assumed he meant that I would enter the human world."

"Yes, well, that explains the foolishness when you arrived. But you know what happens when you assume."

"Excuse me, my Lord, but I do not."

"It's my Lady, not my Lord." She looked down at her body. "Obviously."

"My Lady, yes. You're a woman, like Ella."

Be even as he said it, he thought, *not like Ella. Not like Ella at all*. Ella was delicate and clever and creative. The creature in front of him seemed like she could set this realm on fire with a toss of her dark hair and, worse, would enjoy doing so. PhiTau had never felt anything like sexual interest before, but at this moment, his hearts beat too fast and his toes and fingers tingled in a far off way. He couldn't fathom any sort of physical interaction with this woman, but he knew that he wanted to be possessed by her.

"Ella," she said. Her face went blank for a moment as though she were trying to remember something. "Oh, yes."

She clapped her hands together and suddenly they were standing in Ella's bedroom. The creature plopped down on the bed. "Tell me everything," she said.

PhiTau stared around him. It looked like Ella's bedroom. There was the purple bedspread she'd had since she was little. There the shelf of old toys that had made so many guest appearances in her dreams. He curled his toes in the shaggy yellow rug.

"Where are we? I mean, we can't really be here."

The lady frowned. "I thought you would be comfortable here. I plucked it right out of your head." She mimed snatching something between her thumb and index finger. "Just like that horrid school scene."

"This is Ella's room."

"Good, isn't it? You have a very attentive mind to have noticed all of these details."

"Who are you?" PhiTau asked.

She threw a pillow at him. "Sit down, will you? I made this place just for you. You could at least pretend to enjoy it." Her pout confused PhiTau.

"I'm sorry. I did not mean to make you sad," he paused, "my Lady."

The lady laughed, which confused him even more. First, because he hadn't meant to do anything funny, and second, because when she threw her head back that way he couldn't help but notice how sharp and white her teeth were.

His fear vanished when the lady reached out and clasped his arm.

"We are going to be such good friends," she said. "Now tell me everything." She turned her head, so that only the black eye was looking at him. PhiTau suddenly felt calm. Like whatever had happened couldn't touch him here even though he didn't really know where here was. He told her everything.

The lady listened as he talked about meeting Ella, and her dreams, and how he'd been moved to help and then realized what he'd done and fled. When he finished, the lady tapped one finger to her lips.

"Hmm," she said. "You've come to the right deity, PhiTau. I believe I can help you."

"You'll show me the way home?"

"Home? You mean the Dreaming. Why would you want to go there?"

"Ella needs me. She won't be able to dream without me."

The lady waved her hand in a way that suggested this was an unimportant detail. "Oh, Morpheus thinks dreams are so terribly important. Of course he would." She leaned toward PhiTau and lowered her voice. "Gods have such inflated views of themselves."

As she grinned wickedly, PhiTau shifted on the bedspread. He'd never heard someone speak such blasphemy. Back when he was a harvester he might have secretly agreed with such talk, but at the time, he hadn't even been sure that Morpheus existed.

"Dreams seem so enchanting, but when you get to the core of them, they're nothing but practice runs wrapped up in illusion to make the drudge work seem less dull. The truth is that when human lives get really hard, dreams are useless. Worse than useless because they seem to offer a way out without actually doing anything at all. Humans think they need dreams, but what they really want is me."

"Excuse me, my Lady. But who are you?"

The lady once again ignored this question and countered with her own. "What if I could send you into Ella's world? What would you do?"

PhiTau's hearts leapt in his chest. "Can you?"

"Let's just imagine. What if I could? What would you do?" She was leaning toward him, her eyes bright and wild. Even the black one seemed to glimmer.

"I would help her."

"How?"

"I don't know." PhiTau was mesmerized by the lady's eyes—so bright, so clear, so close.

"Would you take her pain away?"

"Yes, if I could."

"Would you erase her worries, ease her sorrow, shelter her from anything that could hurt her?"

PhiTau felt his eyes water. His gaze was caught in the lady's. He couldn't look away. Couldn't breathe. And didn't care to do either.

"Yes." The word was a sigh, the last breath in his lungs.

A slow smile spread across the lady's face. "Go then."

She leaned forward. PhiTau's vision was fading. He should have been worried about this, but somehow, all he felt was calm. That, and the lady's breath on his face as she leaned forward to kiss his forehead.

PhiTau fell into the arms of Oblivion.

CHAPTER TWENTY-EIGHT

Oneiromancy

Morpheus sat on his blue cushion in the center of the wide open barn that was his workshop, weaving dreams from raw dreamstuff. It was his duty, and more often than not, his sole pleasure. He would reach to his left, pull a tuft of dreamstuff from the constantly renewed pile and shape it into something from his prodigious imagination. Then he would allow it to flap or roll, flutter or fall away as it condensed down to the specks that would become the gleam in a human eye that would grow a dream. Every now and then, an oneiroi would come by with a wide broom and sweep the dream dust into piles for collection and distribution to the tenders.

It wasn't the most efficient way to accomplish this task. Yet Morpheus loved the ritual of dream creation.

He loved to sit in this place, amidst the ribbons of light, and see the dreamstuff piled up beside him. He loved the gentle shush of the broom as it gathered up the processed dreams. He did not love the sound of the door opening, or the purposeful footfalls of AlphaAlpha as they crossed the wide artistically rustic floorboards.

"My Lord, we have a situation."

Morpheus kept his eyes on his work. He was crafting a dog with fur like a cloud and a small, wet nose that could snuffle up the world. "Another one?"

"Yes, Lord."

"Do you know, AlphaAlpha, there was a time when whole centuries went by without any situations at all. There was a time, in fact, when the Lord of Dream could concentrate."

He said this in a calm tone, but the small fluffy dog darkened and lifted, became a storm cloud dog with a bark like a roll of thunder. The effect was slightly marred by the stubby legs flailing underneath. It rose into the air and rained all over AlphaAlpha's fur with a smell like a wet dog.

The oneiroi, who had seen this sort of thing so many times before, only blinked. The rain wasn't even actually wet. "Apologies, my Lord. It's one of the new tenders."

"We dealt with that already."

"This is a different one, my Lord. PhiTau."

"That name . . ." Morpheus snapped his fingers and a cloud of blue butterflies fluttered toward the ceiling. "The sunflower dreamer's tender."

"Yes, Lord."

"An interesting specimen. What has he done now?"

"He's gone."

"AlphaAlpha, oneiroi fade every day. I would have thought he was a little new for it, but he was clearly burning hot in the dreams. These things happen. I would hardly call that a situation."

Morpheus pulled another tuft of dreamstuff from the pile and attempted to get back to work.

"Excuse me, Lord. I don't mean he's faded. He's still very much in existence as far as we can tell. It's just that he has . . ."

AlphaAlpha hesitated as though trying to find the right word. That was unlike him. Morpheus had created him to be a knowledgeable servant, not a kowtowing hesitator. He'd needed at least one person around the place who knew what was going on, so he could focus on creating dreams.

"What does he have, AlphaAlpha?"

"He's run away, Lord."

There was nowhere to run in the Dreaming. It was all fields and harvests as far as any oneiroi could travel. On the very boundaries, for those that had the eye to see them, were the waters of Memory and Oblivion, twin rivers encircling his realm, effectively creating a moat around Dream. Thinking this, Morpheus felt a sneaking suspicion crawl up his neck. He grabbed it off and flung it away. It buzzed in the air for a moment, a grotesque beetle the size of a marshmallow, and then popped out of existence. Morpheus dragged his attention back to the subject at hand.

"He's run to Lethe," Morpheus said.

"We don't believe he did it on purpose."

"You're saying he ran away by accident?"

AlphaAlpha squared his shoulders. "Not as such, my Lord. He ran away on purpose, but he didn't realize where he was going. All the tenders are told is that the Ivory Gate will lead them out of your realm."

Morpheus' fingers moved furiously. He created an angry-faced moon that floated up through the ceiling. A pair of bickering doves followed.

"Why would anyone want to leave my realm? My realm is a delight."

An iridescent river of snakes dried up and disappeared halfway across the floor.

"Indeed, Lord," AlphaAlpha said. "But the tenders are taught to follow some very strict rules while inside human dreams. It seems PhiTau panicked after breaking the most important of these."

"Which is?" Never having been subject to many rules himself, Morpheus was always fascinated to learn of those others had to follow.

"Never interfere with the dream. He told his dreamer that she was dreaming."

"I see." Morpheus had been agitated before. Now he was furious. It was that cold, bright fury that seemed sharp enough to cut. The important thing was to hold the sharp edge in the right direction.

"Leave him where he is."

"Excuse me, Lord—"

"He interfered with the dream. He knowingly broke

the rules of the realm. He has brought down his own punishment. You would agree that exile seems fitting for an enemy of the realm."

"Yes, Lord. However—"

Morpheus clasped a handful of dreamstuff. "You may go, AlphaAlpha."

AlphaAlpha began to speak again, but Morpheus trained both eyes on him, the green and the blue, united in anger.

AlphaAlpha, the wisest of the oneiroi, bowed and went out. Even before the door closed behind him, Morpheus had bent his head over a machine that churned out trick noses in many entertaining colors. His green eye stared intently at the work, while the blue wandered off, to seek the girl, Ella, in her dreams.

CHAPTER TWENTY-NINE

Assisted Readymade

PhiTau, who had never slept a moment in his life, nevertheless found himself woken by a gentle prod to his shoulder.

He opened his eyes to find a little girl staring down at him and withdrawing the bare foot she'd used to poke him.

"Hello," she said. "My name is Ella, do you want to play with me?"

PhiTau sat up so quickly that the girl stumbled backward. "You're Ella?" he said.

He looked around. He was in a field of tall grass with the occasional poppy closed up tight against the darkness. And it was dark. He could only see Little Ella because she was wearing a pale purple nightgown with a ghost on it. The ghost caught and reflected every particle of starlight. No moons though, PhiTau noticed. Not even one.

"Uh-huh," she said. "What's your name?"

"PhiTau. Look, you can't be Ella. Ella is much bigger than you."

Ella drew herself up. "I'm six and a half. And I'm taller than I look."

"No, I mean . . ." He didn't know how to argue with her, so he reached for another question instead. "Where are we?"

"We're sleeping right now. But I think we're going to wake up in a minute."

"This is a dream?" PhiTau relaxed a little. Dreams he could handle. He wasn't sure how he'd gotten here, but at least it was familiar. Maybe the lady had decided to send him home after all.

"No dreams tonight. Just you." Ella spun in a circle then flopped down on the ground. "Shh, it's starting."

"What's—" PhiTau began, but then he looked where she was looking and saw the two lights in the sky. Bigger than the moons in the Dreaming, they started as thin slivers, their light dim and shaded. Then they flickered— bright, dark, bright. At last, they stabilized and light spilled in through two round holes in the sky.

PhiTau had a strange sensation of stretching, even though he hadn't moved. Beside him, Little Ella lifted her arms above her head.

An idea struck PhiTau so hard he almost slumped over. It couldn't be true. Could it? There had to be some more reasonable explanation. This was just a dream. Surely.

"Where are we?" he whispered to Little Ella, who was

still intent on the holes in the sky.

"Inside my head, silly," she said, as though this were the most obvious thing in the world. "Now shh, I'm waking up."

PhiTau stared out through Ella's eyes as they turned toward the bedside table. He saw her arm reach for her cell phone. Huge numbers came into view. They said 6:29.

"Turn it off, before it makes the noise," Little Ella muttered beside him.

Fingers fumbled with the phone, and turned off the alarm.

"She does whatever you tell her?" PhiTau said.

Little Ella shrugged. "Most times. Sometimes I get distracted and she just does stuff."

"And you're Ella?"

"Ella-bella fo-fella, mi my mo mella, Ella." She sang for no reason PhiTau could discern. She even did a little dance with her arms and shoulders while sitting there in the grass.

"I won't be able to think if you talk the whole time," Little Ella said, as though the musical interlude hadn't happened.

PhiTau stopped asking questions and just sat, letting the shock of it all wash over him. He shouldn't be here. He had no right to be here. On the other hand, he'd wanted to help. What better way than to literally get inside her head?

Beside him, Little Ella hummed a song. Outside, Ella

was getting out of bed. He looked out through her eyes. Yes, maybe he really could help her or, at least, convince her to help herself.

~

Ella woke up with a song stuck in her head. She couldn't remember where she'd heard it, it was just a little bit of melody caught on a loop in her brain. She tried to ignore it. Sometimes that worked.

When she got downstairs, Mom was at the kitchen table drinking coffee and scrolling on her phone. Probably reading the news. Adults loved to ruin their day before it even started. Ella stopped at the bottom of the stairs, wondering if there was a way to sneak into the kitchen without having to talk to Mom.

Mom looked up. "Ella, how are we feeling today?"

"I am fine," Ella said, putting an emphasis on the I.

Mom just stared. Ella started to walk toward the kitchen.

"Honey, if there's something you want to talk about?"

The voice in her head said. *I had a fight with Liv. My head feels funny, but not funny haha. I don't really want to talk right now. Shh.*

"There isn't."

"You had a panic attack."

"I know, I was there."

The voice in her head told her to calm down. *Why doesn't anyone ever calm up? Mom's just worried. Mom's such a worry wart. Reassure her.*

"I'm fine, really. I just forgot to eat breakfast and . . ." She trailed off. Mom didn't look like she was buying this story.

Mom sipped her coffee in a totally failed attempt at nonchalance. "Do you think it would help to talk to someone?"

"What kind of someone?"

"A counselor, maybe."

"I'm not crazy." Mom's face flinched. Ella knew she'd struck a nerve. Mom hated the word crazy. It reminded her of Uncle Steve, who had died way before Ella was even born. But Ella knew about him, she'd heard her older cousins whispering the story to each other. He'd self-immolated, like those protesting monks they learned about in history class.

"I know, sweetie," Mom said. "I'm not talking about a therapist or anything. Maybe just a chat with the guidance counselor at school. You know it's totally normal for girls your age to feel some anxiety about the future."

There it was, Mom's favorite word. Normal.

"Ugh, don't remind me." Ella padded into the kitchen, confident that she'd hear no more about this whole counselor idea.

Mom waited until Ella filled her cereal bowl and brought it back to the table. "But if you wanted to talk to someone—"

"I don't."

Mom went quiet. She didn't even look mad, just kind

of small somehow. She must really be worried.

"I'm fine, Mom. Really."

Liar.

That stupid song was still playing in her head. She wished it would shut up so she could think.

~

PhiTau poked Little Ella. "She wants you to stop humming."

"You don't know what she wants."

Little Ella tore a handful of grass out of the ground and threw it at PhiTau. As the blades of grass fluttered down, she said, "She's my friend, not yours."

"I'm trying to help," PhiTau said.

"I can do it." She pouted.

"Sorry."

~

Ella paused with her cereal spoon halfway to her lips. She blinked, feeling like she'd forgotten something. "Oh, by the way, can you take me to school today?"

Mom sighed. "Can't Liv take you?"

Stupid Liv, she yelled at me. Why would she do that?

"She's busy." Ella crunched her cereal and pretended not to notice Mom's concerned look.

Mom checked the time on her cell phone. "You need to be ready in ten minutes."

"Ten minutes?" Ella stuffed an extra spoonful of cereal in her mouth, then jumped up. She rushed toward the stairs, trying to ignore the sweat suddenly dampening her neck. The nerves were familiar, but the feeling that there was more than one voice in her head was new. She didn't like it.

~

Ella successfully avoided running into Owen and Liv during homeroom by getting a bathroom pass as soon as she arrived. The note Mom had written excusing her absence for the second half of yesterday worked wonders for convincing teachers that she really did need to go to the bathroom right this minute. They didn't want "Ella wasn't feeling well" to turn into "Ella has blown chunks all over the classroom floor."

Now she wanted to get to the art room and start working before Owen arrived. Otherwise she'd have to suffer through some awkward conversation about yesterday's drama. Owen would try to smooth things over, to just make peace. But Ella couldn't forget that when Liv had started yelling at her, Owen hadn't done much to stop it. He'd totally sided with his real sister, and of course he would, because Ella, when you got right down to it, was not family, and never had been, while Liv was his actual flesh and blood. Ella knew that, and the knowing hurt. She wished she could just not care about Liv and Owen at all, just like they clearly didn't care all that much about her.

Moving through the halls with purpose and a general disregard for other people's personal space, brought her to the art room before Owen. Good. Now she just had to look busy and maybe he wouldn't bother her.

She went to the cubby wall and pulled out the blue bin with her name on it. The pieces that she hoped would become the head rattled in the bottom, looking even more random and pathetic than she remembered. She sighed and brought it back to her table.

The anime girl, who Ella had realized was named Katherine but went by Kit for some reason Ella hadn't had the energy to investigate, slipped into her seat and flipped open a giant sketchbook. Ella was momentarily jealous. Wouldn't it be great to do the kind of art that you can carry around in your backpack instead of building piles of trash almost as tall as you are? Except that her assemblage would not be as tall as she was if she never finished the damn head.

Kit was working on a drawing that seemed to be the right eye and cheek of some sort of Japanese robot character. As far Ella could tell, the girl's project seemed to be a series of close-up drawings of different anime character body parts. Last week had been particularly embarrassing, because she'd spent a whole class period working on what appeared to be the generously endowed groin region of a very male character.

Over Kit's bent head, Ella saw Owen walk into the room. She snapped her eyes toward the head still in its box. *Shit.* She'd planned to be completely engrossed in her work when he walked in.

Quickly, she dumped the head and all of its detached toy detritus onto the table, and bent to tuck the box down by her feet. As she sat up again, she risked a glance toward Owen's workspace. *Double shit.* He was coming over here.

She tried to pretend that she hadn't noticed and started pulling pieces randomly off the assemblage, grateful she'd at least been smart enough to use a temporary adhesive so she could mock it up before doing anything too permanent. The first version definitely wasn't working.

"Ella," Owen said.

Ella made a noise that was more grunt than hi. She felt blood rushing to her face and knew she must be blushing like an idiot.

"Look, yesterday was . . . Liv was . . ." He paused. Ella wondered if he expected her to say anything. She hoped not, because her tongue felt too big for her mouth. Besides, her teeth were clenching so hard she felt it in her temple. She couldn't decide if she was mad at him, or ready to cry. *Definitely both.*

"I'm sorry. That's what I'm trying to say."

Ella blinked. Her teeth unclenched. Sorry. He was sorry. He hadn't been the one who'd yelled at her, but he was the one apologizing. She let her eyes begin to rise from her project toward his face.

"Liv's just been really . . . well, she's got a lot going

on and she's not feeling super supported right now, but. . . she's my sister, you know?"

The words were rambling, vague, but they hit her like an ice-filled snowball. All her complicated feelings froze. She looked Owen in the eye.

"No worries," she said.

Owen had apparently expected more of a discussion because he just stared at her and said, "What?"

"It's fine."

A smile tugged at the corner of his mouth, but he didn't look like he was ready to be pulled along. "Yeah?" he said.

"Yeah," Ella said, and saying it made it true. "Look, I need to get back to my assemblage now." To make the point, she put one hand on the foam ball, grabbed a random toy and pulled. She didn't even look up when Owen walked away. Head bent over her sculpture, she wondered why she'd ever spent even half a brain cell on Owen Butler.

~

PhiTau let go of Little Ella. It had worked. When Owen had walked over, PhiTau had reacted without thinking. He'd wrapped his long arms around the little girl and put one hand over her mouth to stop her from spouting any nonsense that popped into her head.

Ella had wished that she didn't have to care about Owen and Olivia, and PhiTau could see a way to make that happen, but he hadn't had time to explain. Now he tried.

"I'm sorry, but I needed you to not talk. She was—"

"We don't grab people," Little Ella said. "That's mean. You're a mean monkey." She darted out of reach.

PhiTau felt bad about that. He hadn't meant to scare her. He'd just needed her to be quiet for a minute. "I'm not a monkey. I'm an oneiroi."

"I don't want to play with you anymore."

"I'm not playing."

"Well, I'm not playing with you either. I'm going to watch a memory and you're not invited."

With that, Little Ella turned on her heel and sprinted out across the field of twilight flowers. PhiTau stood and looked after her, wondering if he should follow. They were inside Ella's head right? What could happen to her in here? Besides, she'd probably come back as soon as she got bored of pouting. He'd noticed that her attention span wasn't very long. She'd probably skip back in no time with a flower crown for each of them and suggest a game of . . . a game of . . . you're it, or whatever that game was that little kids played.

In the meantime, PhiTau could focus on helping Ella. Owen had been just the beginning. Now that PhiTau knew what he was doing, now that he understood that his whispers became her thoughts and her thoughts became her words and actions, he could help her in all sorts of ways.

CHAPTER THIRTY

Magic Lantern Show

Art class was quiet. Everyone was focused on their projects. Ms. Beaudry sat at her desk grading papers or whatever it was teachers did when they weren't actively teaching. At her table under the window, Ella sat with her hands on either side of the head. It was supposed to be the focal point of her assemblage, a defiant face looking up and away at something the viewer couldn't see.

She lifted one hand and reached for the dog-chewed foot of a troll doll that was doing duty as part of the cheek. Moving it down a bit might make the expression look less annoyed. She dropped her hand. There was no point. However many small adjustments she made, it still looked like a grumpy frog with a lazy eye.

She'd taken the wrong approach and she knew it. She'd been trying to make the toys fit the sculpture rather than letting their shapes and colors guide her. She wouldn't make that mistake again. She started levering pieces off the foam ball base.

By the end of class, she had something that, if not exactly good, was at least vaguely head shaped. When the ball rang, she started packing up her stuff. Unlike in every other high school class, Ms. Beaudry practically had to kick some kids out to get them to leave.

Owen was waiting for Ella in the hall. "How's your assemblage?"

"Fine."

They walked a few steps in silence. Owen seemed to be thinking and Ella was content to let him.

"The head's kind of the hardest part. Right?"

"Yeah, I guess so."

Again, the silence stretched. Again, Owen broke it. "I'm almost done with the cups. Then I'll just have the swords left. I'm going to do them in a Fauvist style. I don't know if that means they'll go faster than the others or slower."

"I don't know," Ella said as they joined the cafeteria line. "I don't really paint."

Owen stopped trying to talk to her and just stood in line behind her. She grabbed a chicken burger and an orange, paid, and then headed for her usual table without waiting for Owen. He'd catch up if he wanted to.

She noticed that Liv wasn't at the table. A flash of anxiety shocked her body but it passed almost immediately. Liv was probably hounding some teacher about vocabulary words or something. By the time Ella sat down, her equilibrium had returned.

Owen stood a few feet away holding his try out in front of him. Ella looked at him. "What's up?"

"Uh . . ." Owen looked at Ella and then away.

Ella followed his gaze. Liv was sitting at a nearby table with a salad in front of her. Owen took a step in that direction, and stopped.

"Dude, go sit with your sister," Ella said. She started eating her chicken burger. They didn't have very long for lunch, and she was actually hungry today.

Owen's forehead wrinkled. He looked from one table to the other. Then he sighed and walked to the table directly between Ella and Liv. A couple of the kids from art class were sitting there, including Kristen Lund.

"Hey guys, how are your projects going?"

"Hey, Owen," Kristen said.

He sat down and Ella stopped watching. She didn't care what Owen Butler got up to, but that didn't mean she wanted to listen to Kristen fawning over him. Ella finished her lunch alone, thinking about nothing much at all.

~

Little Ella came back, as PhiTau had assumed she would. She didn't bring any flower crowns, but she was carrying something. It looked like a plastic mask, the kind little kids wear on Halloween. She was staring into its eyes as though she expected it to speak to her. PhiTau worried she might trip.

Instead she found her usual spot and lowered herself to the ground, legs crisscrossed beneath her.

"What is that?" PhiTau asked.

"It's Jack and me being Savers of the Universe," she said, barely looking up.

"What?"

She leaned her body toward him, extending the mask in his direction. PhiTau stared down at it. It shimmered. Then he blinked and a memory flashed through his mind. A memory that didn't belong to him.

It showed Ella, maybe five years old as best he could judge human ages, wearing a mask that made her look like Maximus Tron. She posed theatrically while Jack pretended to die at her feet. It was just a flash, no longer than an eye blink, but it was as vivid as any dream.

PhiTau snatched at the mask. "What is this? Where did you find it?"

Little Ella pulled away. "Be careful. If you break it Ella will forget all about this, and then she'll be sad and cry and no one wants that."

That didn't seem right. Why would she cry about something she couldn't even remember? Never mind. PhiTau had already figured out that Little Ella had a bit of Morpheus' magic in her. She was always creating little worlds to live in. The trick was finding a way to understand where her world and yours overlapped.

"Are there more of these?"

"Lots. I could show you."

"Yes."

"What's the magic word?"

PhiTau blinked at her. Magic word? He didn't know any magic words. He tried to think of a word that at least sounded magical. "Um . . . writing."

Little Ella giggled. "No, silly. It's 'please'."

"That's a magic word?"

"Uh-huh."

"Okay then, please, show me where you found that memory."

"Well, since you asked so nicely." Little Ella did a pirouette and headed back the way she'd come, still carrying the mask.

Following her meant responding to her meandering conversations as well. "You have to promise to play nicely and not grab people. If you grab people you have to go in time-out for . . . how old are you?"

"I don't know," PhiTau said. He wasn't sure oneiroi even had ages. They were just made and eventually they faded away with no real marking of time in-between.

"You're supposed to go in time-out for as many minutes as you are years old. You look pretty old. Not like Daddy, but maybe like Jack-Jack. So if you grab people that's seventeen minutes time-out. Okay?"

She stopped. They stood together in the dark for a moment, the memory casting a soft shifting light on Little Ella's chin and nose, before PhiTau realized she was waiting for him to answer.

"Okay."

She kept walking. After a while, PhiTau began to spot

more toys scattered across the grass. He worried whether she'd been disordering them, and what that might mean for Ella.

"I don't like the crying ones," Little Ella said.

"Crying ones?"

She shook her head, apparently unwilling to say more for once. The further they walked, the more memory toys they found. PhiTau inspected them as they passed. Each one gave off a thin white shimmer.

"The blue ones are the sad ones. The yellow ones are the happy ones," Little Ella said. "I like the happy ones best."

What was she talking about? The toys were all different colors, not just blue and yellow. Trying to spot some pattern between them, he stared until his eyes started to water. Then he blinked, and saw it. The toys were all multicolored when your eyes were open. But they left different colored afterimages in the darkness inside your mind. In the group of five he'd been looking at, a single blue star burst among the yellows.

"I see it," PhiTau said.

"These are all the little kid ones. The big kid ones are over there." She pointed into the distance where the toys seemed to cover more of the grass. "There's lots more blue ones if you go that way. So I don't go there very much."

"What are they for?"

"You need to put on your listening ears. I already said, they're for remembering."

"I only have these ones," PhiTau said, touching his own ears.

Little Ella dropped the mask and reached for a small stuffed toy with yellow and green patchwork fur. "Ooh, let's watch this one."

She held it up. The colors shifted. PhiTau watched.

~

Against his better judgement, Morpheus went to call on Lethe. He stepped sideways between worlds, out of his sunny workshop and into the gloomy mist of Oblivion. He hated it here. Not just because it was featureless and gray and empty, but also because it was the one place in all the worlds where he couldn't build a dream. It made him feel impotent. Not that he'd admit that to anyone.

"Lethe." The word left his lips as a firm statement, but shrunk and shriveled in the mist. It didn't matter. He knew she knew he was there.

"You have something of mine," Morpheus said.

"Well, it's not as if I stole him," Lethe's voice came from behind him. He made himself turn slowly, unwilling to give her the upper hand.

"What have you done with him?" Morpheus asked the empty air. Lethe hadn't bothered to take a form. She was just a voice, everywhere and nowhere. It irritated him. He rolled his eyes in a purposefully overdramatic way, knowing she would see. "And why are you hiding from me?"

The mist shifted until the empty space in the air resembled a female form. "You know I don't like going corporeal. It's against my whole vibe."

Morpheus snorted. "Yes, I'm sure it's your vibe that's worrying you."

The form solidified a little more, enough that Morpheus could make out the one black-consumed eye. "Why are you here?" Lethe asked.

"You're meddling."

"Your oneiroi runs into my realm and I'm the one meddling? That's an interesting opinion."

"What are you doing with the girl?"

"It's all completely consensual, I promise you that. She sought me out, just like your oneiroi."

Morpheus itched to craft something spiked and angry that he could fling in her direction, but he couldn't, of course, and it wouldn't touch her even if he could. "You're up to something."

She spread her ghost arms wide and inclined her misty head in a mocking bow. "I live to serve humans, just like you, little brother."

Morpheus touched his fingers to his forehead. "Just give me back PhiTau and I won't bother you anymore."

The figure in the mist waved an airy hand. "I don't even know where he is. He's his own oneiroi you know. Free to do as he pleases." She paused. "No rules. No master."

Morpheus glowered at her. Another moment in her presence and he would do something he'd regret. He could feel it rising in him like a nightmare. He stepped sideways out of her realm, her laughter clanging in his ears.

CHAPTER THIRTY-ONE

Truth in Art

This stupid sculpture was driving Ella crazy. She'd taken it apart and put it back together twice now, and she was beginning to realize the problem wasn't the sculpture. It was her. She didn't have the skill to bring her vision into the world. She was an awkward, sad teenager piecing trash together. She couldn't construct a noble gaze of defiance on a confident young girl. She couldn't even manage it on her own face.

Ella picked up a putty knife and tried to lever a chunk of blue plastic off the sculpture. It was so covered in putty from being stuck on and removed and stuck on again that she couldn't even tell what toy it had originally come from.

She put down the knife. Maybe she should just give up. Some assemblages seemed like a good idea at the time, but never quite came together. This was probably one of them. A better artist might be able to make it work, but Ella couldn't.

Maybe she'd give up art altogether. If she just stopped pretending to be an artist, she could let go and drift through life. Not thinking too deeply, not worrying, not wondering, not trying to see the treasure in another man's trash. She could just walk on by.

It wasn't like she even needed this class. It was only an elective. And she certainly wasn't winning any art contests with this hunk of junk. Some shred of stubbornness tried to tell her that she'd regret it if she quit now, but her more rational thoughts drowned it out. A year from now, this wouldn't matter. Nothing would matter. She'd be six months into the dead-end job that would structure the rest of her life. Liv and Owen would be off living their lives, not that she cared, and she'd be here, in the town where she grew up, too afraid to learn the skill that would help get her out of this place. It was time to just accept her limitations.

Ella picked up the head and walked across the room. A few people raised their eyes to look at her as she passed, but she ignored them. She knew what needed to be done. For a moment, she paused, holding the head between her hands.

It landed in the nearly empty garbage can with a thud. *From trash you were made, and to trash you shall return*, she thought, and almost giggled.

Almost everyone, including Ms. Beaudry, was looking at her when she turned back to face the room. She wondered if this was how Mitch had felt when he'd pissed in the trash can—wild and watched and defiant. Ella tried to keep herself from smiling as she went back to her seat.

She spent the rest of the period cleaning up her workstation, even chipping the dried epoxy and paint from her table. When the bell rang, she stood up, happy to leave her unfinished sculpture in its corner.

"Ella, can you stay after for a minute?" Ms. Beaudry said.

Ella hovered awkwardly while the class flowed out around her. Owen looked over his shoulder at her as he passed, but she barely noticed.

When the other kids had filed out, Ms. Beaudry shut the door. The next class would wait outside. Ms. Beaudry normally had an open door policy. Students could mostly come and go as they pleased, but if the door was shut, that was it. No one in, no one out until she opened it again.

Ella stood next to her headless sculpture. It was going to be about her throwing the head away. She shouldn't have done it in front of everyone. Now they were going to have a talk about it. She didn't know if she'd have the heart to tell Ms. Beaudry that she was really and truly giving up this time.

As it turned out, she didn't have to. Ms. Beaudry didn't so much as glance at the unfinished sculpture. She pulled a stool out from under one of the tables and perched on it. That brought her almost up to Ella's eye level.

"Ella, how are you?"

"Fine." Ella twined her fingers together inside the

pocket of her sweatshirt. Ms. Beaudry was just sitting there, staring at her, a soft smile on her lips. Ella thought about telling her the truth, except she didn't know what the truth even was. She wasn't fine, but there wasn't anything specific. It was just . . . everything was a big cloud of suck and it was sucking her right under.

Finally, Ms. Beaudry said, "I don't think so."

Ella opened her mouth to say, "Well, you're wrong." But she couldn't. Not to Ms. Beaudry. Ms. Beaudry who was so warm and welcoming, who filled the world with color, who really seemed to care whether Ella was okay. Ella bit the inside of her cheek to stop the tears she felt prickling behind her eyes.

Ms. Beaudry must have seen all this, but she didn't push. Instead she said, "Do you know what all great artists have in common?"

Ella shook her head. The second bell rang, shattering the silence and making her jump. Ms. Beaudry didn't flinch. She sat, stoic as a sculpture.

"Great artists tell the truth, their truth, as they see and know it. Van Gogh, Kahlo, Bourgeois, Calder. They told the truth. Sometimes they told truth to power and sometimes they told truth to the public, and sometimes, they just told it to themselves."

Ms. Beaudry's warm brown eyes looked into Ella's. Ella looked away. She couldn't bear the kindness there. It made her feel small and mean.

After a long silence Ms. Beaudry added, "You don't have to tell me anything you don't want to share, but make sure you're at least telling yourself the truth."

Ella nodded, the tears were going to fall and she didn't even know why she was crying.

"I'm going to be late," she said and fled the room.

As soon as the door opened, the next class flooded in around her. She fought against the current mechanically. Most of her mind was caught up in what Ms. Beaudry had said. Truth. What did that mean?

The truth was, she was sad. She felt like she'd been sad for a long time, maybe her whole life. She wished she knew how to just not be sad anymore.

PhiTau, alone in Ella's head, heard her wish. He knew what he had to do.

CHAPTER THIRTY-TWO

Chiaroscuro

Ella woke up feeling great. She wasn't happy about anything in particular. She just felt . . . calm, that was it. Calm, unbothered. She tried not to think about the feeling too much, in case it got shy and ran away. She wondered why she'd been in such a bad mood the last few days. It wasn't as though she had anything to be upset about. Besides, this was much nicer.

She was clean and dressed and smiling when she got downstairs. Mom was rushing around from the kitchen to the bathroom to the front door and then back to the bathroom again. Ella watched as Mom found a pair of flats and attempted to make the left one fit on her right foot.

"Busy day today?" Ella asked.

Mom said, "Do you need a ride to school? Because if you do, we need to leave three minutes ago."

"No, I'm good," Ella said. "Have a good day at work."

Mom had succeeded in getting her shoes on the correct feet. She stood up, kissed Ella on the forehead, and bustled out the door. Ella walked to the kitchen rubbing her forehead in case of lipstick marks.

As Ella filled her cereal bowl and checked out what had happened on social media overnight, she wondered where Dad was. He must have already left for work. She picked up her shiny scoopy thing, spoon, that was the word, right, knew it all the time, and began to eat.

After she'd dumped her cereal bowl and spoon in the sink, put on her own shoes, and sat scrolling for a while, she began to wonder where the hell Liv was. They were going to be late for school at this rate.

ELLA: Hey, where are you?

LIV: School

ELLA: You're not picking me up? :(

LIV: Are you serious right now?

ELLA: Sorry.

Ella lowered her phone into her lap. What was her problem? Maybe she had a big test or something. There always seemed to be something for Liv to be stressed about. Ella wasn't sure exactly what went on in honors classes, because her mind tended to wander whenever Liv started talking about it, but she'd formed the impression that it was all long-answer tests and 5,000 word essays on the symbolism behind that poem about the plums in the icebox.

She grabbed her backpack and walked down to the end of the driveway. Maybe she could take the bus. She knew it was lame for a senior to take the bus, and she couldn't actually remember the last time she'd done so—the experience she could recall at the moment involved pigtails and a *Blue's Clues* backpack, so that couldn't be right—but it would probably stop for her if she waited at the end of the driveway.

Her head felt kind of fuzzy today. Maybe she should start drinking coffee like Owen. She grabbed her backpack and walked down to the side of the road. After just a minute or so, she heard the unmistakable rumble of the school bus. Her road was partially dirt and big trucks never came down it, so it could only be the bus.

It flew right by without even slowing down.

Ella sighed. She'd really wanted to maintain this new chill feeling and not get all wound up about stuff today, but she was going to be late for school. At this point her choices were to bike there, which would take forever and probably be dangerous considering the snow and sand on the roads, or call Dad.

She called Dad.

"Hey, Daddy, sorry to bother you, but I missed the bus. Do you think you could take me to school?"

"Missed the bus, huh, seemed like that happened ten

years ago." He paused for laughter. Ella didn't oblige because she had no idea what he was talking about.

"You really want me to take you?"

"If you have the time?"

"I'm in my truck," Dad said.

Ella, still trying to be chill, bit back the response that she hadn't expected a limo.

"Well, it's too snowy to ride my bike," she said instead.

"Okay then, I'll be over in five minutes. Be ready."

It was more like eight. Ella passed the time by building a three-foot-tall snowman. She was just looking for sticks to use for arms, when Dad rolled up.

He lowered the passenger side window. "Who's that?" he asked, nodding at the snowman.

"Sheldon," Ella said.

"Sheldon?"

"Yeah," she opened the door and climbed into the truck. Suddenly she felt anxious. Why was she so worried? It wasn't like she'd never been late to school before.

"Sheldon Slushman Attorney-at-Thaw."

Dad watched her settle her backpack between her feet and clip her seatbelt into place. He rolled up the window.

"All set?" he asked.

"Yup." She swallowed. There was a sour feeling in the pit of her stomach. Maybe she should have checked the expiration date on the milk before she'd put it in her cereal. Mom had been awfully busy lately, maybe too busy to notice if the milk was going bad.

"You sure?" Dad asked.

"Come on Daddy, I'm going to be late."

"Okay then." He put the truck in gear and pulled out into the road.

"So," he said, "are you and Liv fighting or something?"

"Me and Liv? That's silly. No she just had a test or a presentation or something today. I forget which."

"Okay." A pause. "What about Owen?"

"Her brother Owen? What about him?"

"Right. Okay."

Dad was being so weird today. Maybe he was annoyed that she'd called him at work to take her to school.

"I'm sorry," Ella said.

"For what?"

"You were probably busy at work."

Dad looked at her out of the corner of his eye. "I, uh, wasn't busy. Work's kind of slow right now."

"Oh, that's good."

"It is?"

"Yes, because if you'd been busy at work I wouldn't have had a ride to school."

"Well, that's true I guess."

"You know, I should really get my driver's license, then I wouldn't have to depend on everyone else to drive me places."

Dad slammed his foot on the brake even though they were still a whole car length away from the stop sign. Ella suddenly felt nauseous. It must have been the rocking motion as the truck stopped then lunged forward and stopped again.

"You could do that. Yes," Dad said. "Have you talked to your mother about it?"

Ella scratched her ear. "I think she brought it up once, but I can't remember what we decided."

Dad stared at her. "Are you feeling okay today?"

"Yes," Ella said. But she thought *I'm not sure. Everyone is being weird.* And her head still felt strange, like your mouth after the dentist pulls a tooth and leaves a new hole you can't help but probe with your tongue. That was a very strange way for a head to feel.

"Do you know what we're having for dinner?"

"No, what?" Dad asked. He'd managed to get the truck moving again, and took the last turn to the high school.

"I mean, you tell me."

"Tonight? Are you coming to my place for dinner tonight?"

"It's my place too, right? Or are you kicking me out? It's still a whole month before I turn 18 you know."

Dad's eyebrow furrowed. "Did you have a fight with your mom?"

Ella couldn't understand why he kept changing the subject. "Mom and I don't fight. She gets all spun up about something and I just nod until she gets tired."

"Right, okay. Well, how about spaghetti? I think I can manage that."

"Cool."

The truck drifted to a stop. Dad was still looking at her in a funny way. Maybe he was a little annoyed that she'd called him away from work, but he didn't want to admit it. That must be it. Dad didn't like to argue any more than Ella did.

"Thanks, Daddy," she said and gave him a peck on the cheek.

He twitched like he'd been stung, but then smiled. "Have a good day at school, sweetie."

Ella slipped out of the truck, grabbed her backpack, and slammed the door. Everything was weird today. Maybe she'd drifted into a new reality in her dreams, a parallel universe where everything was the same but just slightly different. Maybe the Ella in this reality wore pastel colors and already had a driver's license. Maybe she was a cheerleader. Maybe she'd never assembled a sculpture in her life. That might be okay.

Ella imagined walking into homeroom and finding parallel Ella already there. Everyone would stare. Someone would scream. Ella would turn and run. But where would she go? If this was another universe, she had no idea how she'd gotten here and, therefore, no idea how to get home. Maybe she'd just have to go back to sleep and hope she woke up in the right place this time. But that was dumb. It was just a normal school day. Mom was busy, Liv was stressed, and Dad was weird.

Oh, and Ella was late. The first bell had already rung and the only kids left in the halls were the stragglers and the slouchers. Ella wondered which one she was. When she reached her homeroom, nobody except Ms. Collins even looked up. Liv was probably off bothering some teacher. Her brother had his head down on his desk. He might have been asleep. Ella slouched to her seat. Announcements had already started. Nothing unusual here. Same old boring school, same old boring life. Ella slipped into her seat and waited for the second bell.

~

PhiTau was pretty sure his plan was working. Ella was clearly bored, but she wasn't sad. She hadn't even gotten upset when Liv refused to take her to school. She hadn't gotten upset about anything.

Sitting alone in one of the circles of light behind Ella's eyes, PhiTau grinned to himself. It was too bad, really, that humans couldn't step inside their own minds and tidy up now and then. They'd all be so much happier.

The tenders had been fed all that puffery about how humans needed dreams to categorize memories and work through challenges, and here Ella was, doing just fine, in fact, better than fine, without any dreams at all.

It was possible that the oneiroi had been going about their tasks all wrong. If they really wanted to help humans, they should be inside their heads removing upsetting memories before they had a chance to become nightmares. Just imagine what they could accomplish.

A high-pitched squeal derailed his train of thought. He sighed and slowly stood up. After one last look through

Ella's eyes to satisfy himself that she'd be okay without him, he ambled into the darkness.

Little Ella was lying on her side. She'd managed to flatten a circle of grass around her as well as several of those red-orange flowers that seemed to grow everywhere. All that thrashing had done her no good. Her hands and feet were still bound together with a jump rope. He'd stuffed a green plush bear into her mouth to keep her from going on and on about what a bad monkey he was and how "breaking other people's stuff is mean."

It wasn't really her fault, PhiTau knew. Human children were still learning. There was a lot they didn't understand. PhiTau may have spent most of his life in the fields, but he'd come to understand a lot since Morpheus had chosen him. Plus, if the Dreaming had any real concept of time, he was sure he'd be much more than six years old.

Little Ella had managed to work the gag out of her mouth. "You're a bad monkey," she said, as soon as he came into view.

PhiTau sighed. "I told you, I'm helping her."

"My arms hurt."

"I can't untie you if you're going to start jumping all over the place and screaming. You know what you do affects how Ella acts in the real world. She's just now getting comfortable. You'll ruin it."

There were tears in Little Ella's eyes. "I'll be good."

PhiTau looked down at her. She was so small and young, no wonder Ella had such a hard time in the human world. It was run by grown-ups, and here she was with a child in charge of her mind. How did that happen?

"What if I bring you over to the eyes and you can see for yourself that everything is okay."

"Okay."

"If you start putting words in her mouth, I'm going to have to stop you from talking again."

"Okay," Little Ella said again.

PhiTau bent down and gathered up the child. She fit neatly into the cradle of his arms. PhiTau felt a momentary stab of regret. He hadn't wanted to tie up Little Ella, but he hadn't had much of a choice. It was her or real Ella. She didn't understand what he was accomplishing here. Well, he'd just have to show her.

He carried her back into the light. Setting her down he said, "Now just watch." He sat close beside her, in case he needed to throw a hand over her mouth. Together, they gazed out through Ella's eyes.

CHAPTER THIRTY-THREE

Reality Check

After Liv blew her off for the second day in a row, Ella started to get worried. She told herself not to be, that everything was okay and why did she care if Liv didn't want to hang out with her? But she did care. It wasn't as though she had a huge circle of friends all fighting for her attention. Without Liv it was just her and her assemblages, and they were starting to lose their appeal. Lately Ella couldn't help but see them as big piles of trash.

For the first time she wondered if maybe she should have made an attempt to have more than one friend. Nothing like putting all of your eggs in one basket.

And of course Liv wasn't in homeroom. Why would she be? That would be too easy. Owen was there though. He smiled at Ella when she walked in. She marched right over to him. "Where's your sister?"

"Hello to you, too," Owen said, his tone smoothing the

edges of his sarcasm.

"Hi," Ella said. She dropped down in the seat in front of Owen's. They were supposed to be in assigned seating in homeroom, because apparently Ms. Collins believed they were all secretly in second grade, but the bell hadn't rung yet.

"Where's Liv?"

"She went to talk to her science teacher."

"Which one?"

Owen shrugged.

"Is she mad at me?"

Owen held up both hands, palms out. "Oh no, I'm not getting in the middle of this."

"In the middle of what?"

"You'll have to talk to her. I'd just mess things up."

Ella rolled her eyes. "You've been super helpful, thanks."

She turned her back on Owen. Her index finger drew boxes on the desktop while she tried to figure out what to do next. Liv couldn't avoid her forever. Could she?

"You really should talk to her, El," Owen's said. "We didn't—"

The bell interrupted his rambling. Ella jumped up and went to her assigned seat. She was not in the mood for a lecture from Ms. Collins.

Ella stewed through the rest of homeroom. *This isn't like her,* Ella thought. *We're best friends. We always have been.* Her thoughts answered, *You don't need anyone else, you have me.* Which, Ella realized, was kind of a strange thing for your own thoughts to say. But she didn't have any bandwidth left over to unpack whatever mental issue was making itself known here. She was busy worrying about Liv.

She must have done something to hurt Liv's feelings without realizing it. That was the only reasonable explanation. She tried to recall their last few interactions. Liv had driven her to school the other day, but Mom had picked her up. Was that it? Had she told Liv she needed a ride home and then forgot about it? That didn't seem like something worth holding a grudge over, not for longer than a few hours anyway. Then again, Ella knew she'd been spacey lately. Maybe Liv was just sick of her shit. That was fair. Ella wasn't exactly enjoying her own company either.

But she could fix this. She just needed to have a calm conversation with Liv and sort this whole thing out.

~

PhiTau shifted from foot to foot as he watched Ella's English class through her eyes. He knew it made her restless when he fidgeted, but he couldn't help it. This class was so boring. Why did humans waste so much of their lives doing things they didn't even enjoy? It was stupid. Ella would never have to know the difference between synecdoche and metonymy outside this classroom. So why bother learning it at all?

In the real world, Mr. Hitchens said, "Let's put this

into practice. I want you to write the first draft of a poem that uses either synecdoche or metonymy."

A couple of students groaned. Riley Perkins raised her hand. "Do we get bonus points if we use both?"

"Let's just focus on one thing at a time for now, Riley."

As Ella stared down at a blank sheet of paper, PhiTau wondered if there was a way he could influence her mind so she didn't have to go to school. Could he make her super smart somehow? That wouldn't help though. Liv was practically a genius and she still went to class.

Outside, Mr. Hitchens said. "Ella, eyes on your own work, please."

"You're making her distracted," Little Ella said. She was lying on her side in the light from Ella's other eye.

"Shh," PhiTau said.

"I wish Daddy was here," Little Ella whispered.

"PhiTau, what have you done?" The voice froze PhiTau's blood. For one wild moment, he thought Little Ella had somehow summoned her father into the mind with them. But he knew that voice, and it was far more terrifying than any human man. The Dream Lord had found him.

Clutching his wings close to his body, PhiTau turned. Morpheus stood among the poppies. He was taller than PhiTau remembered and even more striking. His body seemed to give off its own light. Maybe it was the heat of his rage made visible, because his eyes were blazing, the blue and green both somehow tinged with red.

PhiTau fell to his knees. "How did you . . . Why are you . . . I left your realm," PhiTau's mind stumbled, but a shred of self-preservation prompted him to add, "my Lord."

"But *she* did not," Morpheus bellowed. His finger stabbed toward the lights of Ella's eyes. At the same time, his human-like form distorted, stretched. In the darkness of an eye blink, PhiTau thought he saw claws and rows of teeth. He cowered.

"Shhh," Little Ella said. "You're scaring her."

PhiTau shuddered, shocked that Little Ella had even found the courage to speak. She clearly had no idea who she was dealing with. PhiTau braced himself, waiting for Morpheus to turn on her.

Instead, Morpheus sighed back to his normal shape. He raked twelve fingers through his hair and seemed to collect himself. PhiTau was not convinced. He pressed low to the ground, remembering how peaceful it had been to lie in the cool soil of his first dream with Ella. He wished desperately that he was still there.

"And who is this?" Morpheus asked.

"I'm Ella," the little girl said. Whether it was bravery or ignorance, PhiTau could not tell, but she didn't seem bothered by Morpheus at all. "This bad monkey tied me up." She wiggled and tried to sit up, but couldn't quite manage it.

"Oh did he now?" Morpheus chuckled but his words had sharp edges. PhiTau didn't dare look at his face. "Shall I punish him?"

"I was just helping her." PhiTau recalled the feeling of Ella's memories crunching under his feet. He heard the echo of plastic shattering beneath his heel. At the time, he'd felt powerful and rebellious. Now he trembled. Morpheus wouldn't understand what PhiTau was trying to accomplish here.

"Are you his grown-up?"

PhiTau, face still pressed to the earth, turned his head to look at her.

Morpheus crouched down beside the little girl. He was smiling. PhiTau had never seen such a thing. There was warmth in it, and humor. PhiTau gaped at the sight.

"More or less," Morpheus said. He was looking at Little Ella and she was staring right back at him like he was just another human adult. The sight gave PhiTau courage.

"I only cleaned up a few of her memories," PhiTau said.

Morpheus touched the jump rope around Little Ella's wrists. It fell away.

Little Ella squealed in excitement, then clapped her hands over her mouth when big Ella chuckled out loud.

Out there, Mr. Hitchens gave her a sharp look.

Morpheus touched her ankles, and that knot also disappeared. PhiTau wondered which memory the jump rope had been. Was it Jack's wake, where Ella had cried because she'd expected her brother to be there? Or was it the day her father moved out, when Ella had barricaded herself in the playhouse for three days, living on juice boxes and graham crackers and pretending that she was six years old again? It hardly mattered, but his mind seemed to want to focus on anything but the god looming over him.

"On your feet, oneiroi."

With infinite caution, PhiTau did as he was told. Little Ella was already pirouetting in and out of the light. Free. There went all his work, ruined. What would happen to Ella now?

"PhiTau." The force of the voice snapped PhiTau's gaze back to Morpheus. He watched as his lord pulled a bit of dreamstuff from the air. Eyes fixed on PhiTau, he fashioned it into a tiny sculpture of an oneiroi. PhiTau watched, fascinated. The Dream Lord was creating right in front of him. It was amazing. Sacred. A once-in-a-lifetime experience. For a moment, he forgot to be terrified.

The dream oneiroi was tiny and intricate. Perfect in every detail. PhiTau could see the texture of its fur, the glint of its eyes, the way it struggled when Morpheus suddenly closed his hand around it and squeezed.

"I could unmake you, you know," Morpheus said. His voice was flat, and that, even more than the sight of the dream oneiroi exploding into dust, spilled terror into PhiTau's mind.

"Aww, you broke it," Little Ella said.

"It wasn't very good. I'll make a better one later," Morpheus said, and PhiTau had a sinking feeling that Morpheus was talking about him.

CHAPTER THIRTY-FOUR

Art of Destruction

Ella had written exactly zero lines of her poem by the time the bell rang. She hadn't even decided on a topic. There was something about a toy she'd lost when she was little, but she couldn't remember whether it was a robot or an octopus. She wasn't even sure how a person could confuse the two, but that was about where her head was lately. Hopefully, she'd be able to come up with something at home.

She left Mr. Hitchens' room like a prisoner who had been granted a reprieve, and immediately spotted Liv across the hall. Liv kept walking, but Ella noticed how carefully she avoided looking in Ella's direction.

"Liv, wait up."

Liv stopped, but didn't turn her head. She just stood there until Ella caught up.

"Hey," Ella said.

"Hey," Liv echoed, with about one-tenth the warmth

of Ella's greeting. Ella tried not to take it personally. Liv probably had something on her mind.

"You've been avoiding me," Ella said. "What's up with that?"

They started walking. Owen fell in behind them, as though he wanted to be part of the conversation too but couldn't find an opening. It was kind of sad, Ella thought, the way he was always tagging along. Didn't he have his own friends to hang out with?

"Let's not, okay?" Liv started walking again and Ella kept pace.

"Not what?" Ella said.

"This, this whole thing. Let's not pretend everything is fine."

"Why wouldn't it be?"

"Come on, El. I know it bugged you that Owen took my side."

"Liv . . . " Owen began, but Ella was already talking.

"Took your side on what?"

She rolled her eyes. "Cut the crap, Ella."

"I seriously have no idea what you're talking about. Why shouldn't Owen take your side. He's your brother, right?"

"God damn it," Liv muttered, but Ella couldn't tell if it was about this conversation or because a clot of freshman was blocking the hallway. Liv steered around them, trailing Ella and Owen like ducklings.

"That's what brothers are for, right?" Ella said. "To take your side."

Liv sighed. "Look, Ella, I get it. The thing with Jack really messed you up. It's a sad thing, but you can't let it define your whole life."

"What thing with Jack?"

Liv stopped so quickly that Owen almost tripped over her. Liv jabbed a finger in his direction. "You talk to her."

Ella said, "I haven't seen Jack since . . . he went," Ella's memories were all mixed up again. The first one that came to mind was Jack helping Dad to put the roof on the playhouse they'd built her when she was six. For some reason they'd never finished it.

". . . he went away," she said. Her eyebrows furrowed. Where had he gone? She couldn't remember.

"Ella, are you okay?" Owen said.

Why couldn't she remember?

"She's playing one of her games again," Liv said.

"I don't know what's going on," Ella said.

"I don't think so, Liv. Look at her."

Owen turned back to Ella and looked into her eyes. "El, where did Jack go?"

Ella rubbed her forehead and tried to remember. "He doesn't come home much," she mumbled. "Why are we talking about him anyway?" She loved her brother, of course she did, but thinking about him was making her head hurt.

"This is ridiculous," Liv began. "Jack's d—"

"Shut up," Owen snapped.

Liv looked wide-eyed at Owen. Her mouth hung open.

Owen ignored her. He stared at Ella with an intensity

that made her brain itch. Why couldn't she remember where Jack was? When was the last time she'd seen him? She couldn't recall that either.

Blindly she clutched at Owen's arm. "Owen, something's wrong. I can't remember . . . Where's Jack?"

Liv drew closer. "El, are you okay?"

Tears rose in Ella's eyes, and she didn't have the energy to fight them. "I'm not. I'm not okay. Where's Jack? I want Jack."

"Hey, hey, Ella. Breathe," Owen said. "I need you to breathe."

She did need to breathe, but there wasn't enough air. Black sparkles flitted along the edges of her vision. Owen leaned close. She felt his thumbs on her collar bones, his hands looping over her shoulders. He squeezed gently, anchoring her, but the sensation was muffled, as though she were wearing her winter coat.

"Just breathe, Ella. You're having a panic attack. Deep breath."

She felt the panic welling up, spilling out. The acid flowed out of her, ready to consume everything it touched. She tried to do as Owen said. She tried to breathe. A hand took hers—Liv. But she had no space in her mind for that. The darkness was rising.

"Look at me, El. You're okay. Just breathe."

She swallowed a gasping breath. Owen's eyes had little flecks of gold in them. Had she ever noticed that before? Had she ever looked so closely at his eyes, his face? Had she seen the tired lines, the bluish smudges beneath. He looked . . .

"Are you sick?" Ella asked.

Liv's voice, floating free from her body, muttered, "Now she notices." But it dissipated into mist almost before Ella was sure she'd heard it.

Owen's hands moved, as though he'd shifted his weight onto one foot and back again.

"Just worried about you. I need you to keep breathing. Liv and I are going to walk you to the office."

Owen's hands disappeared. For a moment she was untethered, weightless. She thought she might float up and away, like a balloon bumping across the ceiling. Then, an arm encircled her shoulders. Her hands were tingling stars at the end of her arms and she couldn't tell if Liv was still holding on to her.

"She'll make me go to the doctor," Ella muttered.

"We're just going to the office. That's all we're doing right now." Owen's voice, like a string leading her forward.

"I want to call Jack-Jack."

The prickles at the end of her right arm intensified. Liv squeezing her hand.

"Almost there. Keep breathing. We're almost there."

"Where's Jack?"

Ella was crying but she didn't know why. She felt like the day she'd lost her Baby Sarah doll at daycare. She'd cried herself to sleep that night. She'd found the doll years later in the dirt when they dug up the septic tank. But wait, that couldn't be right. Sarah had been on the shelf in her room for years. Hadn't she?

"Panic attack?" said a voice. "Sit her down there. I'll call her mom."

Owen's arm lifted off of her shoulder. She grabbed at his shirt with numb fingers, clutching the fabric. "Don't leave me."

"We're here, El," Liv's voice said. "We're both right here."

"We're not going anywhere," said Owen.

~

PhiTau knelt in the circle of light behind Ella's right eye watching all of this in horror. He'd allowed Morpheus to distract him, and now Ella was suffering some kind of attack.

"She needs my help," PhiTau said.

"She needs her memories," Morpheus answered.

"They're squished," said Little Ella.

Morpheus looked thoughtful. He plucked some dreamstuff from the air. Everything went dark as Ella squeezed her eyes shut. Between Morpheus' hands, a glowing cat's cradle took shape.

"You can make her new ones," Little Ella said. PhiTau heard her hands clap in excitement.

Morpheus shook his head. "I can't, only she can do that. But I know where we can find copies of the old ones." He grinned at Little Ella. "Do you want to go on an adventure?"

Litte Ella perked up, but then she looked toward Ella's closed eyes and her face crumpled. "She'll be all lonely."

"I'll stay with her," PhiTau said. Maybe with Morpheus and Little Ella out of the way he could regain some control of this situation.

Morpheus laughed, well guffawed really. PhiTau had never heard such a noise, would never have expected such a noise could come from the Dream Lord's mouth.

"You are coming with us." His arm shot out and caught PhiTau by the scruff of his neck. "Bad monkey," Morpheus added. He grinned.

He reached his other hand toward Little Ella. She took it without the slightest hesitation.

"Ready!" Morpheus squeezed her hand. "Steady!" He bent his knees slightly. "Here we go!" Little Ella's laugh tinkled as Morpheus hopped them sideways out of Ella's mind.

~

When Morpheus let go, PhiTau fell in a heap. The ground was cranberry colored, and soft. Carpet? PhiTau blinked at it in surprise. Where were they? He tried to get his bearings while also climbing to his knees. The ground was right here, but the walls were far away. All of them were lined with books, or maybe made of books. It was hard to tell. Tilting his head back, he could see nothing but books arching together high above his head. PhiTau trembled. So many words. So much magic. He yearned to reach out and touch them.

"This is a really big libary," Little Ella whispered.

"Library," a crisp voice corrected her.

PhiTau dragged his gaze away from the books to look for the source of the voice. From this angle all he could see was a massive mahogany desk, made wider by the L-shaped countertops attached to either side. The voice had come from behind it. Cautiously, watching Morpheus out of the corner of his eye, PhiTau stood up.

"And we do not allow pets in here," the voice added.

"I'm not a pet."

The woman behind the desk wore glasses that made her eyes seem too large for her face. They stared at PhiTau as though he were a bug she'd found squished between the pages of her favorite book.

"He's with me," Morpheus said.

The eyes turned to the Dream Lord. "I'm not exactly delighted by your presence either." That wasn't exactly encouraging.

"Believe me, Mnemosyne, I wouldn't have come to you if it weren't urgent. All these dead people give me the heebie-jeebies."

Little Ella crept closer to Morpheus while PhiTau looked around nervously. He didn't see any corpses. There was only one other person in the library. A woman hunched over a book, engrossed in her reading. As he watched, she turned a page. That didn't seem like the behavior of a dead woman.

Mnemosyne rolled her eyes. "And what is so urgent?

Have you misplaced your dream journal? Forgotten the recipe for nightmares?"

Morpheus breathed out sharply through his nose. PhiTau couldn't tell if it was supposed to be a laugh or a sound of annoyance.

"My monkey here has caused some trouble." He made an airy gesture with one hand, and a clatter of pennies fell to the floor. PhiTau couldn't tell if he'd done that on purpose or not. "Now there's a human girl walking around with only half her memories."

"I'm not a monkey," PhiTau muttered. Not that anyone was listening.

"Is that all?" Mnemosyne said.

"All? He destroyed her memory, Meme." Morpheus spread his arms along the countertop. "Doesn't that bother you?"

Mnemosyne shrugged. "I don't get involved with these things. Humans are always trying to forget their memories or rewrite them to be less scary, less ugly, less embarrassing. Who am I to stop them?"

"The Goddess of Memory," Morpheus said, his tone deadpan.

Little Ella set her hands on the edge of the massive desk and pulled herself to her tiptoes so she could see over the top.

"Do you have every book in the whole world?"

Instead of answering, Mnemosyne looked from the little girl to Morpheus. "Who is this?"

"This is Ella, at least one version of her."

"What?"

"I'm not too clear on it myself. But the truth is, Meme, we need you to get involved here. Lethe is meddling."

Mnemosyne's face went pale, and then darkened, as though Morpheus had just told her he preferred folding down the corners of his pages instead of using bookmarks. "Lethe." The name was a curse in her mouth. "Why humans ever made her, I'll never know."

"Oh, there are some things they'd much rather forget," Morpheus said.

Meme cast him a look that said he wasn't winning any allies with that attitude. "I am well aware of that," she said.

But PhiTau barely noticed. He was still stuck on her last comment.

"Humans made her?" He'd never really stopped to wonder where the gods came from, but if he had, he certainly would not have assumed humans played any role in it at all.

Mnemosyne adjusted her glasses, making the lenses flash. PhiTau found himself remembering the feel of raw dreamstuff between his fingers.

"Do you teach them nothing?" she said to Morpheus.

Morpheus shrugged, and pulled a bit of dreamstuff out of the air. A swift motion of his hands turned it into an abacus beaded with peppermints and butterscotches and those strawberry candies that PhiTau didn't know the name of because Ella never had.

"Knowledge just makes them restless," Morpheus said.

"They end up questioning everything. It's hard to rule when your subjects know too much."

He handed the abacus to Little Ella, who stared at it in amazement.

Shaking her head in either amusement or disgust, Mnemosyne set aside the books she'd been working on and then lifted a section of the counter that PhiTau hadn't realized was hinged. She stepped through the gap she'd made, then settled the board back into place.

Meanwhile, Little Ella tugged at one of the peppermints on the abacus. It dissolved into mist, taking the rest of the dream with it. PhiTau expected her to cry, but she just stood there, turning her hands over and over as though she thought the strange toy might be hiding on the other side.

Meme put a stop to that by grabbing her wrist. Then she reached out to touch Morpheus's arm. "Show me," she said.

PhiTau felt a hand on the back of his neck. They stepped.

~

Ella's mind was dark. She was probably asleep. PhiTau felt a stab of guilt. What were her dreams like without him there to hold them together? Were they just colors and sounds? Or was she floating in darkness, silent as the grave and twice as terrifying? He should have stopped to think before he ran. Sure, Morpheus would have punished him, but at least Ella wouldn't have gotten hurt.

Six fingers were still wrapped around his neck. He found himself stumbling forward through the tall grass. Little Ella seemed to be leading them, pulling Mnemosyne along by her hand. The goddess looked out of place here, a librarian in a dark meadow. Tall grass and the occasional poppy flower brushed against her knee-length skirt. It was almost absurd enough to be a dream.

But reality closed in quickly when Little Ella stopped and lifted a shard of plastic. It glimmered faintly in her hand. Mnemosyne took it as gently as one might gather up a small antique volume of poetry, its binding cracked with age.

She turned on PhiTau, and he wished that it were darker, so he didn't have to see the pain in her glass amplified eyes. "You did this?"

He nodded as best he could with Morpheus' fingers on his neck. It hadn't seemed like vandalism at the time. He'd thought he was helping, he really had. Destroy the bad memories, keep the good. Isn't that what everyone wanted, a life without pain?

"Can you repair them?" Morpheus said.

Mnemosyne released the fragment. It fluttered to the ground, like an injured butterfly. PhiTau found himself unable to look away.

"No," she said. PhiTau's heart twisted. He didn't know why what he had done was wrong, but he was beginning to realize that it was. That single word carried the weight of a conviction.

"You did a thorough job, monkey," Mnemosyne said.

"I'm sorry," PhiTau answered. And he was, now, well and truly sorry.

"How do we fix this, Meme?"

"We need the backup copy."

PhiTau's heart leapt. "There really is a backup copy?"

"Of course."

Mnemosyne took Little Ella's hand and touched Morpheus' elbow. PhiTau felt the fingers tighten on his neck just before they stepped.

~

They landed on a catwalk halfway up the side of a giant warehouse. PhiTau shook himself. All this stepping from world to world was giving him a headache. Or maybe that was the noise. It was so loud that it took him a moment to hear the rhythm in it. The staccato wave hit the metal walls of the building and curled back on itself. In its wake, a spray of sound separated into droplets of click and clack, with the occasional ding.

Little Ella wrapped both arms around the pole of a railing and looked down, wide-eyed. PhiTau, finally released from Morpheus' grip, edged forward just enough to see what she was looking at.

"Typewriters?" Morpheus said. He had to raise his voice to be heard.

Mnemosyne crooked a finger and led them along the catwalk.

"Yes, typewriters. We finally got the place upgraded. Isn't it impressive?"

Now they were walking down a set of metal steps, the clangs of their footfalls barely heard against the background cacophony.

"Oh yes," Morpheus said. "I believe the humans would call it retro. What were you using before?"

"Quill pens."

Morpheus snorted, but Mnemosyne ignored him.

"The scritchy noise in here was unbearable. It set my teeth on edge. What was the girl's name again?"

"Ella. Ella Pratt. Seventeen years old, Corinna, Maine."

As they reached the ground level, PhiTau could see that the typewriters were moving on their own. Each one clacking away as though under the hand of an invisible typist.

Little Ella tugged gently on the hem of Mnemosyne's cardigan sweater. "Excuse me Ms. Libarian lady. What are all these things doing?"

Mnemosyne looked down at Little Ella, her eyes suddenly invisible behind her flashing eyeglass lenses. Somehow they reminded PhiTau of the moons in the Dreaming.

"Librarian," she snapped. "They're recording lives, young lady. Every one of these typewriters represents a life in progress."

Little Ella's face scrunched in confusion.

Mnemosyne tried again. "They're writing down what

everyone in the world does and says."

"Even me?"

Mnemosyne glanced at Morpheus who shrugged. He pulled dreamstuff out of the air and made what appeared to be a tiny typewriter with just two buttons. One showed a smiley face. The other a sad face. He handed it to Little Ella. It just fit in the palm of her hand. Enthralled by the toy, Little Ella seemed to forget that nobody had really answered her question.

"You know," Morpheus said, "with parallel processing on modern computers you could probably handle this whole job with one or two million machines. Tops."

"I said we just upgraded." Mnemosyne spun to walk away from him along the aisle between the wall and the typewriter tables.

"I'm just saying, technology moves fast down there. If it weren't for my greenhouse, I couldn't keep up."

PhiTau had no idea what that meant, but he could see that Mnemosyne was angry. She spun around, snapped, "I am not bowing to every passing technology fad." And then continued walking.

Morpheus chuckled and made a pair of mice wearing bright red tap shoes. Hopping from his hand, they did a little dance before scurrying away beneath the tables. Little Ella, who was walking ahead with Mnemosyne, never even saw them before they popped out of existence. PhiTau wondered who the Dream Lord had made them for.

Mnemosyne stopped the little group in front of a

typewriter that didn't seem to be doing anything at all. A piece of paper stuck out the top, but the keys weren't depressing, the arms weren't waving, and the page remained still.

"This one's asleep," Little Ella said.

Mnemosyne looked down at her in surprise. "That's right," she said. "This is Ella Pratt's life, currently on hold as she sleeps an apparently dreamless sleep."

"Don't look at me," Morpheus said. "No oneiroi, no dreams."

PhiTau lowered his head and drew in his wings, trying to make himself as small as possible.

"You really have caused a lot of trouble, haven't you?" Mnemosyne said in PhiTau's general direction. Then, "You're going to owe me, Morpheus."

"I'll make you anything you want. How about a book immune to chocolate-stained fingerprints? Oh, or I could do you a whole room full of chairs that push themselves in as soon as you stand up."

None of those sounded very interesting to PhiTau. Mnemosyne cast a sharp look over her glasses. "We'll discuss it later, shall we?"

She tugged the paper from the typewriter, and then strode off between the rows. Now that he was paying attention, PhiTau spotted other unmoving typewriters. Apparently dreamless sleeps weren't completely unheard of. Maybe he hadn't done any permanent damage.

CHAPTER THIRTY-FIVE

Mark of the Dream Lord

Central Filing was quieter but more crowded. Black, four-drawer filing cabinets filled the large room. They packed in side-to-side, with just enough space in front to open the drawers. From far off in the distance, a figure hurried toward them. It seemed small at first, a child maybe. But soon PhiTau realized that it was just very far away. This room was bigger than it first appeared.

When it got close enough, PhiTau could see a curly haired woman with a wide grin.

"Welcome, my Lady. It's so kind of you to visit us," the woman said, even though PhiTau didn't see anyone else around.

"Lord Morpheus of the Dreaming, may I present Bernice Williams, Central Filing Supervisor."

"She is standing right there," Morpheus said. He inclined his head slightly. "Greetings, Ms. Williams."

Bernice beamed and patted her hair. Then she noticed

Little Ella tugging on the handle of one of the filing cabinets. It didn't open.

Bernice crouched down until she was eye level with Little Ella. "And who is this young lady?"

"My name is Ella. I'm six and a half. We came for Ella's memories but we have to hurry, please, because she's all alone."

Bernice looked up at Mnemosyne, her eyebrows drawn together in confusion.

With a wave of her hand, Mnemosyne said, "I'm afraid it would take too long to explain. Could you just find us a file please, Ms. Williams?" She was so polite to her underlings, PhiTau thought. Lord Morpheus never said please or thank you. He commanded.

"Of course, my Lady." She cast one last nervous smile in Little Ella's direction as she stood up. "Who can I get you?"

"Ella Pratt, 17, Corinna, Maine, United States, North America."

The eyebrows pulled together again. "She said she was six."

Mnemosyne opened her mouth to speak but Morpheus stepped forward first. He was suddenly holding a pink carnation, which he handed to Bernice with a flourish. "Bunny, may I call you Bunny? We really are in a hurry. If you could hop and fetch us that file, please, you'd be doing us a great favor."

Apparently the Dream Lord did know the basic pleasantries, he just chose not to use them with the oneiroi. PhiTau filed that observation away to be annoyed about later.

Bernice blushed and scurried off. When she'd gone Mnemosyne rolled her eyes at Morpheus. "You're incorrigible."

"I prefer the term charming." His grin was as bright as Bunny's.

"Does the file have all of Ella's memories in it?" Little Ella asked.

"You're a perspicacious little thing, aren't you?" Mnemosyne said. PhiTau could tell that she was starting to like Little Ella, whether she wanted to or not.

"That means you're good at figuring things out," Morpheus translated before Little Ella could ask.

"Mommy has a folder she keeps all of my best school papers in and she says it's so when I'm all grown up she can 'member how little I was."

PhiTau realized that Morpheus wasn't paying any attention to him. Could he slip away while everyone was fawning over Little Ella? But where would he go? He didn't know how to step between worlds the way Mnemosyne and Morpheus did. And filing cabinet world didn't seem all that appealing. Besides, he didn't really want to leave the real Ella all alone with a six-year-old and a pair of careless gods as her only hope of regaining her right mind. They didn't understand her the way he did.

Bunny returned still a bit red-faced, with the file in hand. "I'm afraid you'll have to sign this out, ma'am," she said. "We had some trouble with certain deities removing files without authorization."

"Who?" Mnemosyne asked, casting a glare in Morpheus' direction.

He held up his hands. "It wasn't me. The humans bring their own memories to the party. I just do the effects." Red and blue sparkles shot from his fingertips.

Little Ella oohed.

"I wouldn't like to name names, Ma'am. The folder was returned unharmed. But it's the principle of the thing. We've instituted some additional record keeping just to be on the safe side."

"I see," Mnemosyne said. "Morpheus, make your mark."

Morpheus made a sweeping motion with his arm. Letters wrote themselves across the air between him and Bunny, who gaped at them. For the first time, PhiTau realized that he'd somehow picked up the ability to read. It must be all that time in Ella's head. The letters said. "I, Morpheus, Lord of Dream, Shall Return the File of Ella Pratt as Soon as My Quest Is Complete." It was followed by a complex symbol that looked like a poppy plant against outstretched wings.

Mnemosyne groaned. "On the paper, you fatuous peacock."

PhiTau wasn't positive what that meant, but he got the gist. Even Little Ella got it. She giggled, and Morpheus had the grace to look embarrassed. The letters popped and rained down as tiny eggs. As each one hit the ground, it exploded into a miniature quail which ran around peeping for a moment before puffing out of existence.

Morpheus seemed completely unaware of the chaos around his ankles. He busied himself signing the paper with a quill pulled from the air. Little Ella giggled and tried to catch one of the birds before they all poofed.

"Now," Morpheus said, clasping his palms together, "there's work to be done."

Before PhiTau knew it, they were stepping again.

They landed in the meadow of Ella's mind. As soon as Mnemosyne let go of Little Ella's hand, the girl shifted her balance onto one foot and swept both arms into the air. The victory pose of the Savers of the Universe. "We did it!" she said.

"Not quite yet," Mnemosyne said. "Now we have to rebuild all of the memories your little friend destroyed."

"He's not my friend. He's a bad monkey."

PhiTau was getting really tired of hearing that. It had been kind of cute the first time, and even the second, but now it was getting old. Fortunately, he wasn't really listening. He'd noticed the circles of light, which meant Ella's eyes were open. How was she doing?

~

". . . should have called an ambulance," Ella's mother was saying.

"It wasn't like she had a broken leg, Rachel," Ella's Dad said.

They argued over Ella's head in the waiting room of some kind of medical center. That antiseptic hospital smell assailed Ella's nostrils. It wasn't helping her headache at all. Neither was the arguing.

"I'm fine, Mom."

"Passing out twice in a week isn't "fine," Ella, not by any stretch."

"You don't have to yell at her. It's not like she did it on purpose."

"I'm not yelling at her."

Inside Ella's mind, PhiTau sighed, and the air burst from Ella's lips in a kind of exhausted huff. "I just need to eat and sleep better."

"Oh no, young lady. I'm not falling for the 'I worked through dinner' excuse. You ate dinner with me last night, remember? And your art project is at school. You were not up late working on it."

That Ella did remember, but it seemed like a decade since she'd dropped her project off. And the head still wasn't right, was it? *Just like mine.*

Dad's calloused hand closed around hers. "Honey, if there's something going on we want to help you. Are you having trouble with food?"

"Are you saying she has an eating disorder?"

"I'm not saying anything. I'm asking if she needs our help."

"God, Jim, you—"

A voice broke into the conversation. "Ella Pratt." Ella had never been so happy to see a nurse in her whole life.

"Do you need a wheelchair?"

Mom started to say something, but Ella interrupted. "I can walk."

~

Morpheus stepped in front of PhiTau, blocking his view. "Come on, we can't stand around all night, there's work to do."

PhiTau tilted his head back to look up into the Dream Lord's face. He wished he hadn't. Talking back to him was much easier when PhiTau couldn't see the details of his expression, but his anxiety for Ella was crowding out his fear of Morpheus.

"I have to stay here. Ella's in some kind of hospital. She needs me." He thought of Little Ella's magic word and wondered if it would work against a god. "Please."

Morpheus leaned closer, his face now inches from PhiTau's. "This is your mess. You left the Dreaming. You broke her memory."

"It was a work in progress."

Morpheus' voice dropped almost to a whisper. "I am your Lord and you will do as you were created to do."

"AlphaBeta said I was created to help humans." PhiTau heard the whine in his voice, but he couldn't help it.

"You were created to do as you are told." He grabbed PhiTau by the arm and yanked him out of the circle of light.

As he stumbled forward, PhiTau noticed Little Ella watching, eyes wide. Mnemosyne was standing off to the side with her arms crossed in a way that looked decidedly judgmental. PhiTau felt embarrassment smoldering in the pit of his stomach. It made him reckless.

"What were you created for?" he snapped.

Morpheus drew himself up and up, his body stretching until he was twice PhiTau's height. His skin cracked and darkened. Bat-like wings unfolded from his back, making him look even taller. His twelve fingers elongated into talons. And the blue and green of his eyes drowned in a sea of red. Teeth erupted from his mouth, row upon row of them, stretching his face into a gruesome smile.

PhiTau cowered.

Little Ella screamed.

Outside, in the ER room, Ella clutched the paper-covered gurney, her breath suddenly ragged, sweat flooding from her pores.

"Morpheus!" Mnemosyne snapped.

Suddenly Little Ella was standing between PhiTau and the nightmare form of Morpheus. "Stop," she said, in a stage whisper. "You're scaring her."

PhiTau stared at the tiny nightgown-clad creature who stood trembling before the Lord of Dream. She faced Morpheus, and although PhiTau couldn't see her expression, he saw the red fade from Morpheus' eyes.

"How brave you are, little one," Morpheus said, teeth fading from his mouth, claws shrinking.

Little Ella put her fists on her hips. "You can't scare

Ella."

"So I see." The wings disintegrated. The human form settled back into shape. Finally, the green eye found PhiTau. "You could learn from this one."

PhiTau drew his arms and wings close to his body. Lord Morpheus was right. Even a child was braver than he was, and a better guardian on top of that. What had made him think he could help Ella? He was nothing more than clay, to be shaped by Ella's dreams. He wished he'd never left the dream fields.

The tension in Little Ella's back loosened as Morpheus turned away. Then Little Ella turned toward PhiTau. Her face softened. She looked like she might say something to him, but Mnemosyne spoke first.

"Need I remind you we have a lot of work to do?"

"To work then," Morpheus said. "Lead the way, Ella."

Little Ella ran off in the direction of the memories. The others followed at a more sedate pace.

As soon as the first toys came into view, Mnemosyne said, "Something is wrong here."

"Yes, the bad monkey broke the memories," Morpheus answered in a mocking tone. No one laughed, not even Little Ella.

"No, that one wasn't broken before," Mnemosyne pointed, "and neither was that one."

"How can you be sure?"

"I'm the Goddess of Memory. I know what I saw."

PhiTau picked up a dismembered doll with a riot of red curls. He closed his eyes. Just as he'd thought, the afterimage glowed yellow. "I didn't break this one." He looked around for the doll's arms, but couldn't find them. "This one was a good memory."

Little Ella crouched next to a tin top that looked like someone had used it as a soccer ball. It was concave on one side. "This was the time we went to the carousel with Grandma."

"I didn't do this," PhiTau said. "I wouldn't do this."

"No," said Mnemosyne. "There's only one entity I know who would."

"You're sure?" Morpheus said. His eyes scanned the landscape.

"Who?" PhiTau asked.

"What's an intinty?" Little Ella said.

"Lethe," said Mnemosyne, and PhiTau shuddered.

Mnemosyne closed her eyes and tilted her head, as though listening for a far-off voice. When she opened them again, golden light spilled out. For the first time, PhiTau thought she looked like a goddess.

"This way," she said.

They walked deeper into Ella's mind, following the path of broken toys. Mnemosyne strode in the lead, her cardigan flapping behind her like a short cape. As far as PhiTau could tell from behind, she seemed to be staring at some fixed point in the distance. Somehow, she managed to keep up a steady pace without ever tripping on the memories scattered around her feet.

PhiTau wished Little Ella would stop making a fuss over every broken toy they passed. She was darting left and right, picking up memories she recognized and exclaiming over the broken ones. There were many broken ones.

Once, PhiTau closed his eyes, trying to spot the afterimages that would tell him whether the destroyed memories were good or bad. He couldn't tell. The broken memories had gone dull. The sight made his toes curl. This was at least partially his fault.

Little Ella darted toward Mnemosyne, something clutched against her chest. It was a Maximus Tron mask. PhiTau thought it must have been the one that she had brought him when she first told him about the memories, the one that showed her playing Savers of the Universe with Jack. It looked like someone had ground it under their heel. The left cheek was shattered, leaving a gaping hole around the eye. It reminded him of Lethe.

"Can you fix it?" Little Ella asked. She had to trot to keep up with Mnemosyne and almost tripped when a purple and white bicycle basket caught on her foot.

Mnemosyne didn't even break her stride. "Not now."

"Ella needs this one. It's the one when me and Jack-Jack save the world from the hill giants."

"We need to find Lethe."

Little Ella stopped and turned as PhiTau and Morpheus approached. Her lips pursed, her eyebrows drew together. "Can you fix it?" she asked Morpheus.

He released the cat-sized blue whale he'd been shaping. It rose slowly into the sky making a mournful yowling noise. Little Ella didn't even look up. Morpheus took the mask from her. Two of his finger traced the broken eye.

"I can make you a new one." He plucked dreamstuff from the air and handed the mask back to her. "I can make you one in every color." He pressed his hands together, then pulled them apart. A rainbow of masks stretched between his fingers. "But it won't be the same."

The masks turned into butterflies and fluttered away.

"I make dreams. Not memories."

"It was better before you came," Little Ella said. She darted off, carrying the mask.

Morpheus shook his head. "You see what you've done," he said. PhiTau flinched. "If you'd just stayed where you belonged I could be back in my nice sunny barn weaving dreams." He pulled dreamstuff from the air and started crafting something new as they walked.

PhiTau watched him for a moment. It didn't seem so magical anymore. It was almost a tic, like the way PhiTau cracked his toes when he was nervous, or how Ella doodled on her papers when she didn't know the answers.

PhiTau worked up his courage to ask, "Who is Lethe, my Lord?"

"Oh, I'm your Lord now, am I?" Morpheus said, but he didn't wait for an answer before he continued. "I believe you've met her."

"Yes, Lord, but who is she?"

"A god."

"Like you and Lady Mnemosyne?"

Morpheus grimaced. "Like herself. She's the Goddess

of Oblivion."

"What's Obliven?" Little Ella asked. PhiTau twitched. She'd popped up out of the gloom, the mask slung around her neck by the elastic so that it bumped against her chest as she walked. The black eye seemed to wink at him. He looked away.

"Nothing," Morpheus said.

Little Ella pouted. "Is this one of those "grown-up" talk things that I'm not allowed to know until I'm older?"

Morpheus actually chuckled at that. "No. Oblivion means nothing, darkness, forgetting."

"She's the Goddess of Forgetting?" PhiTau said.

"Yes. You ran from my realm wanting to hide, to be unseen, to escape who you were and what you were and you got your wish."

Cold fear slipped down PhiTau's spine. "What will she do to Ella?"

Morpheus shook his head.

PhiTau remembered the first memory of Ella's that he'd destroyed. He hadn't felt any remorse, just a flicker of worry that he might somehow be punished for this. But at the time he'd been certain that he was doing the right thing. The memories were hurting Ella and he was helping. Now he wished he'd left well enough alone.

~

Ella opened her eyes. She wasn't sure how she'd gotten home, but she knew she was. The door was open a crack, letting in enough light for her to see her room. Here was the purple bedspread she'd had since she was little. There was the shelf full of her friends, including Baby Sarah, who wasn't lost at all. Outside, the world was dark. Nighttime. She'd slept so long.

She stepped onto the shaggy yellow rug, feeling its familiar tickle between her toes. Everything looked normal, so why did she feel like someone had popped off her head and scooped out her brain with an ice cream scoop? Her mind was quiet. So quiet that she felt lonely. But that was stupid.

She shook her head, wondering what time it was. Her phone was nowhere in sight. Downstairs, maybe? Oh well, her laptop was in her studio. She could check the time in there.

She padded across the hall. Her studio was dark too, though the moonlight that fell through the windows on this side of the house meant she could see more clearly than in her room. She stood for a moment in the doorway, feeling strangely like a trespasser. But that was silly. She'd used this room as a studio ever since Jack went away to . . . wherever he'd gone. She tried to push the thought from her mind.

Jack was gone. That was the important thing. Nothing to get all worked up about. She could figure out where he'd gone later, when she wasn't so tired. But it was strange, wasn't it, that he'd left so much of his stuff behind? His action figures, no longer mint condition in the box, but standing and sitting free on the shelves. She should pack them away, maybe ship them to him. If she had his address. Mom must have it right?

For some reason, looking at them made her sad.

She walked barefoot across the uncarpeted floor. She'd rolled the rug up years ago so it wouldn't end up full of glue and plastic pieces. She'd hoped to protect it by wrapping it up safe and hiding it in the closet. But that same winter, the mice had found a way in through a hole in the eaves and chewed up the bottom to make their nest. It might have been safer if she'd just left it where it was. It certainly would have been more useful.

At the desk, she opened the cover of her laptop and pushed the button to make it turn on. Then she sat down in the desk chair. Just wandering across the hall had made her tired again. She wondered if there was any point in checking the time. It was clearly night. She could just go to bed and figure everything out in the morning.

Then the screen flared to life, illuminating an action figure seated on the desktop. Red and yellow plastic. No head. Maximus Tron. Ella reached for it . . .

CHAPTER THIRTY-SIX

Enter Lethe

Little Ella spotted it first, a smudge of color on the horizon. Mnemosyne cautioned them all to be silent. Even Little Ella did as she was told, although she also started walking in an exaggerated gait that was apparently meant to be sneaky.

As they got closer PhiTau realized it was a house. A tiny house, perfectly sized for Little Ella, with sky blue walls and a purple roof. Finely crafted pink shutters framed the window. A brass knocker in the shape of a lion guarded the door.

"Should we knock?" PhiTau asked, keeping his voice low. He noticed Morpheus and Meme sharing a glance over his and Little Ella's heads.

"Let's look and see first, shall we?" said Meme.

Ella made it to the window first. "There's a girl in there. A big girl."

PhiTau looked over her shoulder. The room seemed

bigger than should have been possible considering he almost had to duck to look through the window. The girl in there looked like Ella. She had the same angular limbs, the same long blonde hair, even the same slightly slouched posture. But if he hadn't seen it with his own eyes PhiTau would have struggled to envision teenage Ella wearing sparkly shoes and a gauzy blue and yellow princess dress.

She sat on the floor surrounded by a seemingly infinite collection of toys. Dolls, blocks, cars, stuffed animals, games, strewn across the floor and up the walls and even, PhiTau craned his neck to make sure, on the ceiling, as though each surface had its own localized gravity. Ella was sitting in the middle of the chaos, apparently hosting a tea party for a stuffed elephant, a plastic spaceman, a glowing dinosaur and porcelain doll with perfect auburn ringlets.

Little Ella started toward the door. PhiTau grabbed her arm without thinking, or at least, without thinking much further than *this isn't safe.* She immediately began to shriek, "Bad monkey!"

Meme's hand fell on Little Ella's head. "Shh, little one. Inside voices."

Little Ella lowered her voice to say, "He grabbed me." She pouted.

"We're not inside," Morpheus protested.

Meme gave him a sharp look. "I know, but we don't want to upset anyone."

"Well, aren't you just a happy little family?" Someone

had opened the door while they were bickering. She was standing in shadow, but PhiTau knew that voice. So, apparently, did Meme.

"Lethe," she said. In her mouth the name sounded like a curse. Little Ella must have thought so too because her eyes went wide and her mouth made an O of shock.

Lethe emerged, ducking slightly to pass through the door. She stood regal and tall, reveling in their outrage. She was still naked. Still unbothered by it. PhiTau found himself just as awed and anxious as he had been the first time he'd met her. He tried to remember why he would ever have trusted this creature long enough to tell her about Ella.

"You've been meddling where you don't belong," Meme said.

"Oh no, sister mine, I am here by invitation only," Lethe answered. "You're the one trespassing."

Little Ella tugged at Morpheus's hand and said in a stage whisper, "That lady isn't wearing any clothes."

"I know," Morpheus whispered back. They both dissolved into giggles.

Lethe raised an eyebrow. "Sounds like Sandy's been spending too much time with children."

"Focus, Morpheus," Mnemosyne snapped.

Lethe smirked in PhiTau's direction. "And look who else is here. PhiTau the rogue oneiroi. Was it good for you?"

PhiTau stuttered but couldn't seem to find a response, not with that eye looking at him. Besides, he sensed there was more to the question than first met the ear. His toes cracked.

"Let her go, Lethe," Mnemosyne said.

Lethe laughed. "She can go wherever she likes. She likes it here with me."

"She needs to grow up," Mnemosyne said.

Lethe rolled her eyes so hard that her head actually tilted backward, spilling ebony hair over ivory shoulders. "Please, Meme, don't be such an old biddy. You sound like her mother."

"You don't want to fight me," Mnemosyne said.

Lethe's laugh was like water washing over the side of an already foundering rowboat. Keeping her eyes on Mnemosyne, she raised her voice. "Ella dear, these people want you to go with them."

"Why?"

"They think it's time that you grew up and stopped obsessing over childish things."

"I'm having a tea party."

"She's having a tea party," Lethe said.

Little Ella leaned around Lethe so she could see Ella on the floor. "She has so many toys."

Lethe smiled, her gaze falling on Little Ella like the eyes of a cat on the tail of a mouse that doesn't yet know it's been seen. "You like toys, don't you, little girl? I love to give people exactly what they want. Just like I did for your friend here."

Morpheus pulled some dreamstuff from the air and fashioned a beautiful porcelain doll that looked just like

Little Ella. He tried to hand it to her, but her eyes were on the toys stuck to the walls.

"Yes. And that's the whole problem really," Mnemosyne said. "You can't go around giving people everything they want."

"I can and I do." She leaned against the doorway, confident, unconcerned. "You have no power here."

Morpheus squared his shoulders. "Alright, I've had enough of this." He tried to push past Lethe. She stood firm, not even swaying when his arm touched her.

"You think you can just sweep in here and do whatever you want?" Lethe said. "You have another think coming." She raised her voice again. "Ella, shall I send these people away?"

"'Kay," Ella said.

Lethe smiled and lifted her arm. That gesture pulled the darkness in. A black wave poured through the wall, its crest brushing the toys off the ceiling. Ella disappeared within it as it rushed toward them. PhiTau saw the tidal wave approaching, and acted on instinct. As the darkness crested he dove toward Little Ella. He wrapped arms and wings around her just as the darkness hit.

CHAPTER THIRTY-SEVEN

Assemblage Metafisica

The darkness swept over him. PhiTau found himself floating in the dark as though on a warm sea. There was blackness all around and he could hardly tell where his body ended and the dark began. It didn't seem important anyway. He'd been so anxious before. But why? Why worry? Why struggle? He could just float here. Peaceful. Weightless.

He couldn't even remember what had seemed so important. Some person had upset him. But what of that? Come to think of it, what of him? Who was he, anyway, to get upset over things? Just now he couldn't remember.

The darkness brushed against him gently, willing him to give in, let go. It seemed to PhiTau that his body only existed because he believed it did. If that was true, why not just stop believing? Stop thinking. If he stopped, the worry, the pain, the body, the struggle, all of that would stop too, and he could just float here, dissolving in the darkness.

By the time he heard the cry, PhiTau had forgotten where he came from. He had forgotten his companions, and he was making a solid effort toward forgetting even his own name. Then the cry reached the ears he'd nearly forgotten existed. It was soft and distant, but it was clearly the cry of something frightened and in pain. His ears sharpened in an attempt to hear the sound again.

There it was. Definitely a cry. It awakened a feeling in his hearts. Sadness. The darkness wanted him to let the feeling dissolve, but curiosity flared. What was that noise?

A sudden sharp pain in his ribcage. PhiTau was surprised to find that he had a ribcage, and that something had apparently bitten it. "Bad monkey," Came a muffled voice from somewhere near his belly.

Ella. PhiTau thought. He said her name and his mouth filled with darkness. He spat and sputtered, trying to rid himself of the feeling that his tongue was coated in cobwebs.

Suddenly, an owl winged toward them. It's feathers glowed, as though touched by moonlight. PhiTau stared. He'd never dreamed before, but there must be a first time for everything, right?

The owl landed delicately on nothing. "PhiTau. And you have the little one. Good." It was Morpheus' voice. PhiTau blinked stupidly. "What?"

Something was struggling against him. PhiTau looked down and found his arms and wings still locked tight around something. The thing was struggling. He loosened his grip to reveal Little Ella. She rolled away from him immediately.

"I don't like you," she said. Her hair was a tangled mess. Her eyes wide and frightened. She crouched like a startled animal.

"He may be a bad monkey, but he saved you," Morpheus said from the owl's mouth.

Little Ella's eyes took over her whole face, but some of the fear receded. "Hello, birdy."

"Follow me," said the bird. "We have to get you both out of here."

The owl who was Morpheus shrugged and was suddenly airborne. He swept low over their heads.

"Where's here?" Little Ella asked.

"We're in the Lethe," Morpheus said.

PhiTau thought he must have heard wrong.

"We're inside a person?" Little Ella said.

"No." Morpheus sighed. "Lethe is a goddess and a river."

"Like you're a boy and an owl?" Little Ella said.

"So she dumped us in a river of darkness?" PhiTau asked.

"More like she brought the river to us. Now come on. We have to find the other one."

"It's dark," PhiTau said, realizing even as he said it that he was stating the obvious. He could see Morpheus because of the glowing feathers, but now that the bird had taken off, PhiTau and Ella walked in almost complete darkness. He was surprised to find her small fingers wrapped around two of his.

"We're okay," he said softly.

He wished he could see her face. Really, he wished he could see anything. Walking in the dark like this, he found his mind trying to forget who he was and what they were doing. It was like a swarm of tiny creatures nibbling at his memories. He closed his hand around Little Ella's fingers and she didn't even protest.

PhiTau kept his eyes on Morpheus as they walked. There was nothing else to look at. Besides, the sight of the bird overhead reminded him that there was something beyond the darkness.

He felt a tug on his hand. Little Ella had stopped short. "What is it?" PhiTau asked, feeling the fur stand up on the back of his neck. If there was something out there in the dark, or someone, they wouldn't even have time to scream.

"Shh," Little Ella said.

PhiTau hushed, and heard a sound. Not a creeping monster, but a mournful sob, somewhere in the darkness to his left.

"It's Ella."

"I'm Ella."

"It's the other Ella," PhiTau said.

"Let's go find her." He tugged gently in the direction of the sound.

"I wish it wasn't so dark," Little Ella said. "I want the light to come back and I want us all to be together again."

Her voice was sad and small and lonely.

"Me too," said PhiTau and realized he could just see Little Ella's outline in the dark. She was there as long as he didn't look directly at her.

He raised his voice. "Lord Morpheus."

Morpheus banked back toward them. "Yes, PhiTau?" His voice dripped with annoyance.

"Excuse me, Lord, but we're going the wrong way."

"We heard her crying over there," Little Ella said.

PhiTau thought she must have pointed, but it was hard to tell in the dark. Fortunately, Morpheus' eyes seemed to be better than his, because he flew off in a different direction, keeping low.

They plodded along. PhiTau noticed that the ground seemed to be sloping downward slightly underfoot.

They saw the light first. It wasn't the bright light of day, or even the cool glow of moonlight. It was smaller and dimmer than both of these.

As they got closer, PhiTau saw Ella sitting on the same checkered blanket from the playhouse. Her toys still ranged around her with their plastic tea cups. The skirt of her dress fanned out over her knees. The light came from one of the toys, a glowing lantern in the shape of a chubby dinosaur. She didn't seem to notice that anything was wrong. But they had heard her crying, hadn't they? Every one of PhiTau's toes cracked at once.

Ella looked up. "You're late for tea," she said.

Little Ella had gone still next to PhiTau. He looked down at her. He couldn't see her face but something about the set of her shoulders made him think that she had suddenly realized something important. She approached the blanket slowly, drawing PhiTau beside her.

When they reached the edge, she let go of PhiTau's hand so she could kneel next to Ella. They looked like sisters.

"We have to go away from here," Little Ella said.

"Why?"

PhiTau pointed out the obvious. "It's dark."

"I have a light," said Ella.

Little Ella reached over and touched Ella's hand. "We can't stay."

"We're having tea."

"No, it's just pretend," Little Ella said. "There's no tea."

Ella didn't seem receptive to this. PhiTau shifted from foot to foot. He wanted to help, but he didn't know how.

"Mommy and Daddy will miss us," Little Ella said.

Ella pouted and then waved her hand like she was shooing a mosquito. "They're always sad."

Light flickered overhead. PhiTau looked up. The owl Morpheus was circling above them.

"Our friends will be sad, too," Little Ella tried.

"All my friends are here."

"What about Liv and Owen?"

"Liv and Owen?" Ella echoed. Her gaze seemed to pull back from whatever distant fantasy she'd been living in. She looked at Little Ella properly for the first time.

Her head tilted to one side, making her hair fall over

her left shoulder. "I had a mask like that."

Little Ella looked down at the mask around her neck, touching it gently with her fingertips. She'd probably forgotten she was wearing it. "It's broken," she said.

"I don't remember what happened to mine," Ella answered, her forehead furrowed.

"Do you want to try this one?"

Morpheus spiraled down from the sky and landed behind Ella. His form expanded, stretched and became humanoid again. PhiTau could see the edges of a solution. If only Morpheus would follow his lead.

"I know someone who can fix it," PhiTau said.

Morpheus walked to the edge of the blanket and looked down at them. PhiTau, who had never found occasion or faith to pray, found himself mentally begging the Dream Lord to help him understand what needed to happen next.

"My Lord," he said, "you can fix this, can't you?"

Morpheus flexed his fingers. He watched PhiTau's face for a moment, then answered, "I believe so."

PhiTau looked at Little Ella. She frowned in confusion but didn't point out that Morpheus had already said he couldn't do it. Instead, she pulled the elastic over her head to remove the mask. Her blond hair fluttered.

Ella was still staring at her. "You look like someone I used to know."

"Who?"

Ella shook her head. "I don't remember."

Morpheus plucked dreamstuff from the air and pressed

it against the mask. The hole over the eye closed, making the mask look new. He reached to hand it back to Little Ella, but PhiTau intercepted it.

When Little Ella opened her mouth to object, he said, "She wanted to try it on, remember."

PhiTau went down on one knee in front of Ella, scattering toys and tea things. She recoiled, her face suddenly anxious. It was a relief to see real emotion there. PhiTau pressed on, the words spilling out of him like the lines of a dream.

"Ella Pratt, you have been called. Will you be a Saver of the Universe?"

The dinosaur light overturned and came to rest between them. PhiTau, holding the mask out to Ella, looked through its eyes at her face. Her eyebrows wrinkled, her lips pressed together. She reached out, and took the mask in both hands.

She turned it over. Moving like a sleepwalker, she stretched the elastic over her head and settled the mask on her face. Now PhiTau could see her eyes gleaming through the holes.

"I answer the call," she said.

PhiTau felt like he was weaving a dream from invisible dreamstuff, shaping it around the three of them. Out of the corner of his eye, he saw Morpheus pulling dreamstuff from the air. PhiTau's skin prickled. This might just work.

PhiTau stood, and found himself wearing a suit of space armor. He kept talking, bringing the dream to life.

"Our archenemy, Lady . . ."

"Lady Butthead," Little Ella supplied.

Morpheus snorted, but his fingers kept moving. Little Ella suddenly had her own suit of purple armor with a glowing ghost on the chest.

"Lady Butthead has stolen the . . . the—"

"Memory core," Little Ella said.

PhiTau nodded and kept going. "Without it we are lost. Will you help us vanquish her?"

"Yes." Ella, in the red and yellow armor of Maximus Tron, drew her sword. All around them the sky was brightening as the red sun of the Saver's home world rose over the horizon.

"We will recover the memory core," Ella said.

"This way," PhiTau shouted. The dream had taken hold. He knew exactly what to do next.

They ran across the white plains beneath the red sun. The sound of their pursuit flushed clouds of tiny screaming jaja birds from the wiry trees and sent wild android ponies galloping across the plain. Morpheus was going all out with the detail. This really could work.

"There she is," Little Ella shouted.

PhiTau was surprised to realize she was right. For just an instant, Lethe was as naked as the last time they'd seen her. And then she wasn't. Angular white armor encased her body. She wore no helmet. Instead, her long dark hair streamed down around her like a hood. She was on her knees in the river. Both arms plunged into the spray, as though she were holding something down. Or someone.

PhiTau felt both of his hearts stop at the same time. Mnemosyne. Lethe was drowning her.

Little Ella screamed. PhiTau wished they'd left her behind. A child shouldn't see this. He didn't want to see this.

Ella didn't hesitate. She didn't even slow down, just lowered her shoulder and ran right into the river. She tackled Lethe around the waist. They both tumbled into the water.

Morpheus ran to Mnemosyne and hoisted her out of the water. "Who are you?" she asked. PhiTau didn't think that was a good sign.

"Ella, get out of the water!" he shouted.

She was just sitting up. He couldn't see her expression behind the helmet, but from the way her head swiveled he thought she must be confused. Had she forgotten where she was, who she was? Was the water that powerful?

"Help us," PhiTau said.

"Busy," Morpheus gasped. He was doing chest compressions on Mnemosyne. PhiTau couldn't imagine how that would help a god. They didn't even breathe. But there was no time to worry about that.

Lethe was on her knees, laughing. Little Ella ran forward, but PhiTau grabbed her arm, held her back.

"The water makes you forget," he said.

"Ella needs us." She was crying, he could hear it although the helmet hid her face. He tried to think.

This was a dream, right? None of it was real. Morpheus had made it, but . . . PhiTau's breath caught. It wouldn't stay together without an oneiroi. Without him. None of this would be happening without him. Suddenly he knew what he had to do.

With a coughing sound, black water poured out of Mnemosyne's mouth and nose.

"I'm going to distract her," PhiTau told Little Ella. "You get Ella out of the water. Quick as you can."

He didn't wait for an answer. Ella's armor was gone, as though the water had dissolved it away. She was sitting chest deep in the river. Her clothes were different. The gauzy dress was gone, replaced by her normal black sweatshirt. Wet hair was plastered to her face. Blinking. Lethe stood over her, naked, hands on hips. Her laugh made PhiTau want to scream. Instead he leapt.

He jumped on her back and clung. The weight of his armored body pushed her over. She toppled deeper into the river. It was her river. He understood that much. She wouldn't forget, but maybe he could buy the others time.

Underwater he could hear both of his hearts beating. Lethe struggled in his grip. Could she change shape like Morpheus? He couldn't remember. It didn't matter. He'd cling to her whether she was a woman or a . . . what was that thing called? A snake. Right.

"Ella, now!" he shouted, when his head broke the surface for a moment. He didn't know which Ella he was shouting to. Lethe thrashed in his grip. *Hold on*, he told himself. *Just hold on.*

She was slippery and the water was deep, deeper than it should be. This was a river wasn't it? Why had he thought this was a good idea? Ella. The little girl. Right. He was saving her. But that didn't seem to be working. He was drowning. Deep underwater. Why had he thought this would work? *Hold on*, he told himself. *Why?* he answered. He couldn't remember. His grip loosened.

CHAPTER THIRTY-EIGHT

Return to Order

Mnemosyne had thrown up an unreasonable amount of black water, but she was looking better now. "Ugh, it'll be weeks before I get that taste out of my mouth."

"You're welcome," Morpheus said, looking around for PhiTau.

"Monkey!" Little Ella shouted. She ran back and forth along the bank. With the eye of a craftsman, Morpheus noticed that the shoreline was looking thin. Bits of vegetation were peeking through the white sand of the plain. That wasn't good. PhiTau should be holding the dream together.

Morpheus didn't bother to walk, but side-stepped right to Little Ella's side. Overhead, the sun went dark. Little Ella squealed.

"What happened?" Morpheus asked.

"PhiTau jumped in the water to get the naked lady."

Morpheus spotted Ella sitting in the water, she seemed

to be fascinated by the bubbles rising to the surface. That wasn't good either. Damn it.

"Good idea," he said to himself. He snatched up some dreamstuff and fashioned a dam. It was no Hoover, but it would do. Except that when he put it down it immediately dissolved into a wall of bubbles that washed away downstream. Not good at all.

"Stay," he told Little Ella. He waded into the water. There were some perks to being immortal. The water wouldn't hurt him unless he ingested it. He hoped. Even so, he moved fast, scooping Ella up, and depositing her on the grass that had replaced the bank. The dream had dissolved completely. They were back in the twilight of Ella's mind surrounded by rustling grass and bobbing poppy plants. But the river was still there, flowing like oil.

"Meme, I need you here."

Mnemosyne walked over, looking bedraggled but more alert. "This is the girl?"

"Yes, but PhiTau is still in the water."

Mnemosyne shook her head. "Get rid of Lethe and the river will go too. You'll get your monkey back."

"She's drownded," Little Ella said.

"Drowned," Mnemosyne corrected. "And she can't be drowned. The river is a part of her like . . ."

Mnemosyne stopped and stared at Little Ella. Then she closed her eyes, as though she'd just been hit with a migraine. Morpheus reached for her arm. Ingesting the water of Oblivion wasn't good for any god, least of all for the Goddess of Memory. Who knew what it had done to her? She twitched away from him and opened her eyes.

"We're fools," she said. "All this running around and we had the answer the whole time."

Morpheus followed her gaze to Little Ella, standing barefoot in the grass. Her armor had disappeared with the rest of the dream and she was once again a little girl in a purple nightgown.

The teenage version of Ella sat up straighter and pushed her wet hair back from her face. "I don't understand."

But Morpheus did. "She's a part of you," he said.

Ella and Little Ella looked at each other.

"But, shouldn't she have forgotten too?" Morpheus said. "How did she know all the memories even though they were broken?"

"I watched them," Little Ella said. "I like the happy ones."

"She's a part of Ella's self that she kept separate, and she's been here the whole time watching the memories. I don't think Lethe realized what she was." Mnemosyne shook her head. "I didn't even realize what she was until just now."

"I can't remember where Jack went," Ella said. She looked at her younger self with pleading in her eyes.

Little Ella blinked rapidly. She took a deep breath. "He died." Her tone was gentle, as though she were the older of the two. In some ways, maybe she was. "He went to the beach with Anna and their car crashed."

"No," Ella said. She pulled herself to her knees so she

was eye level with Little Ella. "He can't be dead. He promised me we'd have a tea party."

"He didn't mean to die," Little Ella said. She reached her small hand across the space between them and touched Ella's shoulder.

"He said he'd finish the playhouse," Ella said.

"He loved us very much," Little Ella said. "He told me."

"But he promised to come back," Ella said and then she began to cry.

Morpheus looked on, nonplussed. Human emotions were beyond him. His oneiroi faded all the time and he never felt the urge to cry about it, though he was annoyed that Lethe seemed to have claimed PhiTau. The little beast was his. He'd made him after all.

He twisted dreamstuff into a crocodile that grew twelve feet long before disappearing with a sound like an old-fashioned alarm clock ringing. Of course, Morpheus had intended to punish him, but even he wouldn't have gone this far.

The little girl and the big one were crying in each other's arms. Mnemosyne looked down at them, her glasses reflecting the waters of the Lethe.

Really, if you thought about it, it was impressive what PhiTau had managed to accomplish. He'd changed a human's life in a direct way. He'd caused so much trouble that not one but two gods had come to his rescue. That was Loki-level mischief. It would be a pity to lose him now.

"Are we going to rescue PhiTau or not?" Morpheus asked.

"That's up to Ella." Performing that bit of minor magic that allowed a woman to crouch in heels and a skirt without flashing anyone or losing her balance, Mnemosyne brought herself down to Ella's level. "Ella, we need your help."

Ella shook her head. "I can't help anyone. I don't even know who I am right now."

"You can help PhiTau."

"What's a PhiTau?"

"He's our friend," Little Ella said. "He jumped in the river to save you."

"The monkey man? I thought I imagined him."

"No, he's real and Lethe has him." Briskly, Mnemosyne explained who Lethe was and the part she'd played in destroying Ella's memories. "You invited her in. It has to be you who asks her to leave."

Ella curled her fists in her lap and looked down at them. "She took my bad memories?"

"And the good ones too," Mnemosyne said.

Morpheus almost interrupted to say that PhiTau had broken those, but he didn't think it would help their case. Besides, he suspected PhiTau wouldn't have done it if he hadn't already been touched by Oblivion.

"She tried to take Jack-Jack away forever," Little Ella said.

Ella's teeth clenched so tight that Morpheus saw the muscles of her jaw twitch.

"How do we get rid of her?" she said.

~

A moment later, Ella stood on the shore of the river, her arms crossed on her chest, a gaze of noble defiance on her face.

"Lethe!" she shouted. "I want to talk to you."

The river swelled in response. Morpheus stepped forward, ready to pull Ella away, but Mnemosyne caught his arm. He waited.

The water kept rising, not like a flood, but like a waterspout, drawing up and out and taking the shape of a woman, clothed in robes of bubbles and froth.

"Yes, Ella dear?"

"I want you to leave."

The water bubbled with a sound like laughter. "You don't mean that. Without me all that pain comes back. All the anxiety."

Ella shook her head.

The voice bubbled on, "I took your worries, your fears, your sorrows."

The figure in the water raised a hand and reached it toward Ella. But the girl stepped backward, back straight, chin high.

"You took my life. I want it back."

"You were safe here, all quiet and snug inside your head. Wouldn't it be easier to just give in and let me stay?"

"Go away."

"Ella." The voice was soft, a mother talking to a willful child.

"Go!" It wasn't a shout. It was a command.

A small voice beside Morpheus hissed, "Yes."

Lethe stamped her foot, splashing herself. "Fine," she said. And then the river was falling up like rain in reverse, drawing itself into a cloud that rumbled with thunder before rising rapidly out of sight.

Ella staggered and fell to her knees on the now dry ground.

"That was a little melodramatic," Morpheus said.

"You should talk," Mnemosyne answered.

"Monkey!" Little Ella cried. She plunged toward the prostrate form of PhiTau, lying where the river had been.

~

Two rhythmic beats, synchronized. Stillness. It had always been this way. And then it wasn't. First there was light. Then water separated from water and there was sky. Then there was ground, and from the ground, plants, with bobbing flowers. Their redness was a shock after an eternity in Oblivion.

A sound. A voice. "Monkey!"

Meaningless noise. But the voice made the rhythmic beats speed up, just for an instant. A face looking down. Touches eased the fear.

The little hands were pulling, lifting. The little face

making an expression that was joy. People, with arms and legs and heads, but much less fur. All turning to look.

"Your name is PhiTau," said the tall one with extra fingers.

The little one squeezed his hand. "PhiTau," she said.

"You are an oneiroi," the tall one said, "and I am your Lord." He sighed. "This is going to take forever. Meme, have you got a file for him?"

"No records for oneiroi. You'll have to tell him who he is."

"I can do it," the little one said.

"No, you have another task," said the many-fingered one.

The little one wrinkled her nose. "Time to go?" she said.

"Time to grow, I think," said the one called Meme.

The little girl threw her arms around a big girl who looked just like her. For a moment, PhiTau felt like his eyes had crossed. And then it was just one young woman, kneeling in the grass.

She looked up at Meme, "That was right, wasn't it?"

Meme smiled, and put her hand on the young woman's head. Then she was gone too. The young woman looked up at the man.

"You're the sandman."

"Ugh. I suppose. I prefer Morpheus though, or Dream Lord if we're being formal."

The young woman got to her feet. She looked Morpheus in the eye, the green one.

"Do me a favor then, Dream Lord. Let's go easy on the nightmares for a bit."

Morpheus threw back his head and laughed. "I'll see what I can do." He smirked. "Saver of the Universe."

PhiTau saw Morpheus pluck something from the air. It glittered. "Time to go home."

"There's no place like home," said the girl and clicked her heels together.

PhiTau had no idea what that was about, but he didn't have time to wonder, because the young woman's eyes were suddenly on him. In the instant before Morpheus threw a handful of dust at her she smiled.

"Good monkey," she said and disappeared.

A hand closed around PhiTau's arm.

"Come along, PhiTau," Morpheus said. He stepped them into another world.

CHAPTER THIRTY-NINE

Hypnopomp

The first thing Ella noticed when she woke from the dream was something digging into her chest. She had fallen asleep in her desk chair, slumped forward over something hard and angular. Her neck and shoulders didn't want to straighten, but she forced them to. She realized the thing jabbing her had been the Maximus Tron doll, hugged tight to her chest like a teddy bear.

That's when she noticed the second thing, loneliness. Ella woke feeling completely alone. In the moments while she stretched and tried to recover some feeling in her feet other than the pinched nerve tingle, the loneliness settled on her like a blanket. Or more like a second skin, something she couldn't cast aside even if she wanted to.

She set Maximus Tron on the desk and looked at him for a long moment, standing there headless and oblivious. Bits of her dream came back to her: a monkey with bat wings, herself as a little girl, a beautiful naked woman.

Ella blushed at that last thought and hurried to remind herself that the woman hadn't seemed very nice. There had been a nice one, though, a librarian with glass eyes, and a man who turned into an owl?

"Dreams are weird," she told the doll. He, of course, said nothing in return. Ella put her thumb on the jagged edge where his head had been. Her own head felt like an auditorium after the play was over. No audience, no actors, just a custodian with a broom pushing echoes into the wings.

"I miss Jack," she told the doll. Then she laid it gently on the desktop. She stood up. Black sparkles chased each other along the edges of her vision. She waited until they went away. She was hungry, and thirsty, and she needed the bathroom, and possibly a hug.

She went to the bathroom first. In the doorway, she paused. Her reflection in the mirror had surprised her. As though she'd expected to see something other than a skinny, pale, 17-year-old girl with dark circles under her eyes and those weird pink marks you get on the side of your face when you sleep on something that was never meant to be a pillow.

She stared at the girl in the mirror. "You should take better care of yourself, you know." Then she stuck out her tongue. By the time she left the bathroom, she'd gotten used to her reflection again.

In the hallway, she stopped to look at Jack's picture. It was his school photo from junior year. An eight by ten with a simple blue background. He was wearing a green tee shirt that made his eyes seem darker than they were and he was smiling. She smiled back.

The sound of voices, speaking softly, reached her from downstairs. She strained to hear what they were saying, but they were too low. She crept closer to the stairs, wanting to know who was there before anyone found out she was awake. Despite what must have been something like 18 hours of sleep, she still felt shaky and dim. Maybe that was just the lack of food and water.

She hovered at the top of the stairs, unable to see whoever was in the living room with Mom. She heard them though.

". . . of you to come," Mom was saying.

"I feel bad that we didn't say something to you sooner. She's been acting weird lately." That was Liv's voice. Ella's heart leapt. At this moment, she couldn't think of anyone she wanted to see more than Liv. Ella had some apologizing to do.

"Well, she's got a lot on her mind." That was Owen, and Ella realized he was someone she wanted to see at least as much as Liv.

She kept one hand on the bannister as she walked down the stairs as quickly as she dared. When she stopped in the living room doorway, everyone looked up. It wasn't just Mom, and Liv, and Owen, Dad was there too.

Ella looked at the faces of the four living people she loved most in the world and burst into tears.

~

Soon Ella was sitting at the end of the dining room table. Owen was on her right. Liv on her left. Dad had given Ella a big hug and then gone home. She knew he felt uncomfortable in the house that wasn't his anymore. Ella promised herself she'd go see him more often. Dad must be lonely, too.

For now, she focused on her friends. She kept finding reasons to touch them, nudging Owen's foot with hers, plucking a bit of lint off Liv's sweater.

The third time she did it, Owen chuckled. "It's like you're trying to make sure we're real," he said.

"I'm glad you're here," Ella answered. "Both of you." She grabbed Liv's hand and squeezed.

Liv giggled. "Man, someone got up on the right side of the bed for once."

"Liv, I'm really sorry I was awful. You too Owen. I was awful to both of you and you're the best friends ever. You don't deserve me."

"Shut up. We love you and you know it," Liv said.

"I'm glad you're feeling better," Owen said.

Ella smiled at Liv. Beautiful, brilliant Liv, who looked like confidence personified and could solve math problems in her sleep. Liv smiled back and then fluttered her eyelashes. Ella stuck out her tongue.

Just then, Mom came into the room with a platter full of pancakes, butter, blueberries and real Maine maple syrup. Owen jumped up to help, strewing compliments around the room like flowers.

They ate pancakes and talked about nothing. For the next 45 minutes Ella didn't feel lonely even once.

~

Later, after the pancakes were eaten and Mom had refused help with the dishes because the kitchen was too small for more than one person to work in there anyway, Ella went out on the porch to say goodbye to Liv and Owen.

As soon as the door shut behind them, Liv turned on her.

"Spill."

"What?" Ella said.

"What has been going on with you?" Liv asked.

"Liv thinks you have an eating disorder."

"I do not have an eating disorder."

"I know. I saw how many pancakes you ate."

Ella shoved him gently. He made a big show of staggering.

"Owen," Liv said, her voice sharp. "No more games."

Ella felt their love and concern wrap around her. "I've been really struggling with the Jack thing. I'm older than him now. He never even made it to senior year. It felt . . ." She paused, watching their faces. Owen still looked just as tired as he had the other day. She'd have to ask him what was up with him too, but now was not the time. ". . . disloyal, I guess. Like who was I to live and have friends and graduate when he . . ." she trailed off again.

Liv shocked her by throwing both arms around her and

squeezing so hard Ella felt her ribs crack. "You stupid girl," Liv said.

"I can't imagine how that feels," Owen said. His eyes were on Liv as he said it, and Ella thought he might be imagining what it would be like to lose his sister. "It must suck."

"It does suck." Ella had managed to hold it together until now, but somehow admitting that it sucked brought tears to her eyes. "I'm really sorry I was such a bitch."

"I'm sorry we didn't tell you about our fender bender," Liv said. She'd stopped trying to crush Ella's ribs but now held her hand tightly. Even so, Ella noticed she was watching Owen like she thought he had something to say.

"Me too," he said.

Liv sighed and pecked Ella's cheek. "We're going to head out. Text me later."

"Will do," Ella said.

Mom was waiting in the hall when Ella came inside. "Ella," she began.

Ella held up both hands, palms out. "Wait, before you say anything. I know you don't like to talk about Jack, but I need to talk about him with someone. I'm pretty sure all this stuff that's going on with me has a lot to do with that. There's all this stuff," she waved her hands around as though her problems were piled in the room with them. "I don't know how to deal with it on my own, and I don't want to have to. You're right that I should see a therapist or a counselor or whatever, but I think you should too."

The words came out in a rush. Ella hadn't planned to

say all that, especially the last part. It all just spilled out. Mom's face went from anxious to sad and then sort of closed up on itself. She stood there, eyebrows lowered, lips pressed together, eyes narrowed into slits. Ella braced for shouting.

Instead Mom said, "I think you're right. I think we should both talk to someone."

"Really?" The word slipped out before Ella could stop it. She didn't want to press her luck, but she couldn't believe Mom agreed with her.

"Yes, really. Now come over here and hug your mother."

Ella did as she was told.

CHAPTER FORTY

Vantage Point

Soon, life returned to its old rhythm, except that every Wednesday Mom would pick Ella up from school and they would drive into Bangor for their counseling session. Half an hour just for Ella and half an hour with Mom and Ella together. Her counselor, Dr. Kipling, "call me Tricia," had a cozy little office up a flight of narrow stairs above a restaurant in downtown Bangor. Even with all the doors and windows closed, you could always smell pizza wafting up from below, and more often than not, Mom bought them one to share before they headed home.

She'd been watching Ella closely for the past few weeks, making sure she ate regular meals so they didn't have a reprise of the fainting episodes. All the doctor's tests had come back negative, except that she was slightly anemic. So they put her on an iron supplement and told Mom to make sure she ate. Secretly, Ella thought her problems were more emotional than physical. Her fear of growing up and leaving Jack behind had basically given her a nervous breakdown, but if someone wanted to feed her hand-tossed pizza once a week, who was she to say no?

Today it smelled like they were making something with extra garlic. It made her mouth water.

"The deadline for your art competition is coming up, isn't it?" Tricia said.

"Yeah," Ella hugged one knee to her chest. "In two weeks, but we have to have our projects done by Friday so Ms. Beaudry can send them in."

"How are you feeling about yours?"

Ella dropped her foot to the floor. "Good," she said.

Tricia waited. It was her thing. She'd get quiet and wait for Ella to keep talking.

Ella drummed her fingers on the arms of her chair. She liked this chair. It was worn and comfortable, with arms at just the right height for slouching. Tricia was still waiting.

"It's the best thing I've ever made," Ella said.

"You're proud of it." Tricia smiled. She had a smile like the sun coming out. It warmed you. Maybe that's what made her a good counselor.

"Yes," Ella said. And she was. So proud that she almost didn't want to send it out into the world to be judged by strangers. What if they didn't like it? What if they didn't understand it? She felt like she was sending a little girl version of herself into a beauty pageant with a homemade dress and bedhead.

"But . . ." Tricia prompted.

"What if they hate her?"

"What if they do?"

"I'll feel bad."

"Probably." Tricia paused. "Will you still feel bad a year from now?"

Ella bit the inside of her lip. "Probably not."

"Will anyone else's opinion make it not the best thing you've ever made?"

"No."

"Good. We'll come back to this. Now let's go get your mom and head downstairs."

Ella groaned. "The car again?"

"It wasn't so bad last time, was it?"

"No." Last time Tricia had asked Ella to sit in the front passenger seat of Mom's car. Mom hadn't turned the car on or anything. They'd just sat there, until Ella's palms stopped sweating and her breathing went back to normal.

"We'll take it slow, I promise," Tricia said. "You're making amazing progress, Ella. We just have to keep working on it one step at a time."

~

That conversation came back to her mind as Ella stood in the art room looking at her assemblage for the last time before it got packed away for the competition. Another memory stirred as well. Hands with long hairy fingers holding a Maximus Tron mask. A brown eye winking at her through the eyehole. But it slipped away before she could get a handle on it. Maybe it had only been a fragment of a dream.

She picked some epoxy off the neck. It would have been better to build the whole bust on one form and join it to the trunk, rather than jamming a head on at the last minute. But she couldn't turn back time now.

Owen came up beside her. "It's really impressive, El. The face is so expressive."

She grinned. "Thanks. Your cards are beautiful too."

He shrugged. "They came out okay, but they don't have the wow factor this has. You're going to win, you know."

Her smile twinged. "Maybe."

He threw an arm around her and hugged her to his side. "I saw it in the cards."

She shoved him away. "You're a psychic now?"

"Hey, you spend four hundred hours making a deck of tarot cards, and you too will start seeing your fortune in them."

The bell rang.

"Four hundred hours?" Ella said.

"Give or take ten minutes."

They strolled toward the lunchroom. Ella realized she hadn't felt this comfortable at school all year. Maybe it was the upcoming Christmas break making everyone more cheerful, or maybe it was the fact that their projects were finally out of their hands. Nothing left to stress about.

Well, there was one thing. "Owen, can I talk to you a

second?"

She plucked at his sleeve and pulled him out of the stream of bodies heading into the cafeteria. They stood close together. Someone whistled at them, but Ella ignored it.

"What's up?" Owen asked.

"That's kind of what I wanted to ask you," Ella said.

"Just excited to go to lunch."

"Owen, I'm not dumb, just oblivious sometimes. I know you're sick. What is it?"

"I don't know."

She sighed at him. The halls were pretty much empty now. "I promise I can take it."

"Look, El, at this point all I can tell you it's probably not mono, cancer, Lyme disease, sleep apnea, rickets, dysentery . . ."

Ella waved her hand to make him stop. "You really don't know?"

"I really don't. Remember just before summer break I got that sore throat?"

"Yeah."

"Well, I never really got better. Like, my throat is better, but I'm tired all the time and I have all these weird symptoms that come and go. It took me like two months to convince my doctor I wasn't faking it."

"How can they not know what's wrong?"

Owen shrugged one shoulder like it wasn't a big deal, even though it clearly was. "I've been to a bunch of specialists and the tests all come up negative."

Ella punched his shoulder. "You should have told me."

"Yeah, I really should have."

At that moment, Mr. Reynolds, the Vice Principal, came around the corner. "Mr. Butler, Ms. Pratt. Where are you supposed to be?"

"We were just—"

"Going to lunch right now," Owen said. He grabbed Ella's wrist and pulled her toward the cafeteria.

Ella allowed herself to be pulled. When they were out of Mr. Reynolds' earshot she said, "No more secrets, Owen."

He slid his hand into hers. "No more secrets." He squeezed her hand and let go.

Ella heard a burst of laughter. She looked across the lunchroom expecting a glare from Kristen Lund, but Kristen wasn't paying them any attention. She was deep in conversation with Mitch Trasker.

Instead it was Liv who raised her eyebrows at them. Ella shook her head and headed for the lunch line.

~

Morpheus had meant to punish PhiTau for the Ella incident, but there seemed no point when PhiTau couldn't even remember what had happened. Then Morpheus had considered sending him back to the tender's school. After all, he'd done that work exceptionally well until he'd gone off script. Morpheus had never seen such vivid dreamwork between a human and a tender. That would have been a risk of course. There was no way to be certain he wouldn't fall back into old habits. Better to keep him close and keep an eye on him.

Besides, Morpheus had seen how vividly the dream shined when he and PhiTau worked together. Even with Lethe in Ella's head, the scene of the Saver's home world had been a work of art. With a little training, PhiTau might make a competent assistant.

"Observe," Morpheus said. He was sitting cross-legged on his large, round, blue cushion in the center of his workshop. Pale light flooded in from somewhere along the roofline and set the dreamstuff sparkling.

"We move our fingers like so . . ." He made a complicated gesture and the fluffy bit of dreamstuff became a bright red poppy.

PhiTau, sitting cross-legged on a smaller round, blue cushion to his right, tried to mimic the gesture.

For an instant, the shape of a poppy wavered between his fingers. A smile touched the corner of his lips. Then, the poppy burst like a balloon, shooting petals in all directions. They made mournful popping noises, like far-off fireworks.

PhiTau sighed and looked down at his hands. "I don't have enough fingers, Lord."

Morpheus sighed as well. He released the poppy, which disappeared in a puff of scarlet smoke. "It's not your fingers."

He stood without using his hands, or his feet. His body just drifted upward and forward until he could unfold his legs to stand on the wide boards of the barn floor. He knew PhiTau marveled at such tricks and he enjoyed PhiTau's reverence.

"You must understand," Morpheus raised his hands, knuckles outward so PhiTau could see the perfect half-moons of his nails, "these fingers don't even exist."

He closed his fingers. When he opened them again, there were only five on each hand. "None of this exists." He swept one arm through the air and the barn disappeared. Morpheus floated, unperturbed as PhiTau sat in darkness and on darkness.

"We call it into being," Morpheus said. And the world snapped back as vivid and real as ever.

"How?" PhiTau asked.

Morpheus clasped his still five-fingered hands together and gazed off into the distance with his blue eye. The green one stayed on PhiTau. How could he explain it? PhiTau waited patiently.

Finally, Morpheus said, "We shape ourselves, and when we do, we shape the world around us."

PhiTau stared down at his own long fingers. He had five on each hand. Each one long and nimble, with soft fur on the back.

"Will you show me again?" he asked.

And Morpheus did.

Allegory

One Saturday near the end of July, 12 years after Jack's accident, Ella group-texted Liv and Owen.

ELLA: Can you guys come over? I need your help with something.

When their car arrived she was sitting on the steps holding a white shoe box on her lap. She hopped up and went to the passenger window. She gestured for Owen to roll it down. He did, questions pooling between his eyebrows.

"How are you feeling?" Ella asked.

"Fine today," Owen said.

"Really?"

He smiled. "I'd tell you if I wasn't."

"Okay. Will you do me a favor then?"

"Probably. What is it?"

"Will you sit in the back?"

His grin melted at the corners. "You're going to sit in front?"

"Yes. We're not going far."

He looked over at Liv, who shrugged. "Okay." He climbed out, wafting a cloud of black coffee and Old Spice, then held the door for Ella to get in.

"Okay?" he said again.

Ella balanced the shoebox on her knee so she could buckle her seatbelt. She forced herself to smile. Maybe she was freaking out a little bit, but she could do this. Her therapist had told her so, and she'd been practicing. She could do this.

"Okay," she said.

Owen shut the door.

"If you need me to slow down or stop, just say so, okay?" Liv said. "We can pull right over and you can get in the back."

"Got it," Ella said.

Owen slid into the back seat and shut the door behind him. His arm reached between the front seats to grab his coffee from the cup holder. Then he sat back and Ella heard his seatbelt click into place.

"So, what's in the box?" he asked.

"I'll show you when we get to the cemetery."

"The cemetery?" Liv said. "Jack's cemetery?"

"Yes."

"Okay."

She shifted the car into gear and crept to the end of the

driveway. Ella focused on the breath moving through her nostrils. *It's going to be okay,* she told herself. *I'm with Owen and Liv. I'm going to be okay.*

And she was. It helped that the speed limit never got above 35 miles per hour through town, and that Liv made a theatrical show of looking both ways before every turn. They arrived at the cemetery and parked just outside the gate.

"You did it!" Liv said.

Owen reached around the back of her seat to grip her shoulder. "Awesome job," he said.

Ella took a shaky breath. She had done it, and nobody had died.

"Thanks." She grinned.

"So what are we doing here?" Owen asked.

"I have something for Jack."

She pulled the cover off of the box. Inside were two figures, one smaller than the other, both made of red and yellow plastic. They were holding hands.

"I made these from one of Jack's old toys."

Her friends were both smiling at her. She felt a rush of love for these two beautiful people who never shied away from her weirdness. She got out of the car before they could say anything.

Together, they walked through the open wrought-iron gates into the cemetery. It had grown since she was last here. The Cyr family still filled about a third of the plots, but there were more of them now. Jack's gravestone, which had stood alone for the first few years, now had a neighbor on its left. But it wasn't hard to find. Someone had left a bag of gummy worms in front of it, and the yellow and red package stood out against the green grass.

Ella knelt down and wiped the stone clean. "Jack-Jack, it's Ella. I brought something for you."

She propped the plastic figures so they were sitting with their backs against the stone. Then she just knelt there, feeling the damp from the grass seep through the knees of her jeans. She thought she should say something else, but she didn't know what.

Owen and Olivia didn't rush her. They just stood quietly. Finally, she stood up and brushed grass from her pant legs.

Owen reached out and patted the gravestone. "Don't worry, man. We're taking good care of her."

Tears flooded Ella's eyes. Liv shook her head at her brother, and put her arm around Ella. "Come on, let's get out of here."

"We could go for coffee, maybe?" Owen said from behind them.

Ella felt his fingers wrap around hers. Together the three of them walked out of the cemetery, past the Cyr family plots and through the wrought-iron gates, their futures stretching out before them.

A NOTE FROM EMMA

Like Ella, I was born and raised in central Maine. When I was in high school, I shared Ella's belief that my state was boring and lacked culture.

Now I know how wrong I was.

Contrary to her opinion, Maine really is a center for art, including sculpture. I recommend the Colby College Museum of Art in Waterville, the Farnsworth Art Museum in Rockland, and the Coastal Maine Botanical Gardens. There's also the Portland Museum of Art in Portland and the Zillman Art Museum in Bangor. Take a road trip and check them out. (Bonus points if you bring along your copy of the book, take a photo, and tag me! You'll find my social media handles in the next section.)

Also like Ella, I once lost someone I loved. Thirteen years ago, my cousin Nick died by suicide. My family is still learning to live with our grief. I'm still learning.

There was a time when I couldn't talk about him at all, and later, a time when I felt compelled to tell his story to everyone I met.

I started writing about characters living through grief as a way to deal with my own. After *Nothing's Ever Lost* came out, I started hearing from readers and the students in schools I visited. They told me about their own losses and the people they never stopped loving. I wrote this story for them.

What I'm trying to say is: If you're dealing with grief, you're not alone. Reach out. Talking to friends can help. Counseling can help. Assemble a sculpture if you want to. Write a book. Attend a death café. It all helps.

And please know, there's nothing wrong with you. You don't have to get over it or go back to normal. There's no cure for grief but you can learn to live with it.

If you're in crisis, please reach out:

Text: 741741

Call:1-800-273-8255

**A trained crisis worker
is waiting to talk to you 24/7.**

ABOUT THE AUTHOR

Emma G. Rose intended to become a kick-ass girl reporter like Nellie Bly, until the Christmas Eve she stood on a riverbank waiting for rescue divers to pull a body from the water. That's when she stopped waiting and wandered off to explore the world instead.

Facebook: LifeImperative
Instagram: life_imperative
Twitter: emmagwriter
Website: emmagauthor.com
Podcast: Indie Book Talk
Email: emma@imperativepressbooks.com

JOIN THE INNER CIRCLE

Sign up for Emma's mailing list and get an
Exclusive Short Story
available only to newsletter subscribers.

https://dl.bookfunnel.com/fqps8yk4sl

Plus the latest book news, tour dates, and other
super secret stuff.

If you enjoyed this book, look for:

Nothing's Ever Lost–Available Now

Jack and Anna are supposed to be BFF's, but can their friendship survive an adventure through the afterlife?

Near-Life Experience–Available Now

Saving lives is Eric's job. Seeing the dead isn't. Trying to do both might kill him.

And please leave a review wherever you buy books. They help other readers find stories they'll love.

Look for Owen's story–Coming 2022

A mysterious illness. An unconventional solution. Fate has played Owen a strange hand.